THE
BLUE CORN
MURDERS

THE BLUE CORN MURDERS

A EUGENIA POTTER MYSTERY
BY NANCY PICKARD

BASED ON THE CHARACTER CREATED BY VIRGINIA RICH

 Delacorte Press

Published by
Delacorte Press
Bantam Doubleday Dell Publishing Group, Inc.
1540 Broadway
New York, New York 10036

Book design by Susan Maksuta

Manufactured in the United States of America

This novel is dedicated with affection and gratitude to my poetic friends,
Ruth, Tarvi, Pam, Arlene, Barbara, Martin, and Marian.

Foreword

This book is the result of an amazing sequence of events that began in 1983. In that year, I read a first mystery novel called *The Cooking School Murders* by Virginia Rich. I loved it. My own first mystery novel was being published that year, and I felt a desire to write a fan letter to Mrs. Rich, who was, like me, a mystery writer married to a cattle rancher. (I suspected there could not be more than two of us in the world!)

I received a charming note in which she mentioned that she was already working on the fourth book in her series, a mystery to be called *The 27-Ingredient Chili con Carne Murders*. But when I wrote back, her nurse informed me that Mrs. Rich was too ill to correspond. Soon after that, Virginia Rich died. I was shocked and saddened, as were the thousands of readers who had loved her first book as well as the next two, *The Baked Bean Supper Murders* and *The Nantucket Diet Murders*.

After her death, the three books in her series not only remained in print, but grew in popularity. During that time, her husband, Ray Rich, came across a bittersweet discovery: boxes full of her notes, written on yellow legal pads, and newspaper clippings, all related to books that his wife had hoped to write one day. There were even a few first drafts of chapters. Mr. Rich approached her editor at Delacorte Press, asking if the series might be continued by other writers. That editor approached my agent, who subsequently asked me, "How would you like to complete a book called *The 27-Ingredient Chili con Carne Murders?*"

It felt like fate to me.

This book, *The Blue Corn Murders,* is the second "collaboration" between Virginia Rich and me, and a third is in the works. I would like to thank everyone concerned with these labors of love: My gratitude goes out to my agent, Meredith Bernstein; to Mrs. Rich's agents, Susan and Robert Lescher; and to my editor, Jackie Cantor, cookbook collector extraordinaire.

Above all, I thank Ray Rich and Virginia Rich. I am told that Mrs. Rich started writing her mysteries when she was in her early sixties and that she was first published when she was almost seventy. She created a female American sleuth before such a heroine was as popular as she is today. She wrote about an amateur crime-solver when private eyes were all the rage. She set her first story in small-town mid-America when that just "wasn't done." And it was she who started the fashion of printing recipes with her stories.

Working alone at her ranch without the networks of writers to support her that we have now, Virginia Rich became a trendsetter simply by writing what was closest to her heart. I wish I could have met her, to say thank you from all of us who have followed in her footsteps.

Sincerely,
Nancy Pickard

THE
BLUE CORN
MURDERS

One

At the edge of a pasture, where the grass was golden and where it stood high enough to stroke the tips of her fingers, Eugenia Potter heard and felt something crunch under her boots.

"Wait," she asked her companion.

She bent down to part the silky blond grass with her hands, prompting a memory of combing her daughters' long straight hair for them when they were young. In the narrow part she had opened up, down on the ground, something darker than dirt caught her eye. She picked up the object she had broken by inadvertently stepping on it.

"My word, it's pottery."

She glanced up at the rancher standing beside her.

He was seventy years old, tall as a door lintel and broad as the door that fit into it, with a face as lined, brown, and cracked as the bit of ceramic she cradled in her hands. From top to bottom he sported a cowboy hat made of tightly woven and polished straw, an indulgent smile, a white cotton shirt frayed at the collar, a monogrammed leather belt with a silver buckle as big as her hand, thick work jeans, and cowboy boots so worn, they looked as if he had put them on when he came of age and never took them off. A bit shabby around the edges from hard work and long bachelorhood, he didn't look much like the millions of dollars his neighboring ranch would sell for if he ever sold it—which he always swore he would not. He wanted more land, in fact, and specifically hers—Las Palomas ("The Doves"), which abutted his spread in the high Sonoran desert south of Tucson, Arizona. She knew that. And judging from the expression on his weathered face, he was not about to be deterred by a handful of shattered red and buff pottery.

"Why should you keep workin' so hard, Genia?"

His single-minded query completely overlooked the startled expression of joy in her blue eyes. Not that he wasn't aware of the eyes; at sixty-four, the widow now rising to her feet there in the clear hot September morning cut a fine figure in his estimation. He'd known her late husband, too, and in his opinion Lew Potter had been a fool to up and die on this lovely lady eleven years ago; if it had been *him* married to her, instead, he'd of stuck around, that was sure, no early heart attack for him. He approved of the natural look of her, the graying blond hair caught up so prettily in a bun at the top of her head, and the softly tanned complexion with only a touch of lipstick and a bit of some sort of delicate gray color there at the eyelids. She was attired much as he was—boots, slacks, long-sleeved shirt, wide-brimmed hat—and he approved of that, too. In fact, he approved of nearly everything about Genia Potter except for her unaccountable inattention to the important things he had to say. He even approved of the mysterious way she didn't sweat. It was a puzzle to him how she managed to look so crisp and fresh in the middle of a dusty pasture of native grass and cactus, on a morning hot enough to stagger a cow.

Raising his voice, he pressed his case.

"You can lease the whole dang thing to me—land, cattle, and all—and then you can sit up there in your house and needlepoint some pretty little things and play with your grand-babies. I'll do all the work, and you just count the money I hand you ever' month. I'll give you top dollar, Genia, you know I will—"

She interrupted him as if she weren't listening to a word he said.

"Ever since we bought this ranch, I have hoped to find something like this on my property. You can't imagine how much I have longed to find an arrowhead. A piece of an old pot. Something to suggest that prehistoric Indians lived here." The blue eyes that he admired so much were sparkling with an eagerness that all of his fine talk of leases had not inspired. "Just think how ancient this pottery might be!"

"Aw, Genia, it's just an itty bit of old clay pot. Probably not even Indian. Something some settler cooked in, mebbe." He grinned, waggled his bushy white eyebrows. "You're just trying to raise the rent on me now."

She laughed, a most pleasant sound to his ears on a morning that seemed otherwise so quiet, he would have sworn he could hear the cactus grow thorns. Genia's laughter sounded almost as sweet to him as the sound of money on the hoof banging through a chute on its way to a feedlot. He took off his hat for as long as it took to wipe a handkerchief across his brow, and he squinted into the distance behind her. There were black-shrouded Mexican mountains in that direction, and mesquite thickets between here and there. A colony of white-winged doves must have been nesting close by, because every now and then he heard them call, repeatedly, as if they really wanted to know, "Who cooks for you?" The tall old rancher wished this woman cooked for him. He could testify she made a damn fine chili con carne out of more damn ingredients than he had teeth to eat it with. He wished she cooked and washed and cleaned for him and kept him sweet company in the bedroom, too. The day held a faint scent of flowers. Since there weren't any roses around, he had to assume the scent came from her. But dammit, now she was bending down again, scrabbling at the dirt with her fingers.

"Genia, about this lease—"

"Maybe there's more pottery here." She glanced up at him again. "I'm so sorry I stepped on it. Maybe it's part of a—oh! Look at this!" She held up another object for him to see. He feigned interest, then laughed. "A seashell?" His tone was derisive. "What's a seashell doing out here in the desert? Genia, that's some dang souvenir somebody brought back from California. Probably one of your kids. Doesn't your boy live in San Francisco?"

"But look at this." Her fingers, with their nails so nicely trimmed, traced what appeared to be some kind of grooved design in the upper surface of the curved shell. A faint reddish color was visible. "There's something about this that looks very old to me, not modern at all."

He offered a hand to help her to her feet, but she appeared not to notice and got up again by herself.

"It's a seashell, Genia, like you'd buy on a beach at Malibu."

"I don't think so." Her tone was polite but stubborn.

He began to see his lease agreement slipping through his calloused fingers like the reins of a runaway horse.

Genia now held the bits of red and buff pottery in her left hand and the seashell fragment in her right. Slowly she revolved herself in a circle, acting as if she were seeing her own pasture with new eyes, for the first time.

"Why," she said, wonderingly, "I'd never noticed. Look how we're standing in a slightly sunken area. It's almost invisible because of the grass. But it's round, isn't it? And I do believe there's another round place over there, and over there—"

She appeared, to his eyes, to be in the grip of an astonishment. She also appeared to be mightily more impressed by her damnfool discoveries than she was by his business proposition, which he had actually dared hope might eventually lead to something more personal.

"Hell, I don't mind," he said, trying to sound jocular. "They ain't deep enough to lose a cow in."

She turned to face him, looking excited and as determined as a heifer who didn't want to get roped. "We'll have to talk of leases another day, I'm afraid. I'm not rejecting your proposal, but this"—she lifted her finds, like offerings to the sun—"this may change things. I need some time to ask a few questions and to educate myself. I want to think some more about this, before I decide whether or not I want to let this pasture go for grazing again."

"But Genia—"

"Besides, I'm going away for a while."

"You are?" This was news to him, and mighty unwelcome to hear.

It was news to Genia Potter, too, because she had only that moment decided to go.

"Where to?"

"Colorado."

"What for?"

"Something I have to do" was all she would say and the only thing she could say since she didn't really know what that "something" was. It seemed to Genia that mysterious forces were at work in the pasture that morning, revealing long-hidden treasures and pulling her in a direction she hadn't even known she needed to go.

Twenty minutes later, her neighbor found himself waving a frustrated good-bye to her from the rolled-down window of his pickup truck, while she stood in the foyer of her ranch house, firmly closing her front door with her hip, because she was still hanging on to those damn bits of pot and shell. He'd had to open the truck door for her and help her up into the cab and then even take her key from her to unlock her own front door, just so she wouldn't drop any of the tiny pieces. Not that he wouldn't have gladly opened doors for her anyway, and not that he wasn't mighty pleased to finally feel her elbow in the palm of his hand, but hell's bells, she held those little mites of dirt and dust as tenderly as if they were babies.

As he drove away, he wasn't at all sure exactly what had just transpired, but he did suspect that Genia had better not discover any more of those damn pieces of Coney Island seashell on her property, or he might not get the leases he wanted so badly. If she was going to be gone for a week . . . his foot eased on the gas pedal as he realized, *Well, now, that opens up some possibilities.*

After a few miles of thinking things through, the old rancher was smiling again when he turned into his own front gate. Sometimes he just needed to give a stubborn heifer a little push in the right direction at the same time he blocked off her route to the way she mistakenly thought she wanted to go. Yes, sir, he knew a thing or two about cows. And women.

Two

Once her front door clicked shut, Genia put her acquisitive neighbor out of her mind so quickly, he would have rocked back on his boots if he'd known it. With history on her mind, she hurried past her living room with its fine view of mountains and pastures, its grand piano topped with family photographs, and its walls hung with her own original needle-point creations, which Lew once upon a thoughtful time had proudly framed for her. ("Pretty little things, my eye!" she thought in passing.) On down the long hallway she hurried, toward the bedrooms and her home office.

Most ranchers she knew, herself included, conducted most of their business around kitchen tables, but a person did also need a file cabinet and a computer. For that she had an office. Kitchens—Genia had found out the hard way—were not nourishing places for computers, not unless you wanted your mouse pad to double as an absorbent sponge, or your backup disks to be employed as trivets. ("Sweetheart, set your glass of milk on a coaster, please." "Okay, Grandma. Is this a coaster?") She was still very new to the personal computer age, and she felt as if she was learning a *lot* of things the hard way. For such a "labor-saving" device, it consumed tremendous blocks of time, especially now, when she was tediously entering calf weights into a program for cattle ranchers. "Mom," her son had promised her, "it will pay off. You'll begin to chart patterns and trends over periods of years." To which she had retorted, "I should live so long."

The first thing Genia did in her office was to gently lower her treasures onto a piece of paper on top of her desk. Then she rummaged through her wastebasket, looking for a certain colorful brochure. If she remembered correctly, it had been mailed to her from something called the Medicine Wheel Archaeological Camp, and it listed a number of interesting-sounding programs for tourists.

"Yes!" she cried triumphantly, surfacing with it.

She slowly sank down in her swivel chair to examine the brochure more carefully this time. Yes, it was indeed called the Medicine Wheel Archaeological Camp. With the tip of a forefinger, she touched its location on a small map: near Cortez, Colorado. Just west of Mesa Verde. In the so-called Four Corners area, where Colorado meets Utah, New Mexico, and Arizona. That was one of her favorite parts of the country, because it was a land of such dramatic contrasts and scenery.

She opened the brochure to peruse its generous listing of programs that were open to the public. Her glance landed on one that now seemed prophetically clear to her.

"Women's Hike into History," it advertised. "We invite you to join us at Medicine Wheel Archaeological Camp for an exciting program of exploration into the magnificent landscapes and the mysterious and fascinating cultures of the Ancient Peoples."

Genia smiled to herself. Somehow, the first time she read that she had been able to resist "magnificent," "mysterious," and even "fascinating."

She read on: "Join staff archaeologist Dr. Susan Van Sant and other members of our scientific community for five days of hiking into ancient ruins." There, that was what she was looking for—the mention of a real archaeologist. In a program that long, she could surely ask a saddlebagful of questions, possibly learn a lot about the archaeological pedigree of her ranch. Besides, now that she had a reason for going, it sounded like a lot of fun.

But am I up to the physical demands? she asked herself.

Farther down in the brochure, she found the reassurance she sought: "Some of our hikes are in rugged country with no trails and at altitudes over 6,000 feet. A reasonable level of hiking skill and stamina is required, but our pace will be leisurely."

That sounded all right to a sixty-four-year-old woman who spent at least part of every week on horseback and who regularly swam laps in her own pool. She peered closely at the smiling men and women shown in pictures that had been taken amid archaeological digs and ruins, and counted several who looked about her own age.

"While we take every precaution to assure the safety of our guests," the brochure warned, "we assume no responsibility in the event of accident, illness, or injury. Visitors participate at their own risk."

That's all right, too, Genia decided. *Life is risk.*

"For fall hikes, we recommend you bring at least one pair of comfortable hiking boots, sweatshirt, down jacket, long underwear, warm sleepwear and robe, several layers of outerwear including jeans and T-shirts, hat, warm gloves, and rain gear. (Snow is not impossible at this time of year.) Bring also: flashlight, water bottle, backpack, travel alarm. Don't forget camera and film. Bring sleeping bag and rubber mat for one night's camp-out."

Genia mentally reviewed her belongings, checking off the items. Yes, she could pull it all together, if they would accept her reservation into the program. According to the schedule, the next one started . . . she ran her finger across a calendar . . .

Sunday night.

Only two days from now. Could she do it? From her bookcase, she pulled out a road atlas and measured the distance from Tucson to Cortez. Almost five hundred miles, two thirds of it on the interstate. With stops along the way, she was looking at a ten- to twelve-hour drive.

Too much for one day, she decided regretfully.

But what if she started as soon as tomorrow, thereby slicing the drive in half?

It would still be a long haul by herself, and she'd be tired when she arrived, but she thought she could manage it and still enjoy the ride . . . up through the red rock country north of Phoenix, across the desert into Gallup, and then up through the Navajo Reservation, past famous Shiprock and on through Montezuma, into Cortez.

Years before she had gotten over most of her fears of traveling alone. Yes, there were stretches of busy or isolated roads that she'd just as soon avoid, but she'd learned that if she wanted to get from here to there, sometimes she had to grit her teeth and barrel through. Often no friend was available to go with her. But she didn't let that stop her. She had decided, after Lew died, that she wasn't going to become one of those widows who never left home without a man to do the driving or a woman friend to share it. ("Heavens," she warned her own daughters, "you don't want to get to the end of your life and still be waiting for somebody else to do the driving!") Her courage and independence had grown, as a consequence of her daring, and she was glad of her choices. It didn't mean she never worried about flat tires, it just meant she carried an automobile club card and, these days, a cell phone. God bless the twentieth century.

Still, she didn't pick up the telephone receiver to make the call. She forced herself instead to lay down the brochure, sit back in her chair, swivel around to stare out at the mountains to the south, and then argue with herself.

"You're being awfully impulsive," she informed herself,

speaking from the more conservative side of her nature. "Are you sure this is a good idea? Can you afford it?" *Yes,* a knowl-egeable-sounding voice in her head assured her. "All right, but can you afford the time?" *Uh-huh.* The voice sounded amused, which only prompted her conservative side to speak more sternly. "But what do you really know about this Medicine Wheel place?" *Well, dear, it says it's a well-known, reputable, and respected center for southwestern archaeology and scholarship.* "And you believe everything you read?" she demanded of the inner voice. "What do you think it's going to say, that it's a place of *ill* repute? And look here, my dear, according to that brochure, you'll have to share living quarters with three other women, and there are no private baths, only communal showers! You'll hate that!" *I can stand it for a week. Less than a week. Sunday night till Saturday morning.* The inner voice was patient, understand-ing, self-confident. "But why can't you be satisfied with just contacting the archaeology department of a local university? Why do you have to go hiking for a week with a bunch of strangers to find out what you want to know?"

Because, because . . .

Genia let her glance fall once more on the provocative, per-suasive brochure. And there it was, the clincher, the final argu-ment against which no other logic could prevail:

"Our renowned chef," it bragged, "prepares great meals."

"Oh! Well!" said her conservative side, totally capitulating. "Why didn't you say so in the first place?"

Now fully convinced of the intuitive wisdom of her original impulse, Genia picked up the phone to call the toll-free num-ber. A young man on the other end of the line introduced himself as the assistant director and informed her there was still an opening in the program. "Would you please give me your full name?" he asked courteously. "And to guarantee your res-

ervation, I'll need your credit card number and your expiration
date."

"My expiration date?" she asked, amused. "Or my credit
card's?"

There was a surprised silence, then a burst of laughter. "Just
the card's," the young man said, chuckling. "Unless you think
you'll be expiring on our tour?"

"I hope not."

"We discourage that kind of thing."

"I'm very glad to hear it."

By the time she hung up, she already liked the Medicine
Wheel Archaeological Camp. If the rest of the staff were anything like the fellow who took her reservation, they were a
mischievous, good-humored lot. She suddenly felt very good
about this decision to plunk herself down amid the ruins of a
people who had managed to survive for hundreds of years
without a single computer.

"There," she said, pleased. "That's done."

The reasons for her extravagant gesture still lay on her desk.
She felt, oddly, as if some long-buried fragments of her own
psyche had somehow worked their way to the surface along
with these artifacts, although she didn't know what they represented. She suspected that in pursuing the provenance of the
pottery, the shell, and the mysterious sunken circles in her
pasture, she might also be following clues about herself.
Strange how strongly she responded to them. Just looking at
them now, she experienced again the thrill she'd felt in the
pasture. Her heart felt moved by these mysterious connections
to a distant past. Whose hands had formed this clay? Whose
imagination had created the design upon the shell? It shamed
her to realize she knew more about prehistoric Egyptians than
about the prehistoric peoples who had lived in what was now
her own state, her own county. On her own ranch, for

heaven's sake! Now, spurred on by her modest discovery in the pasture, she intended to paint in the blank spaces on the canvas of her knowledge.

Scooping up the artifacts on the paper, she walked to her kitchen for a plastic bag to put them in. While she was there, she also grabbed three sweet dream cookies to take back to the bedroom with her for a packing snack. They were addictive little molasses morsels, frosted to ensure their irresistibility, and named for their alleged magical ability to ensure a sweet night's sleep, if downed by a fretful child just before bedtime with a small glass of milk. She made them as her mother had, with cinnamon, cloves, and ginger. Her grandmother on her father's side had made them first—with lard, of course. Grandma left out the spices, too, and added more molasses, claiming it "ripened" after a few days. Genia didn't imagine she would ever be able to prove that, as they tended to disappear within hours. On second thought, she took a fourth—just a little one—and nibbled her way back down the corridor, thinking.

For her, this particular decade seemed to be turning sweeter by the month. She had finally taken firm hold of the reins of the ranch, living on it for months at a time instead of dropping in for long visits and allowing it to be managed by other people. It was hard work, often difficult and exhausting, but she was also discovering that she loved it and that the days she spent outdoors, on foot, on horseback, or in trucks across rough country, were strengthening her. At a time when many of her friends felt as if they were running down like clocks, guttering out like spent candles, Genia was coming to the astonishing realization that she felt, acted, and even looked younger than she had in years. More and more lately, she was hearing the slightly envious-sounding question, "Genia, what's your secret?"

"Hard work and sunshine," she replied, to which many people seemed to automatically respond by muttering darkly about "retirement" and "cancer."

Retirement? Ranchers like her didn't know the meaning of the word. Cancer? She wasn't a fool—she wore sunblock and big hats and long sleeves and long pants to block out the ultraviolet rays. But beyond taking the ordinary precautions, life was mostly risk anyway, it seemed to Genia Potter. You might as well step out boldly and meet it face-on, instead of allowing it to sneak up behind you and whack you over the head. That, at least, was her modest philosophy.

It had come as a welcome surprise to her to discover that one's life could grow larger and richer and more delicious the farther one moved down its road, instead of narrowing and contracting and growing regretful. She was often simply astonished—and a bit superstitious—about how good it felt to be a woman sixty-four years old in America of the late twentieth century. Because she wasn't callous, she knew perfectly well that her good fortune had a great deal to do with money and health. If she could have bottled them, she would have given those same ingredients in great doses to everyone.

If she felt a shadow, it was only a little anxiousness—usually experienced at about three o'clock in the morning—that all of the new sweetness and glow of her life might vanish, that something might happen to a grandchild, or her children might suffer, or bad health or financial loss might assail her, and that it could all end as quickly and traumatically as the awful day that Lew had been taken from her arms.

Later, when she packed the precious shards of pottery in her suitcase, she placed them inside a down vest, wrapped the vest in her long flannel bathrobe, and placed it in the center, in between all of her other clothes, to protect it on her long ride north.

★   ★   ★

Early the next morning, Saturday, while the desert was cool and dark and the white-winged doves slept in the mesquite, she placed the rest of the cookies beside her on the front seat. "I'd hate for them to overripen," she said to herself as she pointed her headlights toward Colorado.

Three

As Genia traveled toward Tucson, the sun commenced its daily climb up the eastern slope of the Rocky Mountains. From there it rolled over the Continental Divide, then slid down the western slope to illuminate the top of Mesa Verde. Once upon a time prehistoric Indians had dammed streams there, farmed corn and squash, raised turkeys, hunted game. The sun plunged off the precipitous ledges into empty, spectacular ruins of cliff dwellings that those same enterprising human beings had designed and built in an astonishingly short period of time. They had lived in them and had abandoned them after only a century or so, rather as if all of the skyscrapers in Manhattan had emptied a hundred years after first shooting toward the sky. Today the sun, which once had ruled a prehistoric universe, awakened Ute Indians on their reservation exactly as it had once nudged open the eyes of their ancestors. In the humble egalitarian fashion of a former god, it glided on down the valley, through the streets of Cortez, among people who didn't even remember having once worshiped it, and then gently (as yet concealing its full strength) lit the grounds of the Medicine Wheel Archaeological Camp.

Far from being the primitive tent-strewn outpost its name implied, the Wheel was a sophisticated campus, complete with a main lodge and outbuildings set on twenty-five pastoral acres. It encompassed siteworks—or digs—that were spread throughout the countryside and which were the reason for the camp's existence. Visiting tourists stayed either in residential hogans, modeled on the traditional six-sided Navajo dwellings, or in dormers above the dining hall, the kitchen, and the staff offices in the main lodge. An old-fashioned veranda, lined with inviting wooden rocking chairs, ran the entire length of the front of the lodge. At this hour of the morning, only the breeze moved the chairs. They rocked in an irregular creaking line, as if the ghosts of the Anasazi had settled into them.

Below the veranda a young doe stepped out of the golden shade of a grove of aspen trees. The deer walked boldly down a path that wound down from the main lodge and looped around the ten residential hogans (all with their doors facing east, in keeping with ancient tradition). An observer might have thought the animal was headed for the showers at this convenient time on Saturday morning, before most of the tourists were up. But the doe stepped off the path just behind hogan six and trod slowly toward the darker privacy of the far pine trees.

A skunk nosed around the closed door of hogan two.

Several black-chinned hummingbirds hovered near a patch of cardinal flowers. They dived into the sweetness at the heart of the jewellike blossoms, calling, "Tchew."

Out at some of the digs, some archaeologists were already up and working in blissful solitude down in the cool of an excavated kiva or inside ramshackle buildings where the detritus of centuries lay spread out on makeshift tables waiting to be catalogued. At other digs scientists would soon be juggling the physiologically improbable skill of keeping one eye on their own work and another on the well-meaning but frequently clumsy assistance of the tourists and students. The juggling routine would cause a few of the professionals to wonder why they had ever wanted to dig in the dirt in the first place, but most of them would think they were among the luckiest people on earth to be doing what they were doing, where they were doing it. There were no ruins anywhere in the world like the ones in the American Southwest; archaeologists and anthropologists from other countries salivated at the thought of participating in a dig here.

In the main lodge later that day, adult tourists would sit like well-behaved schoolchildren at tables, with pencils in their hands and printed grids and shards of ancient pottery in front of them.

"Oh, boy," some of them would whisper, in eagerness and awe.

Out at the slickrock sites and far up in hidden canyons, other tourists would painstakingly apply trowel to dirt and whisk broom to crumbling brick, as they had been taught. In earthen chambers they would help archaeologists draw maps of the original placement of every uncovered item, every layer, every inch as it was revealed for the first time in centuries.

Around them Montezuma Valley would continue to busily grow its apple trees and other crops. But every now and then the tourists would get a funny feeling, as if they were being watched, and at that moment they would look up to see what had been there for millions of years: the dark, flat-topped, mysterious-looking mesas that resembled low mountains with their peaks sliced off. At such moments the tourists would feel uncomfortably small and mortal. The huge scenery that was always there seemed to hide watchful eyes that looked down at the valley even as the people in the valley looked up.

Behind the mesas, to the east and north, mountains rose to snowy caps; to the south and west lay high flatlands, canyons, and desert. It was a dramatic landscape where human beings had appeared and then vanished over the millennia, leaving behind their pottery where snakes now slept, and hand-hewn caves where mountain lions raised their young, and mysterious pits that gradually filled with rocks and dirt, and strange empty towers where voracious eagles perched.

★   ★   ★

In the boys' dormer on the second floor of the main lodge, a young teenager pulled back a curtain beside the bunk bed to which he'd been assigned and stared toward the east. He'd never been out of Texas before, never seen true mountains before this trip. They scared him. So big. So high and sharp. So easy to fall off of. There was a girl on their trip who called them "those ominous pointy things," and everybody laughed at her, but he knew exactly what she meant. He and she, he figured they'd be quivering on the floor under the seats of the bus if they had to go over a mountain pass.

And what about avalanches?

After a moment he let the curtain fall back into place.

If Mom's parents had never moved to the States, he thought bitterly, *I wouldn't have this problem; I'd be wearing a uniform and walking in a perfect line to class in Nagasaki.* Although, if they hadn't emigrated, he might never have been born. And even in Japan they had mountains; he had cousins who sent pictures of themselves grinning on skis, so even there they might make him go on field trips to Fujiyama or some other ominous pointy Japanese thing.

God. Even those flat-looking mountains here in Colorado— those mesas that looked like you could safely walk all around the top of them without falling off unless you got too close to the edge—even *those* were deceptive. Yesterday they'd gone in vans up to Mesa Verde, and the road to the ruins was so terrifying, so twisty and turny, with sharp curves and deep plunges down the sides of cliffs, that he'd thought he'd die before they got there. He'd stuck his earphones in, turned up his portable CD player as loud as he could take it, squeezed his eyes shut, and held on to the bottom of the seat. He hadn't even cared who saw him do it, and a lot of the other kids were squealing 'cause they were scared, too, so nobody gave him much of a hard time.

When he grew up, he was never going to leave Texas.

The boy lay back on his bunk and stared at the ceiling, willing the time to pass so that the other boys in the dormer would wake up and they could all go down to breakfast. He felt safer inside the big group of them. Lying there awake, the *only* one awake as far as he could tell, he felt very nervous. Too nervous to go back to sleep. Were there grizzly bears in those mountains? he wondered. He knew there were grizzlies in Alaska and in Yellowstone Park, and he was pretty sure they ripped into tourists occasionally. What was to keep them from wandering down here? It wasn't like there was a fence around Yellowstone Park. *Where does a fifteen-hundred-pound grizzly bear go?* the joke went. *Anywhere it wants.* Under a sheet, blanket, and bedspread, he shivered. It was cold here, too. Not like in Farmer's Branch, Texas, where he lived. He had seen snow on these mountains—in September, for crying out loud! Snow was supposed to be something rare in his life, like a C on a report card.

They were all honor students, the six boys snoring around him and the nine girls in the dormer across the hall. All from his prep school in Dallas. Sometimes being smart was dangerous, it seemed to him. First of all, it got you into kindergarten when you were way smaller and younger than everybody else, and then it shoved you into middle school too soon, and by the time you got to high school, you were the class shrimp. You got patted on the head a lot by girls who were older and taller than you and treated you like a mascot or something. Their puppy. And you got picked up and tossed around by guys who were your friends but who acted like you were their personal beanbag. Jumping ahead in school like that meant you weren't bored, but that was mostly because you were too nervous to be bored, because you were always chasing to keep up. Your parents and your teachers all thought you were smart enough to do it, but you knew you were only *almost* smart enough. And being smart—even just *almost* smart enough—allowed you to do stuff like experiment with dangerous chemicals in chemistry class, and it encouraged you to think about revolutionary ideas in political science class, and it got you sent—like live bait—to Colorado, where there were mountains and avalanches and bears.

He was scared but too proud to tell anybody; homesick but too old to go home. At fourteen, he felt too old to cry, but man, he wanted to. The only thing that stopped him was the horror of the other guys waking up and calling him a baby.

Genia, knowing nothing yet of a frightened Texas boy in Colorado, spent a peaceful night at a Holiday Inn in Gallup, New Mexico. She capped off her wearying drive with a tasty restaurant dinner of tamales and enchiladas. ("Someday," she promised herself, "I'm going to learn to make a good *mole* sauce.") Since her sweet dream cookies were long gone, she allowed herself a single cool Mexican beer, to encourage a deep night's sleep.

Four

On Sunday morning, Naomi O'Neal, the executive director of Medicine Wheel, felt exhausted and wished she could manage to get one good night's sleep. Instead she was up and dressed and slouched over her desk at six A.M., feeling lonely and miserable. She could hear the music and clatter of Bingo Chakmakjian and her kitchen staff starting to work. The tourists were served breakfast between seven and nine, not one second earlier or later. It usually took them only one day to find out that Bingo ran a tight ship and you either heaved to or went hungry.

Naomi smelled coffee and bacon.

Her stomach roiled at the thought of food.

She was rapidly losing weight from her five-nine, formerly 175-pound frame, but anxiety was a hell of a way to diet, she thought. Naomi O'Neal—fifty-four years old, divorced, the mother of four grown children, and the director of Medicine Wheel for the last three years—wished she could mysteriously vanish into the literally thin air. She longed to walk away and abandon everything, just as the Ancient Ones appeared to have done eight hundred years ago.

Where's your fightin' spirit? she wearily asked herself.

It was hard to fight when she didn't know what she was battling or even who her enemy was, although she knew a good many people would say it was none other than herself. An optimistic and active person by nature—with hardly a suspicious or paranoid bone in her body—Naomi had a hard time even focusing on such an unlikely word as *enemies*. It was as hard for her to do as meditation had always been. She could never sit still and think of one thing at a time, even a neutral mantra like *om*, much less such a threatening, unlikely one as *enemy*.

Outside the window of her office, the ancient sun was staging an unusually beautiful rising, outlining Mesa Verde in a wide band of pale gold, as if the gods had taken a gigantic felt-tipped pen and were drawing a bright highlighting line around the geological formation. *This is an important place,* they seemed to be saying. *Pay attention, and remember it later for the test.* Naomi stared blindly at her desk, paying no attention to whatever it was that history might tell her.

Nobody knew for sure why the Ancient Ones had left their splendid buildings in Chaco Canyon, Aztec, Mesa Verde, and other sites. But Naomi knew exactly why she wanted to leave the Wheel, and the answer was written on the reservation cards for the Women's Hike into History that started tonight. She stared at the two most recent cards and felt like bursting into tears.

"Dear god," Naomi O'Neal murmured. "Not this, too."

As of Friday night when she'd left work, only five women had been signed up for the hike, but now she'd come in and discovered two new cards that her assistant director had left on top of her desk for her to see first thing. It was a wonder Jon hadn't called her at home to tell her personally, she thought, but he was probably being merciful, trying to give her a couple of days of happy ignorance. The first card reserved a place for someone by the name of Eugenia Potter from someplace Naomi had never heard of in Arizona. Land of the ancient Hohokam, she automatically thought, the people of ball courts, irrigation canals, red and buff pottery, and beautiful seashells etched with cactus acid. No problem with the Potter reservation, as far as Naomi knew. But the second card reserved a place for someone who was a member of Medicine Wheel's board of trustees. To that card, Jon Warren had attached a succinct personal note for her, a note that said it all: "Uh-oh."

"Oh, shit," would have been more like it, Naomi thought, feeling hopeless.

She felt desolate and frightened at the sight of the trustee's name: Martina Alvarez. Why was a board member signing up at the last minute? And why, in God's name, this particular trustee, at this specific time, for this very tour?

A haunting idea occurred to Naomi.

This, she thought, *must be what it feels like to be stranded and lost in the mountains, when nobody knows you're gone.*

She wondered if she should convene a Talking Circle. Should she call the staff together to find out what was on everybody's mind?

"God, no," she said out loud, appalled at the very idea.

Naomi thought she knew perfectly well what was on their minds: she herself; and the possibility that the Wheel might roll more smoothly without her. No, the last thing she needed right now was a Talking Circle, where the people who worked for her might actually be tempted to say what they really thought of her.

She sighed deeply, thinking about her staff and her tourists.

In private letters she sometimes described the Wheel as "home to sun-crazed archaeologists and Indian-crazed tourists." She explained to her friends and relatives that "the scientists come here to sift through red dust—and red tape!—to uncover the secrets of the most ancient of native Americans. The tourists come to peer over the shoulders of the scientists."

In describing her own job, she often wrote, "As director, I'm neither archaeologist nor tourist, neither fish nor fowl, so I don't really belong to either group, but I need both of them and they need each other. Sometimes they all drive me crazy. Ideally, the tourists bring money and the passionate involvement of amateurs, which is urgently required at all times to keep us rolling. The archaeologists *spend* the money and find the treasures that keep the tourists coming back."

Many of the tourists were regulars who came back year after year to spend their vacations or retirements digging in the dirt like delighted overgrown children. Naomi counted several of them among her best friends. It was true that tourists could be unbelievable pains, but Naomi was charmed by most of them, by their wide-eyed pleasure in digging into the past, by their enthusiasms, by their touching generosities, and by their sweet and earnest attempts to follow the rules and to protect the digs. In a way she loved them, just as she had once loved her job.

Not so many years before, the Camp had actually been a camp, complete with archaeologists working and living out in the field in tents, cooking on campstoves, and eking out stipends that, to the proud scientists, felt more like charity than salaries. In fact, that's how rugged and primitive it had appeared to Naomi when she had first accompanied her archaeologist husband to his new post. Sure, the Camp already had buildings by then, but it was only in the past decade—coinciding with Naomi's employment in one capacity or another—that the paying tourists were invited to come. With their introduction, the camp blossomed from a prickly little cactus of an outpost into a major institution. All because of tourists, Naomi claimed. All because of Naomi, other people said, whether in praise or blame. But it was true that the new growth had sprouted during the years of her fund-raising and stewardship.

Naomi recalled an elderly Zuni woman who occasionally accompanied groups on tours. She liked to lecture the white tourists about how nature dictates that all things under the sun have their seasons of fullness and decline. Wisdom, the old woman claimed, lay in walking a straight, unperturbed line through good times and bad, impressed neither by a rise nor a fall in one's fortunes.

Lately, Naomi had a terrifying sense that the Wheel was heading down a precipitous decline, long before it had had a chance to enjoy the fullness of complete success. She suspected others agreed with her. Maybe Jon, her assistant. Maybe even Bingo, the chef and her best friend. She wasn't sure about the archaeologists, like Susan Van Sant. Unfortunately, she *was* sure about a number of her board of trustees, especially those—like Martina Alvarez—who despised the tourists and who wanted to reserve the Camp for scientists only.

And who was there for them to blame but her?

Executive directors don't cry, she reminded herself, as tears began to leak from the corners of her eyes.

At just about the same time that the director of a multi-million-dollar not-for-profit institution was feeling sorry for herself, and a teenage boy was shivering from cold and nervousness, Eugenia Potter was getting up from her bed at the Holiday Inn in Gallup.

After a light breakfast, and with no more sweet dream cookies to carry her north, she felt rather like a member of the Donner party facing that fateful pass. Fortunately, like some of them, she wouldn't starve. She knew of a café in Shiprock where she could stop for lunch. She looked forward to eating a cheeseburger and gazing at the famous desert monolith that gave the town on the Navajo Reservation its name.

When she did reach the café, she bought her hot sandwich and took it back outside to her car, so that she could sit there and stare at the landmark and think about the Tony Hillerman mystery she had just read. It was set all around the great rock. As she pondered it, recalling scenes from the book, she was glad she could leave it to authors like him to find and solve the murderous mysteries of the great Southwest. She'd had her own brushes with homicidal individuals in the past. That was enough—more than enough for a woman who desired only to be a doting grandmother, a good friend, a competent rancher, a bit of a needlepoint whiz, and a plain country cook. Now a few simple pot shards and a bit of shell were quite a sufficient mystery for her, and there certainly wasn't anything murderous about them.

She tossed her trash into a wastebin on the way out.

Five

Martina Alvarez, banker by inheritance, trust attorney by education, and Medicine Wheel trustee by election, was spending the weekend on the telephone in her office at the profitable little bank in Colorado Springs that her family had owned and run since the state first had banks. She was eighty; the bank was older. She was tall, straight, thin, and expensively attired in one of the closetful of identical black wool trouser suits she owned and a white silk blouse. The bank had a similar appearance: tall, thin, and elegant with its nineteenth-century trimmings, which, like her suits, had not changed through the years.

"Have you seen the figures for the last few months' expenses up there?"

She was asking that question of every Medicine Wheel trustee she could reach by phone. Most of them—well meaning but not as fiscally observant by nature or training as she—had to say, embarrassed, that no, they hadn't seen the figures. They'd meant to study the reports, but they were so busy—

"It's criminal," she informed them, choosing her words with care. They counted on her to know, to peruse, to analyze, and then to tell them how to vote when it came to matters of money at the Wheel. "Expenses are rising every month for no good reason. The number of tourists—" She nearly spat the word into the receiver. One or two trustees smiled at the sound of it; they knew Martina's opinions on *that* subject. The majority did not accede to her dictates on that issue, only on money, which was the subject on which she was truly the expert among them. "The number of tourists has not increased, nor the number of scientists." That last word was said tenderly, by contrast, producing one or two more private unseen smiles. "The culprit is sheer mismanagement and overspending, as far as I can see."

"That doesn't sound like Naomi," a few of the other trustees ventured to say in defense of their remarkably successful director.

"Naomi," came the sharp retort, "would give goose-down comforters to her precious tourists if we would allow her such an extravagance. Naomi would take the shovels out of the hands of our archaeologists to pay for gold-plated faucets for her precious tourists, if we let her."

The stronger-minded trustees attempted to defend the sterling economic record of their director, but they didn't persevere for long in the face of Martina's implacable antipathy. To say anything more on Naomi O'Neal's behalf only left them feeling guilty, as if Naomi were a dead horse they kept offering to Martina to flog. Eventually even Naomi's biggest fans among them gave up, and such was the force of Martina's criticism that they even found themselves wondering if there might actually be a flaw in Naomi's character that they had previously failed to detect. She *was* a little flamboyant, they had to admit, what with her trademark serapes and long skirts, her big lush body and her great warmth of personality. Was it possible they had allowed themselves to be flimflammed by her considerable charm? they asked themselves. What if Martina—the upright, the elder, the impeccable trustee—was right? Martina was certainly never fooled by charm; more than a few of them knew from personal experience that Martina responded to charm the way a rattlesnake reacts to a mouse. First came the scornful

pulling back of her head, then the warning rattle of the brace-
lets on her wrists, and then the dart of her poisonous response,
leaving a wounded and paralyzed victim behind her as she
moved on to fresher prey. What if Martina was seeing real
failure, while the rest of them were blinded because they *liked*
Naomi and admired her for making their favorite charity so
successful? Martina could do that—she could weaken the
stoutest faith simply by the onslaught of her always well-
informed self-confidence.

"What are you going to do?" they asked her, naturally hop-
ing she wasn't going to demand any extra time or effort out of
them. They honestly were busy people, and she was a retired
banker, after all. The Wheel was their hobby but her passion.
Let her go looking for trouble there. They did hope, most of
them, that this trouble—whatever it was—would not necessi-
tate an unpleasant showdown over Naomi. They'd hate that.
Fire Naomi? It didn't bear contemplating, for most of them.
And it would mean an extra trip—perhaps more than one—to
Cortez, plus innumerable impassioned and peremptory mes-
sages (like this one) from Martina, and then all the bother of
finding and hiring a new director. Collectively, the other trustees shuddered at the idea. But still they asked helplessly, "What
are you going to do, Martina?"

"I've registered for one of Naomi's ridiculous hiking tours,"
she informed them. "A group of silly women with nothing
better to do, no doubt. But I will go so that I may observe
Naomi's operation closer than I might otherwise be able to do.
I'll find out why we have all this waste, and where all our
money is going!"

The other trustees thought, collectively, well, that sounded
all right. They did pity the other hikers, however, to say nothing of poor Naomi, if it was still allowed of them to feel sorry
for her.

★   ★   ★

It took Martina late into Sunday night to reach all of them. Finally she was satisfied—she had their approval. They could never say she hadn't warned them. But she was exhausted, and her back hurt terribly. Democracy, in her view, left a lot to be desired. Dictatorship, monarchy, even oligarchy were, in her opinion, so much more efficient. The price she paid for consensus was pain.

What no one knew about her legendary rigid posture was that it was held up as much by straps and braces as by strong character. Arthritis was destroying her vertebrae; she remained standing by dint of fiberglass and steely will. The chronic pain made her cranky. She knew she was cranky, but she coldly observed that being cranky got things done in this lazy, slouching world. Her father—a banker of infamous cantankerousness—had taught her that by his example. From him she had learned that if you had to suffer pain, you could ease your discomfort by making the people around you pay for it. Make them do the grimacing for you, make them wince and feebly protest, so that you could maintain a heroically stoic demeanor.

Martina loved pure science and treated the scientists at Medicine Wheel with a respect she accorded no other human beings. She would do anything to assist them in their mission. In another generation she might have been an archaeologist herself, but the times and her father forbade it. After his early death she had gone to law school, then bullied her brothers out of her way in the bank, and now no one dared oust her from her office, which was larger and more centrally located than the president's. She was the majority stockholder. She had outlived her parents, three out of four brothers, two husbands, and a child who had died at the age of sixty, still collecting a weekly allowance from his mother. She'd heard the town's cruel joke: that he had died as a punishment for spending his allowance on comic books.

In the past, fools had learned to their regret not to question her allegiance—her passion—for the Wheel. With her Mexican heritage, they implied, why was she so devoted to the science of digging up *Indian* artifacts? She considered that a racist question and told them so.

She didn't know how she would bear the hiking part of the tour, starting tomorrow. But something was rotten at the heart of her beloved Wheel, and she would find it and excise it, if she had to walk a hundred miles on crutches to do it.

Martina knew that Naomi was popular with the other trustees. But she also knew that popularity is a fickle lover who can desert you for reasons having little or nothing to do with right or wrong, with justice or with truth.

Her responsibility fulfilled, she locked her desk, then her office, and then the bank, thinking she would always rather be right than popular, especially if it meant proving other people wrong. *That* was deliciously satisfying, always. Just look how she had proved her father wrong. *She* was the born banker of her generation, not her spoiled brothers, the boys who had been sainted by their mother and anointed by their father.

She knew she could withstand any degree of physical pain if it was dedicated to the pursuit of the annihilation of her enemies and the validation of her own superiority.

From the look of the sky, snow was falling on Pike's Peak.

She counted on the road to Cortez being cleared by morning and would be on the phone to the head of the Colorado highway department if it wasn't. Assuming clear roads, she would start before dawn. Martina slept very little anyway and loathed wasting time almost as much as she hated wasting money.

At Medicine Wheel a student intern whose mother had practically made a career of yelling at him to close doors and turn off lights delivered two sets of luggage to hogan one: two suitcases, two bedrolls, two backpacks, and a couple of small totes. He piled them on the floor in the middle, right below where the smoke hole would be in a real Navajo home. Then he exited, pushing a luggage cart before him, leaving the lights on and the door open.

A few minutes later, along came a raccoon, chubby and slow as only a coon who lives near tourists can be. Savvy to the ways of college interns, she waddled right into hogan one. After sniffing around the perimeter fruitlessly, she nearsightedly found her way to the leather and canvas mountain in the middle.

The kitchen at the main lodge was always kept shut tight (tragically, from a raccoon's point of view), as were the trash and recycling bins out back. But tourists could usually be relied on for crumbs and for open boxes of things crunchy or sweet.

This hogan was destined to be a disappointment, however, even when the clever animal worked back the zipper of the plastic bag that was sticking partway out of one of the totes.

With her little black fingers, the coon delicately plucked from the bag the first item she came to, sniffed it hopefully and tasted it with her tongue, and then tossed it aside disdainfully.

It rolled until it hit a wall and stopped.

The raccoon heard footsteps and skedaddled away as fast as she could waddle. Maybe pickings would improve at hogan two.

The student intern, delivering the next batch of luggage, spied the broad striped tail, saw the door he'd left open, and thought, *Oh, shit.*

"Git!" he yelled after her.

He was relieved to see nothing amiss in the hogan, except for a cosmetics bag hanging open.

He rezipped it and shoved it back in the tote.

Then he dumped the new load onto the floor against a wall, not noticing the little plastic bottle lying there, which was soon covered by the edge of another backpack.

This time on his way out he slammed the door, thinking how it would please his mother to see him do it. He was half right: he'd still forgotten to switch off the lights, and they glowed hospitably through the windows, giving the hogan the appearance of a cozy haven in the gathering darkness of that Sunday night.

Six

At about the same moment that Martina Alvarez was locking her bank and the raccoon was raiding the hogans, Genia found herself seated on a metal chair placed in a circle at a campfire. She felt tired but exhilarated. Around her, their faces illuminated by the flickering firelight and a harvest moon, sat eight people who were strangers to her. Seven women, one man, one empty chair. She glimpsed one dark complexion among the pale ones, all representing many different stages of life. The smoke from the fire smelled of piñon wood; the sparks climbed so high they seemed, to Genia's willing imagination, to melt into the Milky Way.

The nine people—and one empty chair—sat in a small grassy meadow enclosed by aspen trees on three sides, as if held in their leafy embrace. A few yards behind Genia was a gravel parking lot, and beyond that the main lodge of the campus. Muffled sounds of voices came from up in the lodge, and the fire crackled and popped, but otherwise the night was quiet. They'd convened, smiling and nodding, but not saying much to one another yet. Now they'd fallen into a moment of deeper, expectant silence.

A strongly built woman wearing a colorful serape over a red sweater and long red skirt clapped her hands softly, once, as if to place a period at the end of the silence. To her right sat the only man in the group, a nice-looking bearded fellow, and to her left, a pigtailed girl. Something about the way the three of them related to one another as they sat down caused Genia to think they were all staff people, although the girl looked young enough to be their daughter.

The woman in the red serape spoke.

"Welcome to Medicine Wheel."

Her smile was as warm as her words, and her glance traveled slowly around the circle to include everyone. Genia thought she saw shadows under the woman's eyes and wondered if they were cast by firelight or by something else. She appeared to be in her late forties, maybe early fifties, and she was lushly attractive, with vivid coloring and thick graying black hair that she wore in a French braid that fell to the middle of her back. Her strong-looking hands were clasped in her skirted lap. On her feet were socks under thick, strapped brown sandals.

"I'm Naomi O'Neal," she told them. "I'm the executive director of the Wheel. First, I'd like to introduce Jon Warren, our assistant director." The bearded man on her right grinned at the group of women. "Jon won't be with you on your hike, because he's the lucky one who gets to lead sixteen teenagers on a six-day camp-out, starting tomorrow. But I wanted you to meet him."

He interrupted her by joking, "Yeah, while I'm still alive."

Smiling, Naomi gestured toward the girl in pigtails on her left. "And this is Dr. Susan Van Sant, who will be your own personal archaeologist for the next few days." Genia was astonished that the young woman, who didn't look old enough to have graduated from high school, could be a degreed scientist. "The empty chair represents the final member of your group, who will arrive tomorrow. A couple of you have been here before." The director's warm, if tired, smile focused on two women in the circle, one of whom was seated beside Genia. "But you'll just have to sit still for my introductions one more time."

Genia saw those particular women glance at each other. The one across the circle, a woman with hair so gorgeously silver that it appeared to Genia to be reflecting moonlight, sighed melodramatically. "By now, I think I could give this introduction, Naomi," she said. "You want me to save you the trouble?"

The director laughed. "You don't really know what I'm going to say, Lillian, you only think you do. I have something new to add tonight." She paused—for dramatic emphasis, Genia thought. "Perhaps I should tell you about our mountain lion?"

There were a couple of surprised gasps, and a general stir around the circle. The silver-haired woman named Lillian laughed and said, "Well, you're right, Naomi, I could never have guessed you were going to say that. As opening sentences go, that's a good one."

Everybody else laughed, too, albeit a bit nervously.

"That settles it," one of the other women joked. "I'm not leaving the hogan."

"Does he eat tourists?" someone else asked.

The executive director's tired smile acquired a mischievous twist. "So far," she said, "he doesn't seem to have developed a taste for tourists. But seriously, I do want to advise you that he has been sighted twice, not far from here. Susan here caught sight of him on her way home from work last week. He was just standing on a rock looking down at her truck. That was about a half mile from our main entrance, on the road to Mesa Verde."

As one, the group looked east, where Mesa Verde, with its famous cliff dwellings, blacked out the lower quarter of the night sky. Above its dark flat profile, the heavens appeared to have been painted with the richest, most velvety dark blue color in nature's palette, lightened only by brilliant Venus, a swath of stars, and the full harvest moon. The moon itself could have been a gold coin, tossed into the sky five hundred years earlier by an invading Spaniard.

The pigtailed archaeologist spoke up, sounding as young as she looked. "He's a big sucker," she said in a clear voice with a light British accent. "Scared me half to death when I realized what it was. At first, I just glimpsed this tan thing out of the corner of my eye, and I thought it was a deer. Then I got a real good look at him. And he got a real good look at me. Guess who blinked first?"

They all laughed sympathetically.

"That's the second time we've seen him," Naomi said, taking over again. "The first time, he walked right across the road in front of a van loaded with some of our student interns. That was a month ago. Just as bold as you please, they said, as if they were tourists in a wild animal park. From all accounts he really is a big guy, and just about as scared of people as a house cat might be. If you should happen to see him—"

A collective shudder ran around the circle.

"—please do remember that he is *not* a domestic feline! He comes armed with claws and huge teeth, and he must be considered extremely dangerous."

Lillian murmured, "Here, kitty kitty kitty."

"But I always thought," another woman said, "that mountain lions are shy of people."

"They are," Naomi agreed. "We don't know why this one's so sure of himself."

Suddenly, everyone was talking at once.

"Maybe he's been to an assertiveness training workshop."

"Aren't they endangered?"

"Assertiveness training workshops?"

"As if. No. Mountain lions!"

"Not anymore."

"I read they're coming back all over the United States."

"We're the ones who will be endangered if they catch us."

Genia joined the general hubbub and nervous laughter.

Then somebody asked: "Is that what I heard screaming up in the hills last night?" It was a question that stopped the chatter cold.

"Who heard an animal screaming?" Naomi inquired, looking around the circle to see who had spoken. When the lone black woman in the group raised her hand, Naomi said, "Are you sure it wasn't one of our archaeologists? They go a little loony sometimes, out at the digs." She grinned, as the archaeologist seated beside her poked her in the side with an elbow. "Ouch. No, it probably wasn't our lion. Mountain lions usually do that scary screaming only in the spring when they're courting. You probably heard a coyote."

Genia blinked at that; she'd heard plenty of coyotes at her ranch, and they never "screamed." The other women seemed satisfied with the explanation, however, and she didn't see anything to be gained by debating the point.

The black woman put on a show of sighing in mock relief. "Coyotes, too? Gee, what a relief. I feel so much better now."

Again, the group congenially laughed together. Genia felt herself growing happier and more relaxed with every passing moment around the campfire. She wished she had names to put to all of their faces, but soon, she knew, she would. So far it seemed an unusually congenial group of women, full of good humor and enough self-assurance to speak right up. Lillian, the one with the moonshine hair and outspoken sense of humor, looked as if she might be in her seventies, and Genia was somehow glad to know that she herself wasn't the "elder" of the group.

"A few more words to the wise," the director advised them. "In addition to watching out for mountain lions, that is. This is the part that Lillian and our other regulars know by heart. You'll want to keep your hogan doors closed, because we have little mountain critters who are smart enough to figure out that where there are people, there is food. I'm pretty sure you don't want to walk into your hogan one afternoon and find a skunk inside, or a porcupine, or even a mouse. We've been known to have to chase out the odd stray bird, too, and a couple of years ago, a big stag elk wandered into hogan three and helped himself to somebody's stash of Snickers."

Jon Warren spoke up. "That was interesting, getting him out. Ever try getting an elk with a full rack of antlers out of a narrow doorway?"

Across the circle the irrepressible Lillian pretended to speak seductively to an imaginary animal. "Just bend your head a little to the left, sweetheart, now to the right, now left, now try to slide on through . . ."

The young woman seated to Genia's right got a fit of giggles upon hearing that, and her amusement was so contagious that Genia started laughing, too, and soon they had to wait a bit for everything to settle down enough for Naomi to continue.

"Now then," she said, "let me see. What else do they need to know, Lillian?"

"Flashlight."

"Right. Thank you. Yes, take a flashlight with you if you get up to go to the bathroom at night. That's a small precaution against tripping over rocks or skunks in your way. Oh, and you've probably already noticed that we don't have locks on any of the hogan doors, so please bring your cash and valuables up to my office, if you haven't already, and I'll secure them in our safe for you. Um—"

"Breakfast," prodded Lillian.

"God, yes, breakfast is served from seven to nine, and our chef tolerates no latecomers. Anybody who's late waits for the next scheduled mealtime, with no exceptions. Bingo's not entirely hard-hearted, however. She will leave out apples and oranges and usually some kind of cookies or brownies, and we keep the coffee perking almost around the clock."

She paused long enough to glance at each of them in turn. "That should do it for the rules, for now. We don't want you to think you've wandered into some military camp by mistake." Once again her tired smile warmed the chilly night. "As our regulars know, we have a tradition called the Talking Circle. I always like to start a new group with a Circle. We're just going to go around the campfire and tell what brought us to this particular time and place in the universe. Perhaps we'll begin to understand why this group of people has come together at this specific time, out of all other people and all other times. If I sound a little mystical, it's because I've seen it happen so many times that a group of strangers grow to be good friends over the short time they're together here, and there almost always seems to be some deeper meaning, some profound inner connection, if you will, that draws us together."

She paused long enough for Genia to wonder, what next?

There was a feeling of bodies shifting and settling in, of throats clearing and sweaters being brought up more snugly around bodies. Genia sensed that with just those few sentences, the director had managed to guide the group into a deeper level of being together.

The darkness masked Naomi O'Neal's face, so that her expression could no longer be read easily. "A Talking Circle works like this." Her voice deepened, became calmer and quieter, and now Genia heard clearly a strain of weariness beneath it. "Each person gets to speak without interruption or comment from any of the rest of us. We'll just listen. With compassion, if we can. Without judgment, if possible. We'll begin with a simple ritual of music to set this off as a special time and place."

Genia saw Jon Warren reach under his chair for something. A second or two later, amazing music filled the air. There was a steady drumbeat, like a Native American drum, but also other instruments playing a haunting melody like none that Genia had ever heard before. She closed her eyes and allowed the astonishing music to drift around her, to seep into her. It seemed to tug at the center of her chest, to beat softly, steadily on her heart. A small, long-forgotten grief pulsated briefly in her memory, followed by another memory, of her children, which was accompanied by a sweet surge of joy. She felt almost sorry when Naomi spoke again, over the music, which Jon turned down very low.

"We'll be passing this Talking Stick around"—Naomi held up something that Genia couldn't see clearly in the darkness— "for each speaker to hold, and then to pass on to the next person."

"What is it?" someone called out.

"An ear of blue corn," Naomi said. "Because it connects us to the wisdom of those who have gone before us, and because it will no doubt be here long after we're gone." Her voice trembled on the last word, and as she finished her sentence it sounded as if she were holding back tears. "So it connects us to the wisdom of the future, too."

The director stopped and took several audibly shaky breaths. She pulled her serape closer around her shoulders, as if it represented her own composure that she was trying to collect. It was the music, Genia thought, it was the haunting music that had pulled such unexpected emotion from Naomi. Genia noticed that neither of the staff members on either side of the director looked at her or reached over to touch her. Jon Warren and Susan Van Sant seemed to be staring straight ahead, like seated statues whose heads wouldn't turn. Couldn't they hear her distress? Genia wondered. Why didn't they reach out to comfort her? It was, instead, the woman named Lillian, who said in a concerned and hesitant voice, "Naomi?" and even started to get up from her chair.

"It's okay," the director said, waving her back down. "Really. This part of the ritual always gets to me." Quickly she went on, in a lilting tone of voice that reminded Genia of a parent trying too hard to convince children that nothing unusual had happened. "We usually select a theme for a Talking Circle, and I'd like to suggest a subject." The firelight caught a telltale glistening in her eyes. "When your turn comes to speak, tell us your name, and then answer this question." Her voice wavered again, and one more time she visibly pulled herself together. Softly, tenderly, she said:

"Why have the Ancient People called you here?"

Seven

A sudden wind rustled the aspen leaves, filling the meadow with a sound eerily like clapping. Genia experienced the oddest sensation of being on a stage with an invisible audience watching, listening. Someone in the circle murmured a long drawn-out "ah," for no apparent reason, but Genia felt it, too, an "ah" of anticipation and appreciation. She had the feeling that anything could happen in such a place as this.

"Hello!"

Unfortunately, the first word out of the mouth of the young scientist sounded chirpy and falsely jolly. It was, Genia thought, as if a grinning vaudeville performer had burst onto the scene of a serious drama. The young woman even waved the ear of corn at them, as if to distract their attention from melancholy Naomi and draw it firmly to her cheerful self. Below her blond pigtails she wore a plain white sweatshirt, jeans, and hiking boots. She sat straight against the back of her metal chair, her legs spread slightly apart with her knees sagging in and her feet pigeon-toed. Her posture gave her the appearance of an alert, self-assured child.

"I'm Susan Van Sant, archaeologist and big game hunter."

She laughed when her reference to the mountain lion produced low chuckles. Once again the mood grew light and companionable. All seemed normal again. The breeze died down, and the clapping stopped as suddenly as it had begun.

Genia leaned forward to listen with interest. It turned out that what the young scientist had to say was anything but superficial. She said it in a slight British accent, like someone who'd spent part of her childhood in England or been educated there.

"The Ancient People called to me in a dream when I was ten years old. Honestly, this really happened. I dreamed I was a young woman living in a beautiful empty city that was built into a cliff at the top of a mountain. Mind you, at that age I had never heard of the cliff dwellers. In my dream I was making a great big red pot out of wet clay, and it formed and hardened in my hands, and then when it was finished, it disappeared. I was left holding nothing but air. I woke up crying. It was the oddest thing. So when we moved to America and I came across a picture of the Cliff Palace Ruins on Mesa Verde in a history book, I recognized my destiny."

Genia felt spellbound as she listened.

"I had to find out what happened to the pot," the archaeologist told them. "And so I've been looking ever since."

There was a long moment of appreciative silence, and then the young woman next to Genia whispered, simply, "Wow." That was Genia's feeling exactly. She was rather glad she wasn't the one who had to speak next. In fact, the next woman took the ear of corn and started out by saying, "That's a tough act to follow."

This woman's eyeglass lenses glittered in the firelight.

Everything about her appeared ordinary—brownish hair worn in a short, straight, and simple bowl cut, a square and plain face, a short, stocky body attired in a dark jacket and trousers. Then she spoke. From the first word, her voice flowed out into the circle with extraordinary low-pitched resonance; her enunciation was as precise as that of an actress. Genia found herself reminded of the theater again, and of certain special roles: Lady Macbeth, Hamlet's mother, Medea, all dangerous women adept at disguising their power. *And,* she thought wryly, *the plain face of a nondescript, middle-aged female could be one of the best disguises of all.*

"My name's Judith Belove—Judy—and I'm here with my friend Teri Fox. Uh—" She turned her face toward the woman sitting beside her, as if for confirmation of what to say next. "We're both high school teachers—I teach English and drama—and we're playing hooky from district meetings." A few other women laughed understandingly. Genia, who had never taught anything except games and cooking to her own children, felt mesmerized by the lovely deep voice. Surely this woman could tame the wildest mountain lion, or teenager.

Judith Belove turned again to her friend Teri. "Why *are* we here?" she said humorously, but then she faced the group and said seriously, "We're here—at least I am—because I'm fifty-one years old, and when all of my friends were hanging out in the Haight, I was getting married and working and raising kids. I guess you could say I missed the sixties. So Teri and I, we're making up for lost time. Last year we hooked up with a protest march to Washington, D.C., and a couple of months ago we attended the first rock concert in our lives."

The firelight captured a grin on her plain square face.

"It was the Rolling Stones, who are even older than we are. And now"—she paused, and Genia saw her chew for a moment on her lower lip—"I guess you could say we're doing nature. We thought about signing up for a dig, but Teri doesn't like to get dirt under her fingernails."

Soft laughter circled the fire.

It seemed to Genia that for all the assurance of that remarkable voice, the woman seemed nervous, as most people are—even actresses—when they have to speak extemporaneously in front of strangers. Judith kept shifting the ear of corn from her right hand to her left, then back again.

"I never really thought about anybody 'calling' me here, but maybe they did, just because the places where they lived are so dramatic. Like God was the set designer. I've always thought those cliff dwellings would make perfect stages for Shakespeare. Imagine Hamlet sneaking around among those ruins! Think of his father's ghost appearing at the top of one of those towers. I think I'd have Ophelia throw herself off the edge, provided I could figure out a way to catch her, of course."

She trailed off, to the sounds of quiet amusement from her audience.

When Genia had first glanced at Judith Belove, she had seen only an ordinary middle-aged woman; now she imagined flowing purple robes and a glittering crown transforming the drama teacher into a compelling stage presence. She didn't think she could ever bring herself to call the woman by the diminutive "Judy." This was a full-fledged Judith if ever there was one.

The teacher placed the ear of blue corn into the waiting hands of her friend, who was also the only one of color among the group.

Teri Fox. Her complexion was so dark, it was difficult to see her features clearly in the surrounding darkness, but Genia recalled earlier seeing stylishly short and curly graying black hair, vivid red lips, and wide expressive eyes of an unexpectedly light hazel color, like caramel drops in a chocolate cookie. She was short, like her friend, but more gracefully constructed, with a thinner, more conventionally feminine appearance. Her voice was lighter than Judith's, too, softer and less resonant, so that Genia had to lean forward slightly to hear her, but nevertheless it had the crisp, efficient tone of a longtime teacher. "I can't say I heard the call of the wild, like Judy did. I'll tell you the truth: I don't know exactly why I'm here, except that anything beats faculty meetings. I teach biology to high school sophomores and chemistry to the juniors, and I couldn't begin to guess what that has to do with Ancient People. I'm not athletic, and I'm not really looking forward to these long hikes. And I really do just hate to get sweaty and dirty, and I'd much prefer to have my own private shower and room service."

The litany might have sounded complaining, but she said it with such self-deprecating good humor that the others laughed. Genia did wonder why in the world such a woman would allow herself to be dragged along on this expensive outdoor adventure.

"I don't think the Ancient People called me," Teri Fox said. "I think they called Judy, and I just happened to pick up the phone!"

There was loud laughter at that.

She passed the corn to the next woman, seated to Genia's right. Now that Genia knew the archaeologist wasn't really as young as she looked, it was obvious that this next woman was the baby of the group, probably no more than twenty-five from the looks of her. Even in the darkness, she made a startling contrast to Teri Fox's extreme darkness, for she was as fair and blond as a Nordic princess. In truth, she was attired more like an Indian princess. Genia had already taken note of the beaded headband that held the long blond hair off the pretty face, the fringed leather jacket, the dangling turquoise earrings, fringed leather pants, and even beaded moccasins.

"I'm Gabriella Russell," she said in a voice so whispery that Genia wondered if the people across the crackling fire could hear it. "Although I prefer to be called by my aboriginal name—Gabbling Brook—which I received in a sweat lodge ceremony. And I'm here for the third time, because I just love and respect the original Americans so very much. I just think they're so wise, and we could learn so much from how they treat Mother Earth and Father Sky."

The woman on Genia's left, a participant who had said virtually nothing thus far, suddenly leaned over and murmured cynically in Genia's ear: "And Brother Cloud and Sister Sun?"

The young woman who wanted to be called Gabbling Brook

raised her arms and opened her palms toward the moon, so the long fringe on the arms of her jacket swayed. Raising her voice shrilly, she proclaimed, "I have heard them calling, the Ancient Ones! They have called to me in sorrow! They have called in dire warning to us all! They have called, and I will answer!"

Into Genia's left ear came the words "Repent, sinners!"

Genia glanced at—Gabbling Brook—and saw that her eyes were closed as she lowered her arms slowly. That was just as well, Genia decided, because the firelight revealed that the archaeologist was carefully studying her own fingernails, and the assistant director was trying to hide a smirk, and there was a look of forced empathy even on the director's face. The truth was, the girl's earnest sincerity seemed to be making everybody cringe. Even Genia found herself thinking in dismay, *Oh, heavens, do I really have to call her Gabbling Brook?* A name that might have seemed poetically apposite for a genuine Indian sounded more than a little silly on a blond princess.

Suddenly Genia felt the ear of corn thrust into her own hands.

She found herself stroking the husks, so smoothly ridged and dry. She touched the kernels inside—so miraculous really, when you stopped and thought about it. She loved corn in practically any form, from popped to creamed to chowder to bread. She was surprised to feel her heart pounding; she stroked the ear of corn some more in an attempt to calm herself. It went against her nature to reveal her innermost thoughts blindly to strangers; by habit, she was more reserved than that, good at asking questions that encouraged other people to talk—and that at the same time allowed her to remain unobtrusively quiet. But she thought for a moment about those bits of pot, buried so long and so deep. . . .

"My name is Eugenia Potter, but I go by Genia."

She told them about the exciting discovery of the pot shards and the fragment of colored seashell on her ranchland. "I feel as if some Ancient People have called on me quite directly to get to know them, and to honor their history and their memory. That's why I'm here." It didn't sound very impressive even to her own ears, so she was surprised to see in the firelight that faces smiled at her and looked interested in her little story.

Feeling relieved to have finished her turn, she gave the corn to the woman on her left. Genia felt startled when the woman took it and then tossed it casually into the air and then caught it again. After so much sincerity, Genia thought wryly, the insouciant gesture seemed nearly sacrilegious.

This woman was wiry, athletic-looking, and thirtyish, with dark brown hair cut short and close to her scalp and big hoop earrings and stylish outdoor clothing that looked fresh out of an expensive catalog. Throughout the ceremony she had sat with her right foot propped on her left knee, slouched down on the metal chair as if she were bored or uncomfortable, with her hands in her pockets.

"Madeline Rose," she said, sounding amused. "I go by Madeline," she then announced, leaving the unmistakable impression that she was making fun of the women who'd preceded her: Judith, Gabbling Brook, and Genia. "And I pass."

She dropped the corn into the lap of the next person in the circle, the silver-haired woman named Lillian.

"Oh!" exclaimed Lillian, obviously taken by surprise. "Well, all right. Madeline." A wry tone crept into her own voice, as if to make it clear she could dish it out as well as Madeline Rose could. "I'm Lillian Kleberg, and I'll answer to anything except Get Out of the Way You Old Lady! I have to admit I didn't expect—I wasn't ready . . ." She cocked her head, as if she were trying to hear something faint. Genia expected her to say something tart and amusing, the voice of experience in Medicine Wheel excursions.

But Lillian Kleberg sighed and said, "You talk about hearing a call from the Ancient Ones? I wish they'd call me. I'd go."

She paused. The quiet was deep around them all. "But first I'd ask them, how could they walk away from their own lives and never look back? I wish . . ."

Suddenly, with an unexpectedness that left Genia feeling shaken, the lovely silver hair began to bob in the firelight, and it became obvious that Lillian Kleberg was weeping.

"I wish"—she sobbed—"I wish I could do that, too."

For a moment they all seemed paralyzed.

Then Naomi O'Neal moved quickly, hurrying around the campfire to crouch in front of the older woman. Naomi wrapped her in an embrace and began murmuring to her. Everyone else still sat frozen, although Genia saw the other two staff members exchange glances. Then Susan Van Sant, the archaeologist, came over to the huddled pair. She exchanged a few whispered words with them, then helped Lillian to her feet. With one arm around her, Susan led Lillian out of the circle and walked away with her toward the lodge.

Now there were three empty chairs instead of just one.

The wind blew through the aspens again, but the clapping of the leaves sounded cruel this time, ironic and detached, like a theater critic insulting a poorly acted play. Lillian's sobs had seemed heartfelt and poignantly authentic to Genia; it hadn't seemed like a performance at all. She wondered what the others, particularly the cynical Madeline Rose, had made of it.

Naomi O'Neal resumed her seat but said nothing about what had just transpired. She had a look of ambivalence on her face, as if she were trying to decide whether to offer some explanation. Finally, instead of explaining, she held up her right hand to display the ear of corn she held in it. They were still deep within the Talking Circle, she seemed to be saying, and so they would honor the ritual through to the end. Because the chair next to Lillian was the original empty one, Naomi handed the blue corn to her assitant director.

"My name's Jon Warren," he said. Late thirties, Genia guessed. She thought he might be the amusing fellow she'd spoken to on the phone. He had thick sandy-colored hair that brushed the collar of his yellow turtleneck sweater. His bushy but neatly trimmed beard and mustache were of a sort that adorned many male faces west of the Rockies. They looked like good protection againt the cold, Genia thought, not to mention giving their owners an attractively rugged appearance. Broad shouldered and taller, even sitting down, than all of the women there, he contributed a strong masculine presence. "As Naomi said, I'm the assistant director around here. The Ancient One I hear calling me all the time is Naomi, because she's ten years older than me." An explosion of laughter greeted that jibe, as if they were all grateful to be released from the emotion of Lillian's exit. His boss laughed louder than anybody else. " 'Jon do this,' she calls," he continued, to more laughter. " 'Jon do that.' And I say, 'Yes, oh, Ancient One.' " The firelight caught a glint of the wide grin on his face as he passed the corn back to the woman he was kidding. Naomi took it and mimed bonking him on top of the head with it. Genia admired the way he had managed to defuse the tension, but she also noticed that he hadn't really told them much about himself.

Naomi allowed the hilarity to die down, and then she said into the rather comfortable silence that ensued, "Thank you. We're so glad you're here. We hope you have a wonderful time. I think Bingo left out the remaining gingerbread cake from supper, so help yourselves, if there's any leftover. We do have sixteen teenagers on the grounds, so I won't guarantee there's any food left anywhere in the county.

"Remember, breakfast is from seven to nine. You'll leave on your first hike after breakfast, with Susan. I'll join you whenever I can. Don't forget sunblock, even if it's cloudy.

"You'll find your luggage has already been mysteriously placed in the proper hogans. And there's really nothing more to say, except to tell you that Gabby, Teri, Judy, and Genia are sharing hogan one, and Lillian, Madeline, and our missing member"—she gestured to the empty chair next to Jon—"will share hogan two. If you're having a good time, tell Lillian and Madeline's roommate, because she's a member of our board of trustees. If you have any complaints, tell—Jon."

Amid general laughter, she added, "Hang around the fire as long as you want, but if you feel like carrying a chair up to the lodge, Jon would be grateful. Company! Dismissed!"

It was only then, as everybody was stirring and stretching and getting up, that Genia realized that Jon Warren was not the only person in the Talking Circle who had failed to reveal himself. Naomi O'Neal had not even taken her turn to speak. In the confusion over Lillian's tears, had she forgotten? Genia wondered. Or was it deliberate? And did it have anything to do with the director's own suppressed tears earlier on?

A Talking Circle, she decided, was powerful medicine, as the Indians might say!

Eight

"I just love Native Americans, don't you, Genia?"

"I don't actually know any," she replied tactfully.

She and her youngest roommate, Gabriella Russell, were walking together down the dirt and gravel path toward hogan one, after delivering their folding chairs to the dining hall. In front of them their other two roommates walked in single file, Teri holding a flashlight that adequately lighted the path for all of them, with the help of the great orange moon overhead. The lights ablaze in the first hogan helped to illuminate their way, as well.

Genia's new roommate blinked her lovely blue eyes, as if she didn't quite grasp the advisability of actually becoming acquainted before vowing one's affection for people.

"But I'd like to," Genia added quickly, honestly.

That seemed to satisfy the girl, because she smiled and nodded. Then she said, in the intense near-whisper that seemed to be her usual tone of voice, "It's too bad they didn't kill all of *our* ancestors, instead of the other way around."

A now-familiar cynical voice spoke up behind them.

"Well, that would make it a little awkward for us now." The woman named Madeline Rose laughed. Genia glanced back and saw amused dark eyes set just a fraction too close together over a small straight nose and lipstick so dark, it looked nearly black. "Don't you think?"

Gabriella blinked again. It gave her the appearance, in Genia's eyes, of someone not quite bright, a girl who didn't—in the vernacular of Genia's own grandchildren—"get it." Genia wasn't sure that perception was accurate, but she nevertheless found herself feeling protective, just as she used to feel toward the more socially awkward of her children's friends. That's what Gabbling Brook seemed to Genia to be, really: an overage, overgrown, naive, earnest little girl playing Indian in beads and fringes and moccasins.

Genia and Gabriella followed Teri and Judith into hogan one.

Madeline Rose sauntered, with her hands in her pants pockets, on down the path to the next hogan. She was not exactly the sympathetic roommate one might have wished for Lillian after her tears. Watching the retreating back of the thin stylish woman, Genia thought irresistibly of . . . Custer. General George Custer. That didn't make any sense to her, because he was the one, after all, who was outfoxed by the Indians and not the other way around. So why in the world did the fashionable, sardonic Ms. Madeline Rose make her think of Custer? Genia couldn't imagine a single good reason why, and she was suddenly much too exhausted to care. She only hoped Madeline had a few kind fibers in her body, for her roommate's sake.

"Naomi?" Jon ran to catch up to her in the parking lot, before she could leave for home.

She turned, smiling. "Just call me Ancient One."

He laughed. "If you insist. Sorry. Hope you didn't mind. I thought we needed some levity after Lillian went to pieces." Quickly he added, "Poor thing. Naomi, are we still going ahead with our experiment? Even with Mrs. A. coming?"

"Yes, dammit."

He raised his hands in the air. "Just asking!"

Naomi sighed. "I know, Jon. I'm not mad at you. I'm mad

at her for being such a rigid, unimaginative person that we can't ever plan anything new without worrying that she'll throw a hissy fit over it.''

"She's going to hate it, you know that."

"That, dear Jon, is a given, an absolute, a verity, and not one of the variables of our experiment."

"Tell *her* that." His grin showed through his beard. They were alone in the dark parking lot. "She'd like that. Tell her she's our control group in a scientific experiment. Tell her everybody else is a variable. She'll see it as science, then. Probably give you a grant to repeat it next year."

"Oh, Jon." Laughing, Naomi grasped one of his wrists and shook it as if he were a rag doll. "What would I do without you to loosen me up?" She released his hand with a sigh, and her laughter died. "If only that *would* do the trick with her."

"So it's all systems still go?"

"Yes, dammit!"

"No more changes?"

"Jon," she said warningly, her energy and her patience suddenly depleted at exactly the same time. "No. It's set in concrete, I swear. Just do it exactly as I planned it."

She turned away to open her car door, missing the inscrutable look on his face.

After lights out, Genia overheard Teri Fox whisper to Gabriella, "Do you know that older lady, what's her name, Lillian? You've both been here before, right? Do you know why she was crying?"

"I know why," the girl whispered back. "I heard that her oldest daughter died last year. Some horrible fast kind of cancer. She was only about forty, I heard."

"Wow, that's awful. No wonder. I don't think I'd ever stop crying."

"Really? It's been a whole year, though, since it happened."

There was a brief silence, during which the naive and callous statement hung in the air of the dark hogan like an unpleasant smell. Finally Teri whispered, "That's what you say now. Wait until you're a parent though."

Yes, Genia thought, that was exactly right. Her own heart hurt for the lively, funny woman with the silver hair. To lose a child? A year was nothing, nothing. She added Lillian Kleberg to her silent prayers. And then she added the roommate, Teri, for being kind to the girl. And then Gabriella, who might well need some extra prayers to help her mature into greater sensitivity to other people's suffering. Odd how she was acutely attuned to some suffering—the Native Americans', the earth's—and yet she couldn't relate to so simple and immediate a pain as a mother's loss.

If the whispering continued, Genia didn't hear it.

If the aspen leaves applauded the dropping of the night's curtain on the day, she didn't know it. In the nearby hills, something wild screamed.

Genia, completely worn out by her long day, slept on.

In the bedroom of Susan Van Sant's rented house in Cortez, she reached across the bed, grabbed a book out of Jon Warren's hands, and snapped it shut. It was *Legends of the Little People,* subtitled, *Tales of the Fremont.*

"Hey!" He protested in mock alarm. "I'm studying!"

She snuggled closer to him under the covers. "You're worse than I am, Warren. Forget the damn Ancient People for once and pay attention to this Modern Person."

They smiled at each other.

"What an attitude," Jon teased her, "for an archaeologist."

"Did you find out if we're still going ahead with it?"

"Naomi says all systems go."

"Even though Martina—"

"Even though. Despite, in spite of, possibly *to* spite her."

"She's not going to like it. I'm still not entirely comfortable with it myself."

"Jesus, it's a little late now, Suze. What don't you like? I thought we had it all worked out to please you."

"Jon! Don't make it sound as if I'm a prima donna. I'm protective of the sites, that's all. It's my job."

"And you do it well."

"Was that sarcasm?"

"No, Dopey. *That* was sarcasm." He smiled fondly at her and kissed her forehead where a straggle of blond hair bisected it. "What's still bothering you about it?"

"I'm still afraid you'll disturb things at the site. I mean, kids—"

"They'll be careful, Suze. I'll threaten them with a twenty-mile hike with their backpacks on if they're not."

She visibly relaxed a little. "Okay, then, I guess."

After a moment she repeated, "Martina's going to hate it. If anything goes wrong, it'll be all our jobs."

He threw up his hands in mock exasperation. "Suze! That site has survived for almost eight hundred years. It can tolerate a half hour with a bunch of modern teenagers."

They looked at each other, even his face registering doubt at his last words. When she saw the misgivings written there, she poked a finger into the middle of his bare chest. "See! See? You're not sure either!"

He pulled her face around until it was nose to nose with his and pronounced very slowly and clearly, "Stop worrying." A kiss naturally ensued, but when he tried to sneak his book back from her grasp, she wouldn't let him have it.

"Jon, is Naomi falling apart on us?"

He frowned and sighed, considering the question. "It sure looked like she was going to, didn't it? I don't know, Suze. She keeps holding it together all right."

"How bad are things really?"

"Don't ask me, I'm only the second banana around here. Why do you want to know all of a sudden? What are you hearing?"

"Everybody's complaining. You know, don't you? Or don't they tell you? Not enough supplies. Or the wrong ones. Or too many. Conflicting directions. Mistakes. And she seems . . . confused . . . instead of commanding."

"You'd like it if Naomi left, wouldn't you, Suze?"

"Jon! What a thing to say!"

"Yeah, but if somebody else took over, you could do more work in the field and get stuck less with the tourists."

"I like the teaching."

"Sure you do. But you're a field archaeologist with big ideas to prove." He let the implication hang in the air between them. And then he grinned. "You want me to show you commanding?"

Susan giggled as he pulled her closer. The giggle was a fake. Characteristically, he had avoided answering a tough question. *And if he thinks questions about Naomi are hard, wait until he hears what else I have to ask him,* Susan thought, closing her eyes for his kiss. Her response to that was faked, too, in spite of her hunger for him. It was impossible to feel aroused when all she really felt these days was panic.

She could talk to him about almost anything except what was most important to her. She tried to talk to him about her thrilling discovery and the theory it might prove—and make her famous—but at those times, he always seemed more interested in sex than history. Everything was so lighthearted to Jon, everything had to stay so cheerful and easy. He kidded her that she took life too seriously. "But I'm a scientist. That's what we do, Jon," she'd told him. "We have to take things seriously, otherwise what's the point?"

"You mean I'm not enough?" he'd said, and then laughed at his own outrageous conceit.

Now, even as his beard brushed her face, she was thinking, *Why can't I ask you the hard questions? When am I going to get up the courage to ask you what I really need to know—like, can I have you more often than now and then? Will you divorce your wife for me? You don't love her, do you? How could you, since you don't even live with her? You never talk about her, you won't even say her name. Who is she, where is she, what kind of marriage could it possibly be? Do you love me, instead of her? Will you marry me? What would you say if you knew I'm pregnant?*

She felt a cavernous loneliness and a desperate longing, even as she held him in her arms.

The book about the prehistoric Fremont people slid unnoticed to the floor.

In the morning, when a pair of male and female cardinals showed up at the feeder outside her bedroom, Susan blurted, "Jon, will you marry me?"

"Sure," he said, and then yawned. "I thought you'd never ask."

Completely astonished by his response, she decided to take what she could get for the moment and save the news about the pregnancy for later.

"What about your wife, Jon?"

He groaned in mock dismay and slapped the side of his face as if he'd forgotten that detail. "Damn. She'll be a bitch to divorce. I guess we'll have to kill her."

This time Susan's giggle was real, as authentic as the overwhelming relief that flooded through her body, releasing the desire she felt for him.

Nine

At the approach of seven o'clock on Monday morning, the kitchen staff at the Wheel tried desperately to stay safely out of their chef's way. They knew the signs when Bingo Chakmakjian was in one of her moods. Their boss might be tiny and only twenty-nine years old, but she was ferocious when roused by inefficiency or insincerity. The entire kitchen staff had witnessed an infuriating example of both of those dreaded sins this morning.

Not that anyone blamed Bingo for being upset about it.

Nobody was in a good mood, as a consequence.

And it was all due to the fact that Naomi had done it to them again: laying down certain food service instructions, and then reversing them at the last minute, all the while pretending she had never changed her plastic mind! Sometimes it was just a matter of "Hamburgers? No, Bingo, I said hot dogs." But today it was more serious, because they already had way too much work to do, without also having to save their director's butt—again—because she couldn't seem to remember her own instructions.

Behind Bingo's back, her staff agreed that if she and Naomi O'Neal weren't such good friends, Naomi probably would have had a pan of scrambled eggs dumped on her head when she stuck it in the kitchen this morning. It wouldn't have been the first time that Bingo had flung eggs—or a pot roast—at somebody who angered her. Unfortunately, instead of yelling at Naomi—who deserved it—Bingo had taken out her frustrations on her crew.

They were fiercely loyal to their chef, because Bingo fought like a bantamweight samurai against anybody who got in her staff's way or criticized them. So they tended to forgive her outbursts.

But the incident hadn't made Naomi any more popular.

Today the pink morning memo—which anybody could read, right up there on the kitchen bulletin board—had told them to cook for forty people for dinner tonight, and so Bingo had shopped and planned for just that number. But then Naomi had waltzed into the kitchen not half an hour ago and said in front of everybody, "With seventy-five people tonight, maybe we'd better set up the extra tables, Bingo."

Seventy-five?

While they held their collective breath, Naomi had stood there with her hands on her fat hips, looking as if clarified butter wouldn't melt in her mouth. Bingo had merely stared, and nodded, like she was Naomi's puppet. And yet they all knew—at least, they were pretty damn sure—that Bingo was *nobody's* marionette.

Bingo had exploded, all right, but only after Naomi left the kitchen. Then a knife had been slammed into a cutting board, a cast-iron skillet had gotten kicked across the floor by Bingo's hiking boots, and soprano curses had reverberated from the ovens to the freezers.

A couple of the kitchen workers were pretty annoyed about that. Why hadn't Bingo stood up to Naomi?

They'd all seen the morning memo with Naomi's own scrawl: "Forty for dinner." And they'd all seen her act as if she'd never even written that note and didn't have a clue what sort of chaos she was causing in the kitchen just by changing her mind at the last minute.

After Bingo finished coming apart at the seams, she had announced that she would drive to Cortez as soon as the markets opened, to buy enough poultry and milk to fix Uncle Dick's Chicken, the world's easiest entrée, requiring only those two ingredients plus oil, salt, and pepper. That was vintage Bingo, trying to make life easier for them, even when it was rough on her.

So now they all were even hotter and sweatier than usual and tiptoed around their chef, who was chopping tomatoes as if each one were a substitute for Naomi O'Neal's head:

Whack. Whack. Whack.

All this, and they hadn't even started loading up the food van that was going to transport a week's worth of meals for a camping tour for sixteen teenagers from Texas! Or the portable lunch for the women on the hiking tour. Or the usual preparations for the lunch crowd in the dining hall.

Bingo was, as usual, doing several things at one time: chopping the tomatoes for the breakfast scramble, keeping an eye on the boiling water for the cheese grits, and making sure nobody let the cinnamon rolls overcrisp in the oven.

Above all the labor and clatter rose the music of one of Bingo's damn classical records by that Armenian cousin of hers. It was a symphony this time, with violins and kettledrums sounding all moody and ominous. One of her staff's few gripes against her was that she rarely allowed them to switch to rock and roll or anything anybody else wanted to hear; as long as she was in the kitchen, it had to be that boring classical stuff.

What Bingo needed, they agreed among themselves, was some time away from the kitchen, maybe to go hiking with Dr. Van Sant and that group of women who had arrived yesterday. Because if *she* didn't get away—soon—*they* were going to need some time off from her.

All in all, it felt like a black day in the kitchen.

★ ★ ★

As recorded trumpets soared gloriously above the clatter of food preparation, Bingo was thinking about Naomi, too, although somewhat indirectly. She was thinking about how some women on the Indian reservations still processed corn the old way: pounding it, sifting it, then allotting the smaller kernels to cornmeal, the larger ones to hominy. Naomi's management style was like that: to delegate the smaller jobs to people who couldn't handle anything bigger yet, and the larger jobs to people who could. Some people said Naomi thought *she* was the only one "who could," and that's why so many things were getting screwed up these days.

Once, on a Cherokee reservation, Bingo had watched a Cherokee woman with a North Carolina accent burn a corncob in a bowl to seal in the natural oils so it could be used to hold liquids.

"We're leaking," Bingo muttered to herself, "like an unoiled bowl."

Sweat dampened the white terrycloth band she wore to keep her short black hair back off her face as she cooked. The knife she wielded looked much too large for her hand, but she flailed it with the grace and panache of a samurai, cutting the red meat of the tomatoes cleanly, dicing evenly. Only the barest minimum of juice flowed on her cutting board.

She was also thinking of the food she'd bought Sunday for the menu that now she wasn't going to be able to prepare. Some of it she could save, freeze, and use later, but some of it would spoil if she couldn't use it today. Bingo hated waste. She hated what it did to her budget, much less what it did to the earth.

"We're leaking like a sieve," she muttered. "And if we don't get plugged up soon, this whole place is just going to drain away." Just yesterday one of the housekeepers had told her Naomi was ordering way too much of the wrong cleaning supplies and not enough of the right ones.

Whack!

Bingo missed the tomato and sliced into the cutting board. "Dammit!" she yelled.

As one, her crew flinched, glanced at one another, worked faster.

There was something else Bingo had heard on that Cherokee reservation. The old tribes had a tradition where the widow of a great chief would be designated the Beloved Woman. She got to decide whether they'd go to war, and whether captives lived or died.

"That's power," Bingo muttered. "Life or death."

She sliced cleanly, viciously, through another tomato.

Her crew stayed out of her way. The symphonic kettledrums pounded. The strings wept their dramatic, dolorous song. Bingo glanced up at the kitchen bulletin board, where she posted everything from Naomi's pink morning memos to family photos—her staff's families—and her own personal favorite quotations.

Her glance went automatically to a three-by-five index card that she had thumbtacked in the very center of the board. Once white, but now yellow and greasy from hanging around in a kitchen for so long, the card contained a quote from the jacket notes of an album of music by her very favorite composer in the whole world. The composer was Alan Hovhaness, who was of Armenian descent, just like her. His real last name—Chakmakjian—was the same as hers, so most people assumed he was a distant cousin, or something. He wasn't, but what he said, in the quote on the card, was Bingo's philosophy of life and of cooking.

For probably the thousandth time in her life, she read:

"Things that are very complicated tend to disappear and get lost. Simplicity is difficult, not easy. Beauty is simple. All unnecessary elements are removed—only essence remains."

It made perfect sense to her.

"The essence of this camp is truth," Bingo decided, as she slid the chopped tomatoes out of the way to make room for green peppers. "But if that's the case, why does everything seem so complicated all of a sudden?"

She felt furious all over again and took it out on the peppers.

Ten

The first time Genia woke up on Monday morning, it was to the sound of whispering, but it sounded like an argument.

"How could you *lose* it!"

"I didn't lose it! It's just gone. Maybe it fell out, or somebody took it—"

"Why would somebody take a bottle of shampoo?"

"I don't know! Oh, this is just the worst thing that could happen! Maybe they needed shampoo, for God's sake. I don't *know* what happened to it. It's just gone."

"Are you sure? Did you look?"

"I emptied everything out."

"God, if somebody finds it—"

"Dead. We're dead."

"Not if I kill you first."

"It's not my *fault*—"

It was Teri and Judith, Genia decided, with her eyes still closed. Fighting like children. Or maybe she was dreaming. She turned over under her covers. The whispering abruptly stopped. Genia went back to sleep immediately.

"Genia?" Again a whispery voice roused her. Sleepily, she thought, *Not again! This is getting annoying.* "Do you want to sleep in, or should I wake you up for breakfast?"

"Heavens," Genia said, opening her eyes fast and blinking in the strong sunlight that was now pouring in the windows of the hogan. She looked up into the pretty face and blue eyes of Gabriella, who was smiling hesitantly down at her. "I'll get up. Thank you! How much time have I got?"

"It's seven forty-five." Her roommate gave her a cheery wave, said, "See you later," and exited, leaving Genia alone in the hogan. She hadn't heard Teri or Judith leave, but she vaguely recalled overhearing them argue about something. What was it? Shampoo? Surely not—she must have been dreaming. Once she'd been compelled by nature to get up in the dark, fumble into her robe and slippers, and make her way as quietly as possible out the door of their hogan and down the path to the women's restroom. At first it had seemed a terrible bother, and cold and a little scary to boot. But once she had got outside and looked up at the sky, the sight of all those millions of stars shining just for her had turned her nocturnal errand from nuisance to gift.

Knowing she had over an hour before the kitchen closed, she lay for a few moments in contented comfort, snuggled under two wool blankets. She thought she smelled piñon smoke, again, and garlic. It was that last smell that tugged her out of bed by her nose and got her up and showered and dressed and finally walking down the path toward the dining hall. She was overjoyed to find it was a gorgeous morning. Composing an imaginary postcard to her children, she described the day as "cool and fresh as a glass of orange juice, crisp as bacon, sunny as scrambled eggs." Genia laughed at herself and walked a little faster. She knew she must be really hungry, to be describing weather as if it were food!

Suddenly, from behind her back, came a thundering herd.

"Excuse me!"

"Sorry, ma'am!"

"Pardon us!"

The shouts were from a crowd of teenagers who appeared, running, seemingly out of nowhere, then converged upon her and flowed around her as if she were a slow leaf in a fast stream. The words were loud, but Genia noted they were quite polite, spoken with a pronounced drawl—*"Axcyuze myeh! Sawreh, mayham! Pahrd'n uhyus!"*

Three adults zoomed around her, too—a woman and two men—and the woman grinned at Genia as they trotted by. "Please excuse us. It's a stampede." Genia smiled back at her and came to a snap conclusion: These were the sixteen honor students. Jon Warren, the assistant director, was taking them on a camp-out starting today, and those other two adults must be teachers who had accompanied them—from Texas, judging by the accents.

She watched the kids race up the steps of the veranda to get dibs on the rocking chairs, where they sat chattering and laughing at top volume, while the three adults caught up to them. Jon Warren climbed the stairs to face the kids, but the woman and the other man slumped onto a bottom step and stayed there. With the kitchen open for another forty minutes, Genia decided breakfast could wait a little while longer; she'd find a comfortable rock and stick around to see what was going on here.

Jon wore khaki shorts this morning and a faded T-shirt over well-scuffed hiking boots and thick socks that sagged a bit at the cuffs. Seen now in daylight, Genia decided he was a very attractive man behind his beard and mustache, and she suspected that several of the young girls on the porch would have crushes on him before the week was out. Probably a few of the boys, too, she corrected herself, because that's how the world was and always had been and no doubt always would be. She watched him lean his upper back casually against a post, as if he had all the time in the world to wait for the kids to settle down. On the bottom step, the teachers did nothing to contain the happy chaos but appeared quite willing to turn the stampede over to him.

A couple of kids looked over at Jon, and then shushed their neighbors. Soon they were all looking at him expectantly. Genia thought they were adorable; fresh-faced and rambunctious as the young calves on her ranch in the spring. *Stampede* had been the right word for it.

"Okay, cowpokes," he said casually, in a pleasant, clear voice that carried easily down to Genia's rock. It was, she decided, definitely the same voice she'd heard on the telephone. "First: Remember the names of the three main prehistoric cultures in the American Southwest. Mogollon. Say after me—"

"Mo—gol—lon!"

"Hohokam."

"Ho-ho-kam!"

A few of them got the giggles at that and started chanting "ho, ho, ho" like demented Santa Clauses. Jon Warren merely smiled, as if he'd heard it before, and gave them a bit of time to get it out of their systems. There was a lot of laughter, and Genia chuckled, too. They were an infectious bunch, carrying the germ of high spirits.

Finally, Jon spoke again. "Anasazi."

"An-a-sa-zi!"

"Think of the Mogollon as covering parts of Arizona, New Mexico, and old Mexico. The Hohokam were in Arizona." Genia's ears perked up. A clue! she thought. Maybe it was Hohokam who had made her pottery and seashells. "And this is Anasazi land, which also touched Utah, Arizona, New Mexico, and even Nevada. There was a smaller group, the Fremont, who were also in Utah, and a mysterious little bunch named the Sineaqua down near Flagstaff, Arizona. All three of the main cultures we're talking about go back to about 200 A.D. Say after me—"

"Two-hun-dred-eh-dee!"

He laughed, and so did they.

"Starting about 1150 A.D., the Anasazi, suddenly and for reasons that are still mysterious to us, started building large and sophisticated communities in canyons and up on cliffs. Then an astonishing thing happened. After all that brilliance and effort, they abandoned those sites. By 1250 A.D., only a hundred years later, there was hardly anyone left in any of those places. That's the two-part mystery: First, why did they build them, and second, why did they abandon them?"

Hands shot up, as if he meant for them to answer.

Genia saw him smile and then pat the air with his hands, to calm his listeners. "Wait. Don't jump to conclusions. You'll have the next four days to visit actual sites, examine evidence, and come up with your own brilliant ideas. Maybe you'll think of something no scientist has ever thought of before." Genia saw three or four of the kids look at each other, as if that idea seemed reasonable and pleased them. "Keep in mind that the people themselves did not disappear, as is commonly and mistakenly thought. It's not like they were abducted by aliens." The kids laughed. "Over time they drifted south, mostly, and became the ancestors of some of our existing Indian nations. Direct descendants of the Anasazi are as close to us now as the nearest Pueblo reservation."

One of the hands that had shot up was still raised, and now it waved insistently. Jon pointed to the boy attached to it. "Yeah?"

"I've heard the Pueblos hate the name *Anasazi*. Is that true?"

"Many do, yes, because it's a Navajo word. It was given to that particular group of Ancient People by a man named Richard Wetherill who was the first white man to discover the ruins on Mesa Verde. In Navajo it means "Ancient Ones" or "Ancient Tribe" or "Enemy Ancestors," depending on who's doing the translating. The Pueblos prefer their own name, *Hisatsenom*. Problem is, the name *Anasazi* has caught on with everybody except the Pueblos, so it's probably going to stick. I use the two names pretty much interchangeably, depending on who I'm talking to. What do you think we ought to call them?"

"Hisatsenom" was the boy's quick answer, although he stumbled on the pronunciation, and Jon had to coach him a couple of times before he got it right.

"Heesahtseenome."

All up and down the line of rocking chairs, the kids experimented with the unfamiliar sound of it. It seemed to be settled quickly; these white, brown, black, and golden children wanted to call the Ancient Ones by the name given to them by their own descendants.

That settled, Jon said, "Next: In the early days of discovery and exploration by white people, prehistoric sites were plundered before anybody realized the importance of preserving them. By and large, they weren't in much danger from Indians, because native people tended to consider them sacred or taboo and leave them alone. The Utes lived on Mesa Verde for centuries, for instance, without ever touching the artifacts left in the ruins. But when white people got wind of them—both scientists and amateur pot hunters—it took only a short time to strip them of practically everything that had been left in them. The empty ruins you see now were not always that way. If you could have seen them when they were first discovered, you'd have been amazed: they were full of pots, turquoise, beads, weapons, feathers, blankets, even preserved food and clothing, some skeletons—in fact, thousands of artifacts that were stolen for private collections, or sold, or to put into museums.

"It's very misleading to see the ruins as they are now. It makes you think the Ancient People packed up every single thing and took it with them when they left, but that wasn't so. In fact, when Richard Wetherill and his brother 'discovered' Cliff Palace Ruin, his brother told people that it looked as if the residents had just left only a couple of days earlier and maybe even planned on coming back."

Another hand shot up—again, a boy.

"Is this going to be like a museum?" He sounded disappointed. "Where we can't touch anything?"

"No," Jon answered. "Don't touch the petroglyphs or pictographs, and don't pick up any pots if you come across them. But you can pick up pot shards, just so long as you put them back down exactly where you found them. And don't *take* anything, all right? No Hisatsenom souvenirs. Not even the smallest bit of old pot. It's illegal. Federal offense. Big time. Other than that, don't worry, I'll make sure you get the chance to examine plenty of artifacts very closely."

Sitting on her rock, Genia felt as guilty as a felon.

Oh dear, she thought, *can I put those bits and pieces back exactly where I found them?* A determination began to grow within her to do what she could to preserve the integrity of the little prehistoric site on her ranch.

A girl was waving her hand as if it were a handkerchief.

"Dr. Warren? Don't the Indians hate archaeology?"

Genia watched him shake his head, and she heard the comically rueful tone to his answer. "Why don't you ask me something easy—like who invented the wheel, and is there really a God?"

On the steps below him, the teachers laughed out loud.

But the kids just waited, some of them looking a little smug, some appearing not to get the joke, and none of them letting him off the hook. He freed himself by turning the question over to a young woman who had been listening from the doorway that led into the dining hall.

"Susan?" he called to her. "You want to take this one? Kids, this is Dr. Van Sant, who may look like your little sister but is actually one of those nasty archaeologists you're asking about.

She talks funny, but she's okay, really." He gave her an ironic little salute and said, "Good luck, Suze."

She stepped into the sun at the front of the veranda.

"Thanks a lot, Jon" was her equally ironic retort. Genia thought her slight English accent made her words sound delightfully crisp and amused. In the morning light, with her blond pigtails and freckled face and in her shorts, T-shirt, and sandals, she really didn't look much older than the teenagers in front of her.

"Okay," she began straightforwardly. "I think what you're really asking is, are you going to be offending Native Americans by visiting these ruins? I think you're worried about being disrespectful, am I right?"

Sure enough, heads nodded all up and down the row.

Genia wondered what this scientist would say in defense of her life's work—her "destiny" to find out where the pot in her childhood dream had gone.

"A lot of Native Americans loathe us, yes," she admitted. "They hate it when their ancestral homes are dug up, they are deeply, deeply offended when we disturb the graves, and they just wish we would all go away, preferably back into Europe, where we came from. I have to tell you, that's the truth. I will also say, however, that there are some Native Americans who are themselves archaeologists. And some tribes may despise what they see as the desecration of their sacred trust but they also see the political possibilities our work has for them. It's a very tough call for most of them. But I won't try to hide from you the fact that mostly they don't like it. So why do we do it?"

It appeared to be merely a rhetorical question for her, as if she had long ago worked out an answer that satisfied, for her, any nagging ethical questions.

"I don't know if I can give you an answer that will satisfy you. I could say we do it because that's who we are. We seem

THE BLUE CORN MURDERS 75

to be a people who want to know things. We're driven by our curiosity, half the time. Maybe that's good or maybe it's bad, I'll leave that to you to decide for yourselves. But speaking only for myself, I can swear to you that I love and respect the cultures I am investigating. I believe the work I do helps to encourage the rest of the world to show more respect to the Indians." She paused and cocked her head, as if questioning them. "I don't know if that's a good enough rationalization for you, or for the tribes. I do know that for all the damage we may have done in the last century, we've also saved a lot of important sites that would otherwise have gone under the plow, the bulldozer, or the road grader.

"You want to show respect?" she asked them, looking directly into their young, attentive faces one by one. "Then enter the ruins with respect. Move around—with respect. Touch—with respect. Speak of the living and the dead tribes—with respect. Believe me, if you do only that much, it will be an improvement over the way they have been treated by our cultures in the past."

Then suddenly she smiled broadly at them.

"You ask wonderful questions. Important ones. Absolutely top of the line. Please take these important questions with you on your trip. One day it will be your generation's turn to make these decisions. So if you see things that bother you, go ahead and let them bother you. Feel them. Think about them. Talk and argue about them. Find out what you really think about things like archaeology and restoration and American history. That's what education is all about, learning how to think for yourself while at the same time considering the effects of your thoughts on the whole big picture."

She turned and gave Jon Warren a friendly shove.

"For heaven's sake, don't take *his* word for anything!"

Laughing, he asked the group, "Does anybody have a question that's more interesting than pancakes and waffles?" Not a single hand shot up. "I thought so. Time for breakfast. You've earned it. Be packed and ready to board the vans, right down there in the parking lot, by ten o'clock sharp, or we *will* leave without you. Your teachers and I will be waiting for you." He grinned at them. "Sixteen kids to three adults? Now there's a ratio you ought to be able to work your way around. I have a feeling we're going to have our hands full with you smart guys."

The kids grinned back at him, pleased at the flattery.

On the bottom steps their teachers looked over at each other.

"Now, on your marks, ready, set, go!"

A mad rush into the dining room ensued, and Genia realized that she'd made a tactical error: Now she'd be last in the cafeteria line, following the great ravenous eating machines called "teenagers."

Still, it was worth it, because she had received her first solid clue about the identity of the prehistoric tenants of her land. And she thought she'd detected another interesting clue as well: a clear flash of mutual attraction between the pretty young archaeologist and the handsome young assistant director.

It was only when she walked up behind the teachers on the veranda that she realized they were arguing, in low, furious tones, with Jon Warren.

Eleven

"What do you mean three adults?" The male teacher was right up in Jon's face, keeping his voice quiet but in no way hiding his obvious fury. The kids had all gone inside, but Genia could not avoid the scene; they were blocking the door to the dining room. "You said there'd be at least two student interns going along with us on this trip. I have the letter from your director, saying that. We counted on that, we told the parents—we *promised* their parents—there would be approximately three adults present for every five kids."

"Naomi wouldn't have said—"

"I beg your pardon," the woman teacher interrupted icily. "You want to see the letter?"

"I have seen a million letters just like that," Jon responded, obviously trying to keep his composure and to encourage them to find theirs again. "And it's always the same ratio of grown-ups to kids. Look, we can go to her office and find her copy. I know she wouldn't have said—"

The male teacher was already squatting down on the veranda and opening his briefcase. He quickly pulled out a sheet of white paper, stood up, and thrust it at Jon.

"I'll save you the trouble. Read it."

Jon took it and read it through. Genia, who had walked farther on down the veranda and was trying to appear to be looking at the scenery, glanced over and saw him frown and then shake his head when he reached a certain point in the letter. He looked up at the angry teachers. "I don't know what to say."

"That's easy. Say you'll give us two more adults."

But he looked frustrated and embarrassed and spread out his hands as if appealing to them. Genia didn't feel too bad about eavesdropping, since they were blocking her way into breakfast. She heard Jon Warren say, "I can't. I mean, we'll go find Naomi and ask her, but I know what she'll say. There isn't anybody free this week who can go." He tried smiling at them. "Look, is it really such a problem? These seem like great kids. The three of us can handle them easily, don't you think?"

"The parents expect—"

"This is outrageous, completely irresponsible."

"I'm tempted to say we ought to cancel the whole camping trip and haul them back home."

"Jesus, don't do that. Think how disappointed the kids would be." Jon handed the letter back. "Look, there's got to be a way to handle this. Let's go find our director and talk it over with her."

Genia admired the way he managed to get them in the door and off the porch. She waited a couple of seconds, then followed her grumbling stomach into the dining hall. She saw the three of them marching off toward a door marked "office," while she made a beeline straight for the source of the delicious aromas.

Twenty minutes later, six members of the Women's Hike into History were lingering over their breakfast dishes, arguing happily with one another about what had *really* happened to the Ancient People who abandoned their dwellings by 1250 A.D. Genia had started it all, by repeating for them the brief history lesson she'd heard Jon Warren give the teenagers.

"Drought?" guessed Teri Fox, her hazel eyes eager in her brown face.

"Overpopulation," asserted Judith Belove, her resonant voice giving her slightest opinion the aura of fact, "which depleted the agricultural capacities of the land."

"Disease?" Teri countered. She and Judith both were dressed for hiking in boots, socks, shorts, and T-shirts, with windbreaker jackets laid to the side while they ate. "Like a thirteenth-century AIDS epidemic?"

"War." Judith made that, too, sound definite.

"There *was* a lengthy drought," Lillian Kleberg contributed, obviously speaking as the voice of experience at the Wheel. She looked cool and composed in her neat plaid shirt and loose trousers, Genia thought, with no sign of the tears she'd shed the night before at the Talking Circle. Genia's heart went out to Lillian. One of the hardest things about losing a child, she had always suspected, was that people might never look at you the same way again. You might always be, forever after, the parent whose child had died, and an object of secret pity in the eyes of other people. That fact alone might be enough to make you want to start over again, anonymously, somewhere where nobody knew you. What was it Lillian had said before she burst into tears? Genia tried to recall: *Something about wishing she could walk away from her past and never look back?* Genia thought she could understand that longing, although wouldn't that mean giving up memories of the lost child, too?

"They may well have overused the land above the cliff dwellings," Lillian was saying, with one finger in the air as she made her point. "But those factors alone are usually not considered sufficient to account for such a complete and permanent exodus. There aren't many signs of armed conflict, so most archaeologists think war is an unlikely cause of the abandonment. And there aren't any indications that rampant disease wiped them out. They weren't wiped out, anyway; they just moved south." She grinned. "Aren't you impressed by how much I know?"

"I certainly am." Genia smiled back at her.

"Aliens," said Madeline Rose, and they all laughed—even Genia, who'd heard more or less the same joke from Jon Warren.

At the side of the dining hall, where she was seated on the sill of an open window, Naomi stared outside, watching for a car to arrive. Some people might have thought that her morning couldn't possibly have gotten any worse, but she knew better. Indulging a masochistic urge, she was just going to sit there and wait for it to arrive.

She was also half-listening to the women talking.

At the Talking Circle last night, she had thought Teri and Judy seemed like nice people. Madeline Rose could prove to be a pill—one of those people who joined a group only to make a point of not participating in it. But she seemed to be getting along with everyone this morning. She certainly looked like a catalog-order fashion plate, safari jacket and all. Naomi recalled Madeline's response to the Talking Circle, but thought, trying to be fair, that instant self-revelation wasn't for everybody. Eugenia Potter seemed pleasant, too. Interesting, about her finding those artifacts at her ranch. Hohokam, no doubt. She must be tougher than she looked, to be a cattle rancher. Would cows, Naomi wondered as she stared unhappily out the window, be any easier to herd than tourists? Or trustees?

God, those Texas teachers!

What a mess.

Between Naomi and Jon, they'd been able to appease the angry teachers somewhat. Enough, at least, for them to agree to continue with the trip. Now they were eating their breakfasts, a little apart from their teenagers, and talking together with an intensity that made Naomi feel nervous just to look at them.

How could I have made a mistake like that?

Naomi felt bewildered. She honestly didn't remember writing the letter that way. What in the world could she have been thinking? Her problems felt like such a vicious circle: Typically, she was accused of giving orders (or writing letters!) that she didn't remember issuing, and then her frustration over *that* left her so preoccupied that she made other mistakes.

Naomi had never minded confessing to her faults, but she felt so damn innocent of most of them these days. Jon had been great with the teachers, she thought gratefully. He even told her, "I'll bet I distracted you when you were writing the letter, Naomi. It's really my fault." Absurd but sweet, bless him. At least he wasn't mad at her this morning. Bingo was, again, and Naomi didn't know why, and Bingo didn't seem to want to talk about it. And the housekeeping staff were ticked off, claiming they were out of toilet paper when Naomi swore she'd ordered a month's worth only two weeks ago. Could somebody be stealing supplies? she'd asked them. That had only insulted and incensed them further, of course.

It seemed she couldn't win.

A whispery voice recalled her attention to the table of women.

"The Native Americans know where the Ancient Ones went, and they know why, too!"

Reluctantly, Naomi turned her head to search out the source of the defensive-sounding whisper, and then she watched as Gabby Russell spoke heatedly to her tablemates. "I don't know why nobody ever listens to them!"

What Naomi knew, and what the tourists didn't know, was that Gabby was infamous around the Wheel as a member of a dreaded tribe, the Indian Wannabes. This morning, Naomi saw, the ersatz Pocahontas wore her usual surfeit of symbols—

beaded headband, fringed vest, turquoise earrings, squash blossom necklace—and that was merely what was visible from the waist up. Naomi wouldn't have been surprised to see the girl stand and show off a turquoise belt buckle, her ridiculous fringed leather trousers, and, of course, those damn moccasins. The ensemble was worth about a hundred times more money than most real Indians could ever afford. Didn't the girl ever stop to think how she must appear in their eyes? On top of which, Gabby exhibited one of the major propensities of Wannabes—a hair-trigger defensiveness on behalf of any Indian who had ever lived.

Naomi had met tribal *chiefs* who didn't spring to their people's defense as rabidly as Gabby did; she'd met celebrated Native American revolutionaries and modern warriors, and not even they claimed that every single Indian was perfect in every way. It was only Wannabes who insisted on the romantic ideal of the "unspoiled native." It was a dangerous obsession, Naomi thought, because idealists tended to get so furious when reality failed to meet their impossible expectations. They could go from "loving" Indians to hating them, the instant any real Indian behaved like a real person. Gabby was one of the most extreme versions of the breed that Naomi had ever encountered.

At her perch on the windowsill, Naomi sighed. She was almost amused at the clear sound of martyrdom in her own breath. But Lord, Wannabes were such a pain in the ass. Generally she found them to be ignorant of their own culture, whatever that might be. They usually hated their own history without even understanding it, and so they wanted to adopt somebody else's. But they wanted only the beautiful and noble parts of Indian civilization, not the dark parts like internecine warfare, slavery, human sacrifice, even cannibalism—all those nasty little habits that made the American aboriginals strictly human, just like everybody else on the planet at those particular stages of development.

Naomi knew that Susan Van Sant—even more than most archaeologists—hated Wannabes, had no patience with them, considered them to be among the most annoying and silly creatures on the face of the earth. Unfortunately, this beautiful phony Indian maiden was a prime example of the species, and Gabby simply *loved* signing up for programs at the Wheel. Naomi thought sympathetically that Susan was going to have her hands full, what with Lillian's fragile emotional state, Madeline's sharp tongue, Teri's avowed aversion to dirt and exercise, and Gabby's tiresome earnestness.

Naomi already felt so miserable that she might as well just really rub it in. So giving in to a wicked impulse, she called over to the women's table: "So tell us, Gabby, what really *did* happen to the Anasazi?"

"There's a Navajo legend," Gabby said—but then all of a sudden she stopped in midsentence. Naomi looked at the mulish, nervous expression on the girl's face and came to the amazing conclusion that Gabby was afraid of her. *Well, well,* Naomi thought, *and is that because of my supposed archaeological authority? Or is it because she foresees the entirely likely probability that I will think she's a fool and an idiot?*

"Yes?" Naomi prodded mercilessly.

Gabriella Russell set her jaw and carried on. "I'm writing an article about it." She made it sound as if that fact alone proved its truth. "I'm going to get it published in a major magazine. Or maybe a newspaper syndicate will pick it up."

She looked satisfied to have all of their attention now.

"Well, according to the legend, there was a great gambler who won all of the people and took them north into slavery. You've got to understand that I'm not talking about modern-type gambling; gambling was a sacred activity for the Ancients, as it still is for some Indians today. This great gambler was a cruel and powerful man, however, and he forced them to build all of the great houses at Chaco Canyon, which were actually fabulous gaming palaces for him. But finally, after the people had suffered a great deal for many years, another gambler came along, and with the help of the gods, he won the people back their freedom. And that's why they left this area so suddenly, and moved back to their original homelands."

A few feet away, Dr. Susan Van Sant, who was just entering the dining hall, dropped her breakfast tray. Silverware flew. Hot scrambled eggs covered her sandals, but she didn't flinch. Tomato juice ran like a thick stream of blood down her left leg. The clatter of the fallen tray echoed in the large room like gunfire.

Twelve

When Susan dropped her tray, Genia noticed several things about the moment, flashing pictures that she would vividly recall later.

There was a look of shock on the archaeologist's face.

There was the alacrity with which Jon Warren jumped up to grab paper napkins and how he crouched on the floor to wipe off Susan's bare legs and her feet in their sandals. Naomi also went over to help, although more sedately.

There was the way everybody at her table jumped, and the way Madeline Rose then frowned and glared, as if the entire incident had been designed to annoy and offend her personally.

And not least, there was the hateful glance that the executive director of Medicine Wheel had cast in the direction of Gabriella only moments before.

But most of all, there was the dramatic entrance into the tableau of someone entirely new.

"Well, Naomi," said an elderly and elegant woman standing in the doorway with her hands on her hips, "I heard things were a mess, but I didn't expect to find our director and our assistant director down on their knees cleaning the floor." Her hair looked as black as Colorado coal, and it was stiffly coiffed to frame a face that had a stretched look around the mouth, as if a plastic surgeon had pulled the skin a bit too tight, or too often. Her voice, harsh and commanding, made Genia think of ravens and crows. The fact that she wore a black trouser suit only perfected the impression of a black bird. "Are we broke? Did you fire the maintenance people? And what in the world happened to you, Dr. Van Sant? Is that blood? Are you hurt? Did you cut yourself?"

"No," the archaeologist said slowly, in a hollow-sounding voice. She stood looking down at the heads of the people who were helping her. "I dropped my tray."

Naomi O'Neal, who was on her knees with scrambled eggs in both hands, flushed nearly as red as the tomato juice running down the archaeologist's leg. "Martina," she said, stumbling over the first letter of the name. "Hi." She looked as if she knew exactly how foolish she sounded. "I'll be right with you. Why don't you help yourself to breakfast, while we clean this up?"

Genia watched the haughty newcomer stride toward the cafeteria and was positive she heard the woman mutter, "It's going to take more than a rag and mop to clean up after you people."

Judith Belove said to the rest of them, in her low vibrant voice that could carry across an auditorium, much less a dining room that had been shocked into silence: "Somebody please tell me that woman won't be in our group."

Lillian grinned. "Sorry, she's the empty chair. That's Martina Alvarez, she's on the board of trustees. I'm surprised she signed up. I've never known Martina to walk any farther than it would take to go from her limousine to her bank. And by 'her bank,' I do mean *her* bank. Just a little bitty modest thing in Colorado Springs that's been owned by her family for three generations." Lillian grinned and looked as if she were thoroughly enjoying the chance to gossip. To Genia, her hair looked as soft and natural in the morning light as Martina Alvarez's had looked dyed, stiff, and unnatural. Lillian and Martina must be about the same age, Genia decided, although the haughty trustee might have the edge on being older. She certainly had the edge on trying to *look* younger. "She's so rich, she could probably build her own ruins to live in."

Madeline Rose laughed. "And call it Archaeology World?"

Just about the time the dining room had settled back into normality, the swinging doors into the cafeteria slammed open and the trustee stalked out again. "Naomi!" Even the teenagers across the hall looked up. "Tell that chef of yours to serve me breakfast! She says it's after nine o'clock and I'm too late to eat!"

The beleaguered executive director got slowly to her feet, after having swept bits of egg, toast, and bacon back onto a tray. She brushed herself off before she answered the woman. "Martina," she said with surprising dignity, considering the circumstances, "given a choice between making you angry or making Bingo mad, I'll take my chances with you. The breakfast doors close at nine. That's the rule, and we all have to follow it, even members of the board of trustees. You can still get coffee, and maybe I can scrounge up some cereal for you. Will that be all right?"

The dark-haired woman fumed, "I can't believe this."

She turned on her expensive-looking heels and walked out of the dining hall, exiting through the front door, without another word to anyone there.

After a long moment in which even the teenagers were quiet, Genia heard the sound of soft clapping.

It was Jon Warren, applauding his boss.

"Go, Naomi," he cheered in a quiet voice that everyone could hear. At Genia's table Madeline Rose also began to clap, and soon the large room was ringing with whistles and applause. Genia observed that Susan Van Sant had long before left the room, without helping to clean up any of the mess she'd made.

★   ★   ★

Susan leaned heavily against the back wall of the lodge. She felt sick enough to throw up but prayed she wouldn't. She told herself to calm down. She was being hysterical, she thought; she was making much of nothing. But still she felt ill, queasy with panic.

If somebody saw her like this, what would she say?

"I look like death warmed over because I just saw my whole career flash before my eyes?"

No, she couldn't say that.

She couldn't say she was frightened of the damage one *stupid* little Wannabe could do to all of her secret ambitions, hoarded and nurtured for three years. She couldn't say it, because then she'd give it all away too soon, even quicker than that *stupid* girl could do.

Susan made herself take long, deep breaths, forcing the air past the knot of nausea. She made herself slow her breathing again . . . inhale . . . exhale . . .

Dammit!

She whirled around and slammed her open palms against the wooden planks of the building. If Gabby published that crazy gambler story, no reputable scientist would ever believe anything like it. She'd ruin everything, everything.

Susan's hands stung.

She bent over and threw up into the closest bush, just as Bingo Chakmakjian walked out the back door.

"Suze!"

She felt the chef's small hands on her bent back, patting her, trying to soothe her.

Susan finally straightened up, avoiding Bingo's concerned gaze.

"What's the matter, Suze? You got the flu? Couldn't be food poisoning, not from my kitchen."

The archaeologist said the first truth that popped into her head.

"I'm pregnant, Bingo."

"Ohmigod. Jon?"

"Jon."

"Do I congratulate you?"

"Don't buy any strollers yet. He doesn't know."

"You going to tell him?"

"When he gets back from this trip with those kids. Don't say—"

"Anything to anybody. Of course not. But you're sick— how are you going to manage . . ."

"It usually passes. Literally."

"Tell 'em you're hung over."

Susan nodded miserably.

"I'll get you a glass of water."

But when the chef returned, the archaeologist was already gone. Bingo stood for a moment listening to the strains of Alan Hovhaness's Exile Symphony no. 2, played by the Seattle Symphony, Gerard Schwarz conducting. It sounded as if he were conducting it in her kitchen. *Beauty is simple,* Bingo thought, *and if that's the case, this situation is not beautiful.* Because it wasn't going to be simple. Jon Warren was married. Separated. They'd never seen the wife, he never talked about her, Bingo didn't even know the woman's name or where she lived. But Jon never claimed to be divorced. And now with a pregnant archaeologist girlfriend throwing up in the bushes.

Bingo shook her head in disgust. *You'd think a scientist would be more careful. You'd think a scientist would know better. You'd think a scientist would know how to control her experiments. You'd think!*

Teri Fox, who had left pancakes on her plate, sliced into them, saying, "I've waited long enough. I'm hungry again." But when she lifted a bit toward her mouth, she exclaimed, "My God. They're blue!"

Lillian laughed at her reaction and hurried to explain that

they were made from blue cornmeal. "One of Bingo's favorite ingredients."

Teri made a face and joked, "My great-grandmother always said, never eat blue food."

"Your great-grandmother," said Gabby archly, without appearing to think first, "was not a Native American."

"Boy, is that ever the truth!" was Teri's ironic, good-humored reply. She was wearing a white baseball cap and a white T-shirt that made the rich walnut shade of her complexion look even darker than usual. "My ancestors were definitely imported, not native."

Gabby's face reddened, and she tightened her lips. "The Native Americans," she said angrily, "have suffered more than anybody, and they still suffer more."

The black schoolteacher looked astonished, as if she couldn't believe that Gabby had pushed even further into her original faux pas. Anger crossed her face, too, but then she merely said, even rather gently, "Well, it's not a contest, is it?"

Gabby shrugged with an ill grace that made Genia want to grasp her firmly by the shoulders and pack her off to her room and leave her there until she found her manners again. There seemed to be two Gabbys—a sweet thoughtful one who made sure her roommate didn't miss breakfast, and a rude fanatical one.

The awkward moment passed quickly, because Teri kindly made it so, by steering the conversation along other lines. Gabby, however, remained stiff-jawed and silent as the other women went on getting to know one another. "Where are you from?" Genia asked. She learned the answer to that was Salt Lake City for Lillian, Tulsa for the teachers, Denver for Madeline, and Santa Fe for Gabriella, who didn't answer for herself but allowed Lillian to answer for her. It turned out that Madeline was in real estate, Lillian was a retired government employee, and that Gabby truly was a freelance writer specializing in stories about Native Americans, mainly for "alternative" magazines.

"Ah," said Judith, as if that explained something.

"Do you have children?" It was Lillian who bravely asked that question, and it was Madeline who said, "Not a one, thank God. How about you, Lil?"

Genia felt herself holding her breath. It was clear that Lillian had not confided in her roommate last night. Madeline obviously didn't know about the tragic death of Lillian's daughter this past year. Genia sensed that Judith and Teri were also waiting tensely.

"Two boys," was the soft reply, and then after a slight hesitation, "and I have a daughter."

"Me, too," said Judith, quickly, and went on to tell them all a funny—and distracting—tale about her youngest child. The delicate moment passed without causing any obvious problem among them. Genia thought that the two teacher friends were being very kind and gracious to everyone this morning. She was proud of them and felt glad they were her roommates. After that, the women talked and laughed about many things, until they realized how little time they had left to get ready to leave for their first hike. One by one they dumped their dirty dishes in the tubs labeled "paper," "silver," and "plates and cups," and followed each other out the door. Genia thought it amazing that she could already feel so fond of this disparate group of women, when they'd all known one another less than twenty-four hours. Even Madeline had her good points, namely a sharp sense of humor and a lively intelligence, and Gabby was, well . . .

Sweet, Genia thought lamely, trying to come up with something nice to say about the difficult child. Yes, sweet. Sometimes.

"You know," Madeline remarked to all of them as they briefly gathered again on the veranda, "we tell each other we're this, or that, or the other. But the truth is we could be any-body. We could be crooks or liars or thieves. Nobody knows us here. Even the ones who've been here before—you don't really know each other, do you? So we could give any name, and we could say we had any occupation—doctor, lawyer, Indian chief—and who's to know if we're telling the truth?"

There was a moment of nonplussed silence as the truth of what she was saying sunk in among them. But then Lillian grinned at her roommate. "If that were true of you, Madeline, why would you choose to tell us you're a realtor?"

Madeline laughed. "Lack of imagination, Lillian." Then she grinned wickedly. "But I never said *I* was lying, only that any of us *could,* and that none of the rest of us would know."

Teri smiled. "I think we're all pretty sure I'm not an Indian chief."

Madeline winked at her. "Yeah, Teri, good thing you didn't try to get away with that one. But are you *really* a high school science teacher, as you claim to be?"

"You'll never know," declared Teri, with mock haughtiness, as she stepped off the veranda onto the stairs. She accidentally tripped and had to grab hold of the railing, completely spoiling her dramatic moment but giving all of them a good laugh once they knew she wasn't injured. All of them, that is, except for Gabriella, who frowned disapprovingly at them from the door-way.

Thirteen

After breakfast, Genia found herself walking up the path with her youngest roommate. Soon she was scurrying to keep up, because the girl's long-legged stride was more like an angry stalking than a simple walk.

Gabby's silence finally ended halfway to their hogan.

"She doesn't understand! Her people wouldn't even *be* here in this country, there wouldn't have *been* slavery, if the Native Americans had killed all the Europeans. That's what they should have done. They should have killed all of us. They should have wiped us out the first time they laid eyes on any of us."

Gabby broke into a run then, as if she could no longer restrain herself. Genia watched her race toward the shadows beneath the pine trees above the hogans.

Feeling winded in more ways than one, Genia took the first bench she came to and sat down.

She intended to sit there only long enough to catch her breath and to admire the view, east to Mesa Verde. But the bench had one other occupant, a teenage boy, who also seemed to be mesmerized by the horizon. He looked about fourteen, she thought, and there was an Asian cast to his handsome features. He wore baggy blue jeans, hiking boots, and a plaid flannel shirt that looked about five sizes too big for him. His black hair was cut to about a three-inch length, and all three inches stood up straight on top of his head. Not being entirely conversant with current teenage fashions, Genia couldn't be sure if he'd styled it that way or if he'd just gotten out of bed.

"May I share your bench?"

"What?" he asked, with a perceptible drawl.

He looked startled, as if he hadn't even noticed that she'd sat down there. Genia was sorry she'd disturbed his reverie.

"I was asking permission to share your bench."

"That's okay." She didn't really expect him to say anything more, but he spoke right out, sounding frustrated. "We're all supposed to do this imagination thing. It's like an exercise. We're supposed to pretend we're ancient Indians and try to see everything through their eyes. Like, you see a bird, and instead of thinking, 'Wow, bird,' you think, 'Wow, food.' "

Genia inwardly smiled. It had always amazed her how her children, as teenagers, would just start talking right in the middle of one of their own inner dialogues, as if they assumed she always knew, at any time, what they were thinking. They had been so impatient, too, when she dared to inquire, "What is it we're discussing?"

The boy ran his hands through his hair, making it stand up even straighter. "Yeah, and it's like, 'Squirrel! Yum!' And like, 'Pond! Fish!' You know? But I mean, so what? Like, what's the point?"

Somehow, she was able to translate the idiom.

"You make it sound," she said, smiling, "as if they were thinking about food all the time."

He mused on that for a moment, and then his face cleared and he burst out with a laugh at his own expense. "I guess that's the point." He whacked the side of his own head, to demonstrate his own obtuseness. "Duh. To experience how different their life was, even at the most basic levels. Yeah, I guess they'd have to be thinkin' about food all the time, 'cause it's not like they could cruise on down to the grocery store or order out a pizza, you know?"

"That's true."

"Although"—he grinned at her—"if they thought about food all the time, how's that so different from me?"

She laughed with pleasure at his perception. He had, she thought, the most wonderfully lively and intelligent face. She recalled her own Benjamin at that age, disguising his natural sweetness behind cynical jokes and a deadpan expression. This boy didn't seem to hide many of his feelings. "Are you here with that Texas group?" she asked.

"Yes, ma'am." Suddenly he sat up straighter, as if he had just realized he was dealing with a grown-up. Genia rather regretted the change. She couldn't remember the last time she'd heard a child address her as "ma'am," unless it had been during a trip to his home state of Texas. It seemed that children there continued to be schooled in "yes, sir" and "yes, ma'am."

"We go to Longhorn Prep School in Dallas," he told her formally. "There's a whole bunch of us. We're all honor students"—she detected a hint of swagger to the words—"and we earned almost all the money to come up here. We're going to hike and camp out and explore . . . Hisatsenom . . . ruins for six days."

"That sounds wonderful."

"Yes, ma'am."

There was something new in his tone, a shading of doubt, that made her ask, "Isn't it?"

"I guess. I'm kind of scared," he confided, glancing at her, then quickly away. His eyes were gracefully slanted, and the irises were nearly as dark as the pupils. She saw him look around, as if checking to make sure that none of his friends could hear his admission. "I have this feeling that something awful is going to happen."

Genia took her time before replying. "It's normal to be

scared, if you've never done anything like this." She thought about what might be frightening him. He seemed such a sturdy, confident young fellow. "Have you ever camped out before?"

"Oh, yeah, sure, lots."

A bit of bravado there, she thought.

"What scares you, especially?"

He shifted uneasily on their bench. "It sounds so stupid." He rolled his eyes, as if to say he knew he was being really dumb. She didn't think he was dumb at all. "The deal is, I'm kind of scared about sleeping out at night in the mountains. You know, they've got wild animals in Colorado."

At least one mountain lion, Genia thought, but didn't say it. She found it easy to imagine how miserable a person could be, lying in a bedroll in the darkness, away from home, far from his parents, and hearing strange animal sounds in the night.

"Well," she said, "most wild animals are scared of us, especially when we're in big noisy groups. Can you think of a noisier group than sixteen teenagers?"

He laughed at that and looked a little more relaxed.

Genia suddenly thought of something that used to work with her own children, even when they were nearly as old as this boy. She put a forefinger up in the air, as if she had just then had a bright idea. "I know what will help."

"Really? What, you got some pepper spray or something?"

"No, better than that." She dug through the pockets of her utility jacket until she came up with an item that might work for the purpose she had in mind, and she held it up for him to see. Mentally she crossed her fingers and hoped she could be persuasive. "Now I know this looks like an ordinary key chain. Just a silver circle. But it is not. Believe me, it is not. It was given to me, for luck and safety, many, many years ago." Her tone was extremely serious, as befit the importance of what she was saying. "And as you can plainly see, I'm still alive and kicking. I'm going to remove my keys"—she struggled to match the deed to the words—"and present this to you. Put it in your backpack, or keep it in your pocket. With this to protect you, you won't have to be scared anymore."

He looked torn between skepticism and a wish to believe. "You really think that's true?"

She looked at him as if she could hardly believe her ears.

"I have never," she said emphatically, "had a single accident in any car I drove using this key ring. Never."

It passed from her hand to his.

"You're really giving this to me?"

"I want you to have it. These sorts of things have to be passed on, when the time is right. What's your name, by the way?"

"Hiroshi Hansen."

"I'm Mrs. Potter."

"Okay. Well, thanks. It's really a good luck charm? I mean, it really worked for you?"

"As I said, I'm still here."

"Yeah." He nodded, smiling at her. "Okay."

She couldn't help but ask him, "Do you feel a little better now?"

"Yeah. Kinda. Although I still have this weird feeling . . ." He glanced at her. "It's like, one time I had this same sort of feeling, it's like in my stomach, almost like I'm going to be sick or something, and one time I felt like this, and I found out my uncle died. He'd been sick. And he died, right at the same time I was feeling like . . . this." He touched the key chain to his abdomen, to indicate where the bad feeling was. "It's like, something bad is going to happen, or it's already happening, like right now. What if it means somebody else has died? Like, what if it's somebody else in my family?" He swallowed so hard she could see it. "What if it's my mom or dad? Or what if *I'm* gonna die? On this camping trip? I hate this feeling, I really do." He stared down at the key chain in his hand, took a deep breath, and then shrugged. "Maybe this'll help." He stuffed the talisman down inside the pocket on the front left side of his shirt, then changed his mind, took it out, and placed it into one of the tighter, more secure pockets at the back of his jeans, as if he didn't want to take a chance on losing it. Then he looked at his watch and reacted with almost comical panic. "I gotta go!"

Quickly she held out her hand to shake his, which was firm and smooth. "Hold on to the key ring, Hiroshi, and make a lot of noise in the woods. I hope you have a great time."

"You, too."

He trotted off toward the lodge, and Genia got up and headed off in the opposite direction, toward the hogans.

Maybe, she thought, as she approached the closed door of hogan one, Hiroshi had only humored an "old lady," as she knew she probably must look to him. But on the other hand, if he woke up in the middle of the night and started to feel afraid, maybe he would find the little silver circle and hold it and feel better. She didn't know if there was actually any such thing in the universe as good luck or bad, but she had seen plenty of proof in her lifetime that a strong belief in either one of them could produce a particular *attitude* that almost ensured one or the other. A positive, confident attitude seemed to make "good luck" more likely; a negative, tentative attitude almost guaranteed "bad luck."

She reached for the iron door handle.

If he had been her son, she couldn't have done more.

Sometimes, Genia thought, as she started to pull the door open, the only thing that adults can give to children, as they go off into the world, is their own sense of confident trust in the future. She hoped she had passed that on to Hiroshi. She decided not even to think about the fact that it was a *sterling* silver key ring.

Fourteen

"Oh, Genia, hi!"

She walked into the hogan to discover that Teri Fox was down on her knees looking under Genia's own pillow. And that Judith Belove was quickly moving her hands away from Gabby Russell's cosmetics kit. Judith started straightening things here and there, as if she were trying to pretend that she hadn't been doing what she had obviously been doing.

They both looked flushed.

"I lost some shampoo," Teri said from her crouched position.

"We were just looking for it," her friend said, with a nervous smile.

"I thought it might have fallen onto one of the beds."

"I thought maybe Gabby picked it up by mistake."

Genia acted as if she hadn't noticed anything out of the ordinary about the little tableau she had just walked into. "I have plenty of shampoo," she offered, "which I'd be glad to share."

Teri quickly got to her feet, brushing off her hands.

"Thanks a lot," they chorused.

Genia crossed over to her own belongings, to gather together the water bottle, camera, and few other things she wanted to take on the hike. She hoped it was only her imagination that made it look as if her possessions had shifted slightly, as if someone had picked through them in her absence.

Conversation in hogan one was a little stilted after that.

When they all walked back toward the main lodge together, Genia felt the two friends were practically stumbling over themselves to be congenial to her. It was clear they were horribly embarrassed, which, Genia thought sternly, they richly deserved to be. Did they honestly think she would hide shampoo under a pillow?

But by the time they reached the long veranda, she was ready to give them the benefit of the doubt. Maybe they really had been innocently—if rather tactlessly—searching the room. Genia's initial feeling of suspicion and indignation softened into amusement. *That must be some great shampoo,* she thought.

Gabby had descended from the woods and was sitting in a rocking chair off by herself at one end of the veranda, looking moody. Lillian and Madeline were rocking side by side, carrying on an animated conversation. Genia regretted to see that the two Dallas teachers had cornered the irascible trustee and appeared to be giving her an earful about something—no doubt the tale of Naomi and the letter with the misinformation in it. The trustee appeared to be taking it all in with a look of profound satisfaction that Genia found unpleasant to gaze upon, so she looked away.

Susan Van Sant stood alone and quiet just inside the doorway, but then she stepped back out of sight, into the dining hall.

After that, the group was all there, except for Susan, to wave a merry good-bye to the kids, who were all piling into three big golden vans. Naomi O'Neal came out of the dining hall to see them off, too.

A tiny woman wearing a white apron came around one corner of the building in time to join the impromptu farewell committee. At first Genia mistook her for a child who'd better hurry if she wanted to catch the vans. Then she saw the "child" was wearing a chef's apron, and only then did it sink in that she was staring at a petite adult, a woman under five feet tall. Her black hair, cut boy-short and pushed off her face by a white terrycloth headband, only heightened the impression of extreme youth. Staring a bit, Genia decided she was probably closer to thirty years of age. It was only the woman's small stature that might cause one to confuse her with a child; in fact, she had an adult body and an interesting face, bony and full of planes and shadows, that appeared almost somber. Unlike most of the other adults gathered around the veranda who were grinning and waving madly, the one in the apron stood silently, her arms folded across her chest, frowning in concentration. Genia glanced quickly away when the woman suddenly looked around and caught Genia staring at her.

From the driver's seat of the lead van, Jon Warren waved back at everyone, flapping a sheet of what looked like computer printer paper out the window. He yelled to Naomi, "Are we sure about this schedule now, Naomi?"

"We're sure!" she yelled back.

"You're sure?"

"I'm sure, Jon!" She sounded embarrassed at his insistence, and in front of so many people. From his window he grinned appeasingly and nodded. "Just checkin' one last time, chief!" He glanced back at the two vans behind him. "Okay! Round 'em up, and head 'em out! Ride 'em, cowboys!" In a cloud of gravel dust, Jon pulled away, followed by the other vans, each driven by a teacher who didn't look very happy to be behind the wheel.

In the back window of the second van, Genia glimpsed a handsome boy with black hair standing on end. She waved at him and got in return a big grin and then a flash of silver held up for her to see.

"Bye, Hiroshi," she called, and sent him a wish: "Be safe."

When the dust cleared from the road, Naomi O'Neal called out to all the women on the porch, "Is everybody ready to go? Take your last trip to an indoors bathroom, grab your packs, and then let's take a hike into history!"

Genia saw she had remembered the water bottle but neglected to put water in it. She hurried back through the dining hall into the L-shaped alcove where the food was laid out cafeteria-style for meals. There was a soft-drink dispenser there, where she pushed her empty canister under the water spigot.

On the opposite side of the now-empty and gleamingly clean food trays was the kitchen, entirely open to her view and hearing. While she waited for the water to trickle down, she counted five kitchen workers, all in white aprons, and all gathered around a handsome woman who was perched regally on a high stool. It was, Genia saw, the Medicine Wheel trustee, Martina Alvarez. Her black trouser suit fit her elegantly, her dyed black hair sat atop her scalp like a permanently styled wig, and her back was straight as a cookie sheet. In contrast, the kitchen workers generally looked as if they'd been steamed over a pan of boiling water. Genia saw red faces, flyaway hair, and the respectable disarray of people who have been laboring hard under pressure.

They were all talking at once.

The trustee appeared to be taking notes on a pad she held in her left hand.

Genia overheard the words "morning memos," and "always changing her damn mind," and "drives us crazy," and "waste and expense." She heard Naomi O'Neal's first name repeated, and there was no doubt about the object of the anger boiling out of the kitchen workers.

Just as Genia's bottle topped off and cool water spilled down her wrist, the same petite, aproned woman she'd seen outside entered the kitchen by the back door. Young as she was, from her first stern words it was clear this was the redoubtable chef, Bingo, of whom Genia had heard so much praise.

"What's going on here?"

Her kitchen staff looked as startled as birds and flew off in all directions to their posts.

Genia shook water off her hand and slowly and with great care and conscientiousness began to screw the lid back on the bottle.

The chef strode over to stand directly in front of the stool where the trustee had enthroned herself. Even sitting down, the older woman loomed taller than the younger one. Still, it looked to Genia like a dead-equal standoff of intimidating personalities.

"What are you doing, Mrs. Alvarez?"

"My duty as a trustee." The reply was dry and cool, clearly and deliberately enunciated. "I am interviewing employees on the subjects of waste and mismanagement. It is, I am sure you will agree, Ms. Chakmakjian, congruent with my fiduciary responsibility as a member of the board."

"We're busy in here, Mrs. Alvarez. You need to interview my staff, you tell me about it first, and we'll make an appointment, assuming I can manage to find the time for it. You're about to miss your tour, you know. The van's ready to depart."

"I am not going with them this morning."

"Is that right? We packed your snacks and a lunch for you. You want to talk about waste? How about starting there? Next time you decide to cut out of a scheduled meal, you let us know ahead of time, how 'bout that?"

Genia, who hoped she was invisible, saw the trustee look down at her notebook. "Your people tell me that Naomi—"

"You want to talk about Naomi, we'll do it when she's around to hear it. Otherwise I've got nothing to say"—Bingo gestured toward the ovens behind her—"and a lot of work to do." Pointedly, she added, "Should we expect you for dinner?"

Martina Alvarez stood up, getting down from the stool carefully, as if she didn't want to muss her suit. In a carrying voice, which Genia was sure she wanted everyone in the kitchen to hear, she said to the chef, "You may want to remember, Ms. Chakmakjian, who your real employers are. Naomi may be your day-to-day boss, but she is not, ultimately, the one who is in charge here."

"Bingo! Can you come here?"

One of the kitchen workers called out so urgently that Genia half-expected to see the sink on fire. Bingo responded immediately, leaving the trustee and rushing to the side of her employee. They entered into an intense, hushed consultation, although there didn't appear to be an actual emergency. It occurred to Genia that the kitchen worker had managed, in a quick-thinking and kind of desperate way, to prevent his fiery little boss from shooting back a response they might all have lived to regret.

Genia watched Martina Alvarez turn and walk with measured dignity toward the very alcove where she stood with her overflowing water bottle in hand. The trustee walked into the area, noticed her presence, smiled coolly, and said merely, "Hello."

Genia called upon her own reserves of sixty-four-year-old dignity and responded in kind. "Good morning."

As she followed the trustee out, a few steps behind, she heard the chef call out in the kitchen, *"Who turned off my music?"*

Bingo encountered Susan Van Sant again, this time at the coffee machine only moments after her own confrontation with Martina Alvarez.

"You're having coffee?" she asked meaningfully.

"The doctor says decaf's okay."

"That's what they said about—"

"Never mind, Bingo. One cup of caffeine-free coffee won't kill me or the baby."

"Why weren't you outside waving good-bye to—"

"Daddy?" Susan's smile was impish, pleased. "Because Jon and I try not to be too obvious in front of the tourists. We're going to be married, Bingo! He said so this morning, but I'm not supposed to tell anybody yet."

"Oops."

Susan grinned. "Oh, you won't tell."

"I thought there was the small detail of a wife."

"Oh," said the archaeologist, blithely, breezily. "Her?"

Bingo laughed and shook her head. "You guys are trouble on wheels, you know that?"

The other woman looked hurt. "You think so? We can't help it if we fell in love, Bingo."

The chef merely shrugged. "Let me know what flavor to make your wedding cake."

"Almond," said Susan, taking a sip of coffee.

"The fragrance of cyanide. I know that from reading old Agatha Christie novels. You planning on poisoning the wife?"

Susan looked a bit nonplussed. She thought of Jon's joke that morning: *We'll have to kill her.*

"Don't be silly, Bingo." Susan took another sip. "I'm an archaeologist. The last thing I need is more dead bodies."

Fifteen

Housekeeping swept—literally—through the hogans with cheerful efficiency that morning, starting about the time the women boarded their van.

Two women and a man, armed with brooms, bags, rags, and cleansers, started together on hogan one, familiarly and quickly working their way around the various messes left by the tourists, like droppings from big birds. One of them dusted, another one picked up wet towels and hung them up to dry on wall hooks and then swept the floor, and a third checked for burned-out lightbulbs, empty tissue boxes, litter on the path, and flowers that needed watering around the outside of the hogan.

The designated duster was by nature an incorrigible "neatener," and so when she saw the little green-and-white-plastic bottle lying under Gabby's belongings—and assumed it belonged to that particular tourist—she picked it up and went to the trouble of thoughtfully putting it into Gabby's pink cosmetic case. She tucked it way down at the bottom, so it wouldn't get loose again.

"Come on!" her compatriots called to her from the doorway when they were finished. "Will you stop straightening everything up? They'll never find their stuff if you keep moving it."

She hurried after them, making sure all the lights were turned off and the door was firmly snapped shut behind them.

No money ever got wasted on electricity and no raccoons ever got into a building after *she* cleaned it. If Naomi wanted to run the place like a spendthrift, that was her business—and that's exactly what *this* member of the housekeeping crew would tell that trustee at their appointment this afternoon.

Only one full-size van was required for the small group.

The archaeologist drove, and Lillian rode in front with her. On the bench behind them were Genia, Madeline, and Gabby, while Teri and Judith had the back bench all to themselves. Their feet rested on coolers that were reported to hold a picnic lunch. Additional coolers of beverages were stuffed into the space behind the last bench and the back door.

As they bounced along, driving farther and farther down unmarked dirt and rocky roads, the cool morning air blew pleasantly through the open windows, keeping the van comfortable in spite of the rising sun. They were going, first, to Half Watch Tower and the Two Spruce Settlement, or so Susan had informed them as they boarded. After lunch, the women would climb higher, she promised, up to some petroglyphs she wanted them to see at a ruin she called Last Man Standing.

"I'm already hungry," Madeline Rose remarked in the van.

It did, in fact, already seem a long time since breakfast.

Genia wondered, only half-facetiously, if Teri and Judith could be trusted not to sneak into the coolers and eat the food. If they got caught with a cooler lid up, would they claim they were searching for shampoo?

The women rode in the van for more than an hour, first past farm fields that were still green even in late September, and then climbing higher into Gambel oak and aspen forests that were starting their swift turn into autumn colors of rust and gold. The women talked quietly to their seatmates and pointed out sights of interest to one another.

Genia learned that Madeline Rose, a real estate saleswoman in the Denver suburb of Aurora, was thirty-eight years old, married to a man whom she described vaguely as being "in management," and had no children, nor wanted any. She let drop hints that of the two of them, husband and wife, she was the real moneymaker, the more successful one, and that he had to be constantly prodded—by her—to get ahead in life. Genia would have been willing to reciprocate by sharing bits of her own history of a long, happy marriage, children, and the years of widowhood since Lew Potter had died eleven years ago. Her seatmate didn't, however, ask any questions that might elicit such responses, and Genia didn't want to bore her if she wasn't interested.

So she contented herself with admiring the scenery while listening with half an ear to Madeline's tales of the effect of hordes of Californians moving to Colorado. She gathered it was good news for realtors.

On the other side of Madeline, Gabby had entered one of her quiet, pouty spells—Genia was able to recognize them now—when she seemed entirely self-absorbed and oblivious to the people around her. She came out of it only long enough to interrupt Madeline by saying once, "The Indians know that private property will not endure," and then later, "The earth cannot be bought or sold."

To the first comment, Madeline laughed. "It only has to last until I cash the check for the commission," she said. And to the second comment, she said, "Try telling that to somebody from L.A." Otherwise, she ignored the girl to her right and talked only to Genia.

At some point in the drive, an air of companionability descended firmly among the occupants. It was then that Genia and the others learned that Teri and Judith were both married to much younger men. "It's the first thing we had in common"—Teri laughed—"namely, what to say to people who think we're their mothers!"

"That happens?" Madeline looked horrified.

"Well"—Teri cast a sly glance at Judy—"it happens a lot less since we left them."

Lillian laughed at that, but Madeline still seemed appalled at the notion of being mistaken for your husband's mother. "Well, that's the best argument for divorce I ever heard," she said. "God. I'd die." She shook her head. "Or find a very good plastic surgeon."

The two teacher-friends took it good-naturedly, even when Madeline fixed them with a stare and demanded to know, "Did you leave them for each other?"

"No, no." Judy laughed out loud. "We're not *that* experimental. Heck, we haven't either of us even had enough experience with *men* in our lives."

Teri sighed. "And probably never will."

"It's never too late," Genia heard herself blurting out and then, to her embarrassment, found them all turning toward her with interest. Lamely, she added, "So they say."

Madeline arched an eyebrow. "Do tell, Genia."

Lillian turned around in the right front passenger seat and grinned at her.

Here she was again, Genia thought, at a crossroads similar to the one she'd experienced at the Talking Circle. A lifetime of the habit of personal reserve made her want to hold her tongue, but a few halting words worked their way to the surface anyway. "I thought I was finished with romance, too, and I'm much older than you two. Then a few months ago, my very first real love walked back into my life again."

She stopped; it was hard to reveal herself. Why did she want to? she wondered. She never had before, except sparingly and only to friends she had known for a long, long time.

"And?" Madeline prodded her.

"And it's never too late."

No more than that could they get out of her, not Jed White's name, or that he was divorced, or that he lived in Boston and that he never complained about his long-distance telephone bills to Arizona. Genia, having gone as far toward self-revelation as she was willing to go for the moment, became aware of Teri Fox gazing at her with an unreadable expression. Genia cocked her head at Teri, as if to ask her, "What are you thinking?"

"Nothing." The younger woman smiled and shook her head. Her expression was . . . soft, that was the word for it, Genia thought. "I'm just paying attention, that's all, to you and Lillian, so I'll know how to be when I'm your age."

Touched and surprised by that, Genia felt rewarded for speaking up so personally and for giving them more of herself than she normally might have. Maybe, just maybe, extreme personal reticence was not *always* the virtue she had long believed it to be.

"I keep learning," she said thoughtfully to Teri.

"See?" Teri responded. "That's what I mean."

Then, in the sort of instant, humbling moment that often made the universe seem so comical to Genia, she observed that Madeline Rose was staring at her with an expression of anything *but* admiration. Madeline seemed to be taking in Genia and Lillian's "natural" look and thinking, *No way, not me, not ever!*

"So you divorced them?" Madeline asked Teri and Judy, turning the conversation back onto its previous track.

"No, we're just kind of running away from home," Judy said, "like so many women did back in the seventies." To which she hastened to add, "Our kids are all grown—it's not like we left infants in cribs."

"We're still a bit scandalous though," Teri said, as if she didn't want their "escape" to be taken too lightly. "At our churches and in our neighborhoods. People just don't know anymore when we'll show up, or where—"

"Or with whom," Judith chimed in.

"We wish," Teri added sarcastically.

"You look so *average*," Madeline said rather insultingly.

"I know." Teri didn't look insulted. "We hate it."

"What do your children say?" Lillian asked from the front seat.

"Children," Judith said, with the air of making a pronouncement, "do not need to know everything about their mothers."

"Amen," blurted Genia, and then laughed as hard as the others did.

They had been talking for some time, and only Susan and Gabby had said nothing. Susan concentrated on the driving, and Gabby stared out a window, appearing to ignore them entirely.

Finally the archaeologist turned the van off the paved road and onto a rutted dirt lane, where they continued to bounce along for another twenty minutes, driving deep into the forest. When the van came to a stop, the women alighted in a sunny glade ringed by white-trunked aspen and slop-armed spruce trees. On the ground wild yellow sunflowers poked through the green and golden grass.

Sixteen

It was warm, and swarming gnats were visible.

The air was scented with the fragrance from a thick layer of pine needles that carpeted the shady forest surrounding the little meadow. Genia got out of the van, stretched, breathed deeply, looked around, and felt enormously glad she had come to Medicine Wheel to spend almost a week with these women.

"Is anyone starving?"

It was Susan asking the question.

A chorus of "I ams" rose up.

"Well, we won't set up lunch for another hour, but merciful Saint Bingo does provide for the in-between times."

Susan opened the back doors of the van, then reached in and hauled out a large orange plastic beverage jug that held iced tea. Next came paper cups. After that she surfaced with a big opaque plastic bowl with a blue lid on it. She gestured for the women to gather around her, and then she smiled and held the bowl high in the air with both hands, as though it were a votive offering.

"This is one of Bingo's sacred snacks."

Removing the blue lid and passing the bowl to the woman nearest her, Susan instructed, "Take one and pass it around, but don't eat yours until everybody has theirs."

When the plastic bowl came by Genia, she carefully lifted out of it a perfect, puffy, yellow stick of cornbread.

"This isn't merely cornbread," Susan avowed as they all held on to theirs, as directed. "According to our Bingo, it's a taste of history. She likes us to pause before we go tromping through other people's ancient houses, and to try to commune with them by partaking of something we still have in common with them."

She raised her delicate stick of cornbread, as if in a toast.

"Corn has been around for at least five thousand years, starting out in this hemisphere, and as cobs no bigger than your thumbnail, if you can believe that. So here's to us and to the ancient ancestors as well. Whoever they were, we are now linked through the millennia, by the simple and familiar taste of corn."

"I'm allergic to corn products," Madeline Rose objected. She tossed hers onto the ground for the squirrels to eat. Genia thought it was a remarkably selfish and insensitive thing to do, especially when she got a look at the expression of horror on Gabby's face. The girl looked as if Madeline had spit into holy water. If Madeline didn't want to participate, she could have given her share to someone else or tactfully held on to the corn stick without actually eating any, like a nondrinker joining a toast.

All of the other women bit into the cornbread and seemed to appreciate the touch of ritual and solemnity that the chef had provided for them. Genia made up her mind that Bingo Chakmakjian—was that the unusual name she'd heard the trustee use?—must be quite a remarkable woman.

"Hey!" Teri looked pleasantly surprised. "I hate cornbread, but this is good. What's Bingo done that's different?"

"It's not dry," Judith observed, her theatrical voice making the simple pronouncement sound like solemn oratory.

"Cream cheese," Susan informed them. "Bingo's secret ingredient is cream cheese. If you like these, just wait until you see her cornbread cake."

"Why?" Judith asked. "What about it?"

"You just wait," Susan teased them. "Here, there's more."

There was enough for two sticks for everybody, and a third for Gabby, who took the one Madeline didn't want. And two were leftover—the two intended for Martina Alvarez, Genia surmised, as she accepted Lillian's suggestion that they divide the remainder among them.

Gabby was the last to finish eating.

At first, Genia was under the impression that Gabby wasn't going to eat the third stick. For several moments the girl cradled it in her hands, closing her eyes and murmuring something over it as if she were a priest, it was the host, and their little ceremony had been a Holy Communion. Finally, she brought it slowly to her mouth and ate it prayerfully, as if it were indeed sacred.

Genia happened to look over at Madeline Rose.

The realtor shook her head, and then Genia saw Teri Fox and Judith Belove give each other an eyerolling glance. Genia felt another stirring of concern for this odd, impressionable child who wanted to be known as Gabbling Brook. Was this normal behavior, she wondered, and merely the expression of a sincere devotion to a cause? Or was there some danger that Gabby might be going off the deep end?

A quiet voice spoke near her left ear. "Is she all right, do you think?" It was Lillian Kleberg, staring over Genia's shoulder at Gabby. "Is this normal behavior?"

Genia turned her back to Gabby, so there was no chance she would be overheard. "I was just asking myself the exact same thing, Lillian. You know her a little, don't you? You've been here at programs with her before this one?"

Lillian nodded, looking grave. "Yes. She was a little strange then, always spouting off about the Indians, but she didn't seem so—obsessed. I'm worried about her." She looked into Genia's eyes. "If you don't count Martina, I'm the great-grandma of the group, so I guess that makes you the grandmother, Genia. And she's the baby. Let's keep an eye on her together, all right?"

"Yes, let's."

Lillian let out a sigh. "Thanks," she said, as if Genia had just done a personal favor for her. It seemed natural to Genia that Lillian, who had recently lost a daughter, would transfer some of her motherly concern to this possibly troubled young woman.

When the van was locked up again, Susan advised them to split into two bands, so that half of the group could visit the tower while the other half went to the settlement.

"Then reverse directions."

Hearing that, it seemed to Genia that there could not possibly be a nicer way to spend a day. When Lillian Kleberg came over to her again and suggested, "Come on, I'll show you the way to the tower," Genia happily followed along behind.

As they set out, she knew she wouldn't have to worry about whether her boots would fit or her socks would rub. Everything she had brought for this adventure was well loved for being well worn. Her sturdy old brown ankle-high boots were well broken in. Her down vest and jacket were fluffy and familiar. Her shirts, trousers, even undergarments, all were soft and easy to get in and out of. It was a good thing to be free of the worry and pain of blisters, stiff fabrics, and unforgiving zippers. She felt at home in her clothes. As for her body, this was a slimmer, definitely tougher version moving along the trail.

In a word, she thought, *I'm prepared.*

So much of a successful life *was* preparation, she had come to believe. Preparation made spontaneity, even impulsiveness, possible. It made her life feel like previously tilled earth into which she could plant any new flower on the spur of the moment.

And so here she was, and grateful for it.

She turned to look for Gabby, to invite her to come along with them, only to discover the girl was already right at her heels. So Gabby—who seemed to be sticking closely to her, as if the girl felt comfortable only with Genia—tagged along, and the archaeologist made up their fourth, after pointing Teri, Judith, and Madeline in the right direction for the other destination.

It was only when they heard tramping footsteps behind them that they realized somebody had ignored Susan's instructions.

"It's me," called out Madeline, as she approached their single-file march through the woods. When she caught up, she said, ironically, "I don't do old houses. Just new, expensive ones. But I figure, where there's a tower, there's a view."

The tower, what was left of it, stood three times as high as Gabby, who was the tallest woman in the group. The base—its mortared stone walls a good two feet thick and with a diameter of about fifteen feet—was still intact for the first three feet or so. But above the base the front of it was gone, its stones having long ago tumbled down the thousand feet to the valley below. Only the long, gracefully curving back climbed skyward, until it ended in a jagged row of stones and broken mortar.

It looked almost Gothic, Genia thought.

On a cloudy day it would have looked quite sinister.

It was perched about as close to the edge of the dangerous cliff as could be, a gray skeletal finger pointing up, and it was surely visible for miles. You couldn't look at it, Genia thought, without marveling at the courage and skill of the ancient builders who must have had to balance so precariously to complete it.

"What was it for?" Madeline asked Susan, as the five of them cautiously poked around the talus pile at the bottom. "Defense?"

Susan shrugged. "Maybe."

"A lookout," Gabby said in an authoritative voice, as if she were privy to insider knowledge. She ventured so close to the cliff's edge that Genia felt nervous.

"Could be," Susan agreed.

"A landmark?" Genia suggested, still keeping an eye on Gabby. "For travelers?"

"Possibly."

Gabby stepped back, and Genia breathed more easily.

Madeline laughed and said to Susan, "I thought you were supposed to be the expert archaeologist who has all the answers."

"I wish I did. I do have an excuse in this case, because this tower has never been officially investigated. It's not a dig, it's just a place that somebody built a long, long time ago. There are literally thousands of anonymous sites like this all over the Southwest. Not all of them are towers, of course. Some of them are cliff dwellings, some are caves, and some are mysterious stone walls that don't appear to have any good reason to exist. Most of them just look like big mounds covered with rabbitbrush, but if anybody ever dug into them, they'd find rock walls, or earthen berms, or kivas, or middens, or any number of things."

"Well, do you know *anything* about it?"

"I can guess that it's probably from the early Pueblo period of Anasazi development—before the multiple cliff dwellings on Mesa Verde, to give you a context. Although I'm not even sure of that, because what most people don't realize is that there were people living in pit houses on Mesa Verde even before the construction of the great houses. It's difficult, for many reasons, to place this tower exactly in time."

"Food storage?" Genia wondered aloud, her curiosity well aroused, like everyone else's, even Madeline's. "Like a silo."

Susan nodded. "It could have been a storage tower."

"Not for food, though," Gabby stated.

"Possibly not," said the scientist, "although the so-called Fremont people used towers for storage in Utah and northern Colorado. You should make a trip to see one someday. The towers have little bitty doors in them, so for a long time people thought they had been built by a race of tiny people!"

"It's a lookout," Gabby repeated, speaking much more authoritatively than the official archaeologist of the group. "So when the people were traveling to the great gambling houses in the south, the Gambler would know they were coming."

Susan turned to stare at her. "Is that what you're going to put in your article, Gabby?"

"Definitely. And I'll write about the religious significance of gambling, too."

Susan's lips appeared pale, as if she were feeling ill again. "You can't prove any of this, can you?"

"I don't have to," the writer said dismissively. "The Navajo say it's so, and that's all I need to know. I couldn't care less what you archaeologists can 'prove.' "

"It's not a new idea, you know," Susan said weakly.

"Well, of course it isn't, not if the Navajo have been saying it for centuries!"

"No, I mean quite a few archaeologists and anthropologists have tossed it around for decades, too."

"So?"

"So maybe it's not news, that's all, as you think it is."

Gabby looked angry, defensive. "What do you care? Besides, nobody but the Navajo have ever really believed it, so trust me, it's still news to white people."

She didn't get an argument to that, because Susan turned and walked away from her.

Genia, who had been listening with interest, now saw that Lillian Kleberg had paused in her "investigations" to sit down on a rock and appreciate the view. Genia went to stand beside her. Plains, riverbeds, mesas, mountains, all measure of geological wonders met her gaze. Sensing the presence of the archaeologist, she asked, "Where are we, exactly, Susan?"

"We're more or less equidistant from Utah—over there—and Arizona, over there—and New Mexico, down there. Hovenweep National Monument is due west, and Shiprock is down that way on the Navajo Reservation. There are a couple of Ute reservations over there, and way over east of them is an Apache reservation." Indicating a mountain shaped like a recumbent human form, she identified it as Sleeping Ute Mountain. "The Dolores River is off yonder, and the La Plata Mountains are way back there, behind us." Susan smiled at Genia, who was charmed by hearing so many words of the American vernacular spoken in a British accent. "That's about as 'exactly' as I can do for you. Do you feel oriented now?"

Genia smiled back at her. "Yes, I do. Thanks."

"It's against the law to divulge the location of ruins on government land," Susan said with mock severity. "We had to get permission to bring you up here. Promise you won't tell anybody, Genia?"

"Susan, if someone had to find this place based on my directions, it would remain protected until the end of time."

The other two women laughed quietly.

All three of them simply stared at the landscape for several moments. Then Genia murmured, "So beautiful."

The archaeologist said softly, "Maybe *that's* the reason."

But Madeline had overheard them, for she spoke up loudly, saying, "Location, location, location. Of course! I should have guessed that, right off the bat."

Susan allowed them to prowl around the tower for a while longer, before shooing them off in the other direction. Midway the two bands of women passed each other, with comments of "You'll love it" and "Wait till you see." The group following

Susan had already come upon the first indications of Two Spruce Settlement before they noticed that Madeline wasn't with them any longer.

"She wanted to return to the van," Susan told the others. "I gave her the keys."

Sure enough, when they returned from their expedition, they found Madeline seated in the van with the engine on, the windows closed, and the air conditioning running. She was already eating a plateful of sandwich meat, bread, potato salad, and pie. She had a cup of iced tea, and her bare feet were propped on the dashboard.

"So much for fresh air," Susan said with resignation.

"I could learn to dislike that woman," Lillian remarked to Genia.

"What's to learn?" asked Judith, walking past them. "It just comes naturally. Do you suppose she left any food for us?"

Seventeen

A surprise waited for them after lunch, when they traveled to the location of their afternoon hike. There both the executive director and the trustee joined them.

As Susan Van Sant pulled the van off the blacktop highway, Naomi O'Neal and Martina Alvarez got out of a blindingly clean four-wheel-drive vehicle with a Colorado license plate. Martina had driven, and now she stood beside her car, regally erect, her hands in the pockets of her black jacket, looking—thought Genia—like a queen waiting for all of the peasants to approach her.

Naomi, dressed in a bright yellow peasant blouse, loose blue trousers, and hiking boots, left Martina and trudged over to the window of the van and leaned in to greet the seven women.

"Hi. How'd it go this morning? Any chance I could enlist you guys in helping me to push an elderly trustee off a high cliff?"

An explosion of tactless laughter greeted that remark.

In the front seat of the van, Lillian Kleberg said, sounding astonished, "Martina's actually going to hike, Naomi?"

Susan's question was a sardonic one: "Did you tell her to *take* a hike, Naomi?"

Naomi snickered but then shushed them, with a terrorized look over her shoulder back toward where the object of their spite was waiting. "Just shut up and get out of the van, Dr. Van

Sant. Take the other ladies up the hill, will you? I have to go back to meet my doom."

Susan smartly saluted her.

"It's been nice knowing you, Naomi."

The director trudged back to the car where the trustee waited.

They had been brought to a location which took Genia's breath away, and not only because it was another thousand feet higher in altitude. Right in front of them lay a vast expanse of slickrock—a hard, unforgiving, monstrous slab of red rock laid down like the floor of the world. Genia thought it was spectacularly beautiful but unnerving. It appeared to her as the Creation must have looked *before* God said, "Let the waters pour forth."

At one o'clock the slickrock was hot beneath the soles of their boots.

As they moved forward behind Susan, small lizards scurried into sight and out again. Dozens of long, hot yards away, a sheer red cliff rose to a flat top. They were headed, Susan told them, even beyond that monolith, into the rugged, rocky canyons, where there would be amazing hideaways, petroglyphs, and pictographs.

After only a few yards, Genia wasn't sure it was worth it.

She felt sweaty, awkward, and uncomfortable.

No one talked much, not even Gabby, who had been on one of her periodic talking jags back in the van. Now, halfway to the canyons, a large dark bird flew in toward them and circled overhead. Madeline pointed up and said, "Buzzard."

"Hawk," Susan corrected her. "After lizards, probably."

"I feel like a lizard," Teri said, her words sounding sluggish and forced, which was also the way Genia's legs felt, moving over the flat expanse. "I feel just like a tiny inconsequential creature crawling along the ground, where giants could step on me. An ant. I am nothing but a tiny black ant."

"Termite," said Judith. "If you're an ant, I'm a pasty white termite."

"Mosquito," said Teri.

"A spot of grease on the rock," said Genia.

"I am wind!" sang Gabby. "I am the hot, hot wind!"

"I guess that would make you a Santa Ana then," Madeline said nastily. "The kind that makes everybody so irritable, they want to kill you."

Somebody chuckled. Nobody else had the energy to respond.

Far behind, Naomi walked with the trustee, who appeared to be having no problem in finding the energy or motivation to talk. The other women couldn't hear what was being said, but Genia looked back at the way Naomi's head and shoulders were slumped and the manner in which Martina held her own head upright, and she guessed the words were not friendly. The queen appeared to be reprimanding her prime minister.

Their moods lifted ten minutes later, when they reached trees and a path where rocky overhangs provided periodic shade along their way. They paused to drink from their water bottles—and some of them slipped behind the trees to answer the call of nature—and then they continued single file, except for Martina.

"I have overestimated my ability," she announced. "And my stamina. I will sit here in the shade and wait for you."

When Naomi, looking resigned, started to move with her toward some rocks in the shade, the trustee stopped her. "No, Naomi," she said in a martyred tone, "you go on with the others. I'll wait here alone."

When they were safely out of the trustee's earshot, Genia overheard Naomi whisper furiously to Susan, "Why did she bother to come at all? She should have known she couldn't do this! Look how she's dressed—in black wool, for God's sake! She's eighty years old, and her bones are as fragile as dinosaur eggs. And she makes it sound as if I twisted her arm and forced her to come."

"The only dinosaur eggs I ever saw were petrified. Watch where you're stepping, Naomi!"

"Oh! Thanks. I would hate to please her by tripping and knocking my head on a rock. How am I going to push her off a cliff, Susan, if she can't climb up where it's high enough?"

Genia heard the two staff members giggle together at that.

The director's mood seemed to lift the higher they climbed and the farther they hiked away from the woman in black. Eventually Genia found that she and Lillian were outpacing everyone except, surprisingly, Naomi, who was stepping right along, nimbly, up the incline and over the rocks.

"Thanks a lot, Naomi," Lillian said wryly, as she spoke to the director's back, "for giving me Martina as a roommate. I thought you liked me."

Naomi looked over her shoulder briefly, with an apologetic smile. "Do you want to kill me? It's okay. I don't blame you. I had to put her in *somebody's* hogan, Lil. Genia, Teri, and Judy are newcomers. Martina might scare them off, and they'd never come back again. And can you even imagine her rooming with Gabby?"

Lillian made an appalled sound in her throat.

"No, you can't. Neither could I. Gabby would be shredded meat by the end of the week. So that left only you and Madeline Rose. Madeline is a tough cookie, and I know Martina respects you at least as much as she respects anyone. So that's my excuse. Forgive me?"

"All right," Lillian granted her. "We'll manage. But if she gives me any lip, I'm going to tell her you let tourists camp overnight in the ruins."

"Lillian!" came the protesting cry from the director. "I never! You wouldn't!"

"Hah!" The woman behind her laughed. "Just sharing the pain, my dear."

"Oh," Naomi moaned lingeringly as she trudged ahead. "Don't even say such a thing as a joke to that woman. She'd have my job *and* my head, probably on an ancient woven Indian platter!"

Soon the drop-off to their left became precipitous. Genia didn't really feel afraid, but she started to pay more than casual attention to where she placed her feet.

The awful moment occurred an hour and a half into their excursion. All of the women were gathered around Susan as she lectured about prehistoric art. They'd already had their sacred snack for the afternoon—a moist, tangy zucchini bread, "to remind you of the importance of squash in the diet of prehistoric people."

Madeline, Naomi, and Gabby stood closest to the pictographs they were all studying. Genia sat on a fallen oak limb, Lillian squatted on some rocks, and Teri and Judith had their backs propped against a wall of the tiny pocket canyon where Susan had led them.

"The Hopis don't call this art," Susan was saying. Behind her on the flat rock wall, a dozen figures had been painted onto the stone or pecked out of the black patina: three pairs of handprints, a goat, two human figures with lines of dots rising from their heads; the skin of an animal, flattened as if viewed from above. "They say it's writing, that these are historical documents written by their ancestors to mark their migrations. They say a wall like this tells who the people were—which clan—who passed by or stayed here, and where they came from and even what important spiritual events happened here." She shifted her feet on the canyon floor. "So when something like this is vandalized, to the Hopis it is a desecration of an important historical document—and a one-of-a-kind document, at that. It's as if someone scribbled on the Magna Carta or cut a piece out of the original copy of the Declaration of Independence."

Just then, Madeline, who was closest to the handprints, held up her left hand and splayed out her fingers in just the way the fingers on the wall were spread. Before anyone grasped what she intended to do, she leaned in and placed her hand against one of the painted prints.

Like a tiger, Gabriella sprang on her, screaming, "No!" With a full swing of her right arm, she knocked Madeline's hand away from the wall, which knocked the other woman off balance and sent her sprawling face forward onto the sharp rocks at their feet. "Don't you touch that! It's sacred! It's a bridge to the spirit world! You've contaminated it!"

Madeline cried out in pain and shock.

The others reacted first with gasps, and then there was an instant of stunned, disbelieving paralysis.

Gabby faced them all, her back to the wall as if she intended to guard it with her life. The expression on her face was thunderous, her eyes looked wild with fury and intention.

Naomi was the first among them to spring to Madeline's aid, followed quickly by Genia, and then Teri and Judith.

Lillian, meanwhile, went up to Gabby and gently took one of her hands and pulled her away, assuring her that no one would go near the wall again. Wisely, Genia thought, she led the girl away from the others, out of the pocket canyon, and back along the path they'd come.

Madeline was sitting up by then and cursing, as she checked herself for torn clothing or bloody scrapes.

"Lunatic!" she said with venom.

It was difficult to feel entirely sympathetic toward Madeline, Genia thought, even as she helped to dust her off, because the woman was so very wrong to have touched the vulnerable treasure. They'd been warned not to; they all knew better.

And yet what stuck in Genia's mind afterward was not Madeline's arrogant, self-centered gesture of curiosity but the extreme violence of Gabby's reaction. She had the uneasy feeling that a border had been breached, and that it was one of the invisible, important borders that kept civilized people safely on their own proper side of the line.

"She'd better not touch me again." Madeline's lips tightened in pain as she allowed Naomi and Teri to help her to her feet. One side of her face was raw from the force with which she had landed on the rocks, but amazingly, there wasn't any blood. "She gets near me again, I'll sue her ass."

Genia nearly laughed with relief.

A lawsuit! What a day and age we live in, she thought, although she supposed it was an improvement over the age when revenge meant more violence. The word *sue* nearly managed to transform the event from melodrama to mundane.

Their afternoon hike aborted, the women retraced their steps back to where Martina still waited for them. Her response, upon hearing of the contretemps, was a single, sneering word: "Tourists!"

They returned in uneasy peace to the main campus. For the sake of that peace, Madeline rode back with Naomi and Martina in the trustee's car.

In the van Lillian kept firm hold of one of Gabby's hands, which lay limply in her own. Genia, Teri, and Judith talked quietly of other things—teaching, ranching, normal life.

A wind had picked up, seemingly out of nowhere. It buffeted them about on the blacktop and heavily dusted the van with red dirt. Genia noticed that Susan's hands on the wheel looked white, as if she were holding on tight to keep them all safely on the road.

Eighteen

In hogan two Martina Alvarez lay on her bunk in agony. The middle of her spine was aflame with pain; she could think of almost nothing but the torture of it. She hardly knew how she had managed to drive to the slickrock site with Naomi, then walk those hideous broiling hard yards across it. Somehow she had endured the cruel wait for those fools, and then the drive home with that idiot of a woman, her other roommate, Madeline. The one who ought to be hanged. Despoiling a site!

On top of all of that, once they arrived at the hogan, she had been forced to wait while the idiot woman and Lillian had changed clothes, taking their moronic time about it. Only after they had both left the hogan could she allow herself the excruciating luxury of shedding her own attire, bit by painful bit. She wouldn't have dreamed of asking for help from her roommates; the idea of anyone seeing her in her vulnerability was repellant beyond imagining.

She had once heard it said that nothing repelled God; that having granted human beings free choice, the Godhead could not very well then condemn them for using it. If that were the case, Martina had decided at the time, then she and God had nothing to say to each other. She was repelled by many things; at the moment by her own weakness most of all. Nor would she care to know a God who felt sympathy for her rather than disgust at her capitulation to the pain.

It had taken her an infinitely long time to remove her brace and then to lower herself onto the bunk bed. But then the medication for pain, which she rarely allowed herself, had begun to reduce the flames down to mere small, aching embers of suffering. She was used to that; that, she could bear. If only she could sleep through the dinner hour, she felt she might regain enough strength of will to get up out of her torture rack and attend the advisory meeting this evening.

It was an important part of her reason for coming.

Indians, Martina believed strongly, were their own worst enemies. If they would only leave the scientists alone, their sacred sites might be preserved for all time. Granted, they would not themselves then be able to use them for their ceremonies, but Martina had no more patience for shamans and medicine men than she had for priests, rabbis, or ministers. It was the churches that deserved preserving, not the foolish humans who frequented them, wearing them out with their foolish theologies. It was architecture, whether natural or man-made, that Martina loved, not the architects or the patrons of that architecture. She loved only the buildings, and the pure science that designed them, analyzed them, and saved them for future historians and investigators. (She had admired the neutron bomb from the first moment she read of it and could not fathom the sentimental objections to the fact that it killed people but left buildings intact.)

A brief flare of the worst of the pain returned.

Death would be preferable to this, she thought.

Black, blank, nonexistence.

She would have chosen to be anywhere but here on this hard bed, with no privacy for her suffering. But she could not give in now. The Wheel, the scientists, depended on her and only on her. Who else did they have to defend them against Naomi, who was bleeding them dry for the sake of tourism? Of all the superficial reasons to spend a dollar!

Martina's only distraction, her only real consolation in her agony, was her fury, which equaled her pain in fire and intensity. She pictured that idiot's palm pressed against the ancient art. The human sweat eating away at the vulnerable design! She recalled the indignation of the two Texas teachers, and Naomi's culpability in *that* mistake. If anything untoward happened to those children now, the blame would be easy to place! Even in her pain, Martina's lips curved in a secret, satisfied smile at the thought of such a consequence.

And that insolent chef!

Martina reviewed with a sort of pleasure the litany of complaints, large and small, that she had sought out and attended to since she had arrived last night.

It was unconscionable. It was malfeasance or worse.

Something had to be done.

The tourism must cease immediately.

Naomi must go.

Martina's eyes closed as the medicine worked its soft fingers into her brain, easing away the worst of the pain. She disciplined herself, as always, to go to sleep at once. There wouldn't be much of it; she needed what little she could obtain.

Her last thought before sleep was that by this time tomorrow, *there would be changes.*

"Chef! Chef!"

The teasing, flattering cry rang out from the table in the dining hall that evening, where five members of the Women's Hike into History sat together. They applauded, whistled, and shouted irrepressibly, and all of the other tables quickly caught on and joined the ruckus.

A tiny, dark-haired woman finally came out of the kitchen,

wearing tennis shoes, blue jeans, a T-shirt, a white apron, and a grin.

"You like Uncle Dick's Chicken?" she asked, prompting hollers of "Great!" and "Yes!" and even more wild clapping. Bingo picked up the ends of her apron skirt, lifted them, and neatly curtsied. Then she flapped the apron at her audience, as if dismissing them, and disappeared back into her domain, leaving even more laughter and bonhomie in her wake.

"I swear to God, this is the best chicken I ever ate." Judith Belove looked blissful as she stabbed another tender piece of chicken awash in creamy juice. "What do you think she puts in it?"

"Milk," Lillian Kleberg said.

Judith, Genia, Teri, and Madeline looked at her expectantly, waiting for more. When Lillian noticed, she smiled, and said, "Salt and pepper."

"And?" Madeline prodded her.

"That's all. I swear. Chicken. Milk. Salt. Pepper. Oh, and a little oil to brown the chicken in."

"That can't be all," Teri protested. "She may be a culinary genius, but nothing this good can be that simple."

Judith laughed at her. "How can you say that, you science teacher, you? Have you forgotten H_2O, for instance? Lots of the best things are the simplest." But then she turned a doubting face to Lillian, too. "Really? That's all?"

"Really." Lillian put down her own fork—reluctantly—and raised her right hand, palm out. "That's what she claims. I watched her make it one time, and I didn't see her slip in any secret ingredients."

"Yes," Judith said darkly, "but would you tell us if she did?"

"It's all in the wrist."

They looked at her inquisitively.

"When she stirs it."

Genia cocked a skeptical eyebrow. "No doubt."

"Salt and pepper," Judith murmured, her eyes glazing over as she chewed. "Amazing."

After Madeline and Lillian had departed from the table with their dishes, which looked so clean no one could have told they'd ever held food, Genia asked her remaining tablemates a question.

"That shampoo bottle you were searching for. What does it look like?"

Judith looked startled to be reminded of it. "It's just a little thing, one of those freebies you get when you stay in a hotel. This one says Sheraton, I think."

"Holiday Inn," Teri corrected.

Her friend looked doubtful. "Are you sure?"

"Yeah, 'cause don't you remember where we got—it?"

Genia wondered at the sudden guarded expression that crossed Teri's face between the words *got* and *it.*

"Oh. Right." Judith nodded seriously at Genia. "Holiday Inn. If you see it anywhere—"

"I'll hand it right over." She couldn't help but smile when she said it.

Judith's expression turned a little sickly, Genia thought, while Teri jumped right in to say, "You probably think we're making an awful fuss over a bottle of shampoo, but it's—"

"A souvenir," Judith said quickly.

"Uh-huh. Of our first protest march."

"Oh?" Genia said agreeably. "What were you protesting?"

"French atomic testing in Polynesia," said Judith. "Japanese whale slaughter in the Pacific," Teri said.

Genia nodded, keeping her facial expression carefully neutral. "Both good causes, I'm sure." It was a struggle not to laugh, so transparent was their prevarication. "And so geographically proximate, latitudinally speaking." She bit down hard on her lower lip.

"Well," Teri said, sounding defensive, while Judith's face turned a bright sunburn red, "there were two marches on the same weekend."

"Educational," Genia said smoothly, as she pushed back her chair and picked up her dinner tray. "I'm sure."

After dinner she went onto the veranda where she joined Madeline and Lillian gazing idly toward the moon rising over Mesa Verde, and soon Teri and Judith joined them, too. Although Madeline now and then had made cutting remarks about Gabriella, who had not come up for dinner, the incident in the canyon seemed to have released some of the natural tension in her. Strangely, at least in Genia's view, Madeline seemed more relaxed and easier to get along with now, and not quite so quick with her usual, rather off-putting sarcasm. It almost seemed as if she were trying harder to be part of the group.

Various vehicles were pulling into the gravel driveway.

Genia was fascinated to see that almost every person who got out of the cars and trucks was obviously of Native American descent. And they were all heading up the stairs, onto the veranda, and into the dining hall. One of them, a short, swarthy middle-aged man wearing a business suit, cowboy boots, and a ponytail, glanced their way, and then smiled.

"Lillian?" he called out. "Is that you?"

"Hello there, Robert. How are you?" She stepped forward, holding out her right hand, and he came toward them to shake it. "What's going on? Some kind of tribal confab?"

He grinned. "Anytime you get more than one Indian together, it's a tribal confab. No, this is just the regular monthly meeting of the Medicine Wheel Native American Advisory Council. They tell us what they're up to out at their digs and what they think they want to do next. We tell them what we think about it."

"They're actually asking your opinions?"

He shook his head. "I know. Pretty amazing, isn't it?"

"Robert, let me introduce you—"

There were names, smiles, and handshakes all around. Genia thought Madeline looked defensive, as if the touch of Robert's hand reminded her of the ancient prints she had touched. It turned out that Lillian had met Robert several times over the many years of her attendance at the Wheel, and that he had long served as an unofficial liaison between the scientists and certain contemporary Pueblos.

"Now I'm official, I guess," he said with a slight smile.

"What's on the agenda for tonight's meeting, Robert?"

"The council itself." Suddenly his broad, dark-eyed face turned serious. "It may disband."

"Why, Robert?" Lillian looked appalled. "After you finally get some influence, why would it disband?"

"Not everybody likes our connection to this place, Lillian," he said. "Some of my people." His smile was unapologetic. "Some of yours."

"Don't call them mine," she snapped. "Do you mean Martina?"

He grinned and shrugged, but Genia thought she saw many strong emotions in the dark eyes. "You know Martina, she's of the old school, Lillian. She thinks the only good Indian is a dead Indian." When he saw the shocked reaction on Teri's dark face, he hastened to explain, "I don't mean she wants to exterminate us, I just mean she's really only interested in ancient Indians, not living ones. We get in the way of archaeology, don't we, Lillian? We're a nuisance, from Martina's point of view. She liked it better when nobody ever asked us for our opinion about anything." He sighed. "And frankly some of our people liked it better that way, too, because this way feels to them like compromising something sacred."

The parking lot was quieter now, because most of the visi-

tors had gone inside. Robert noticed. "I'd better get in there."
He tipped his head to the other women. "Nice meeting you."
They reconvened their study of the rising moon.

In hogan two the trustee carefully raised herself from the
bunk bed and reached for her back brace. She was still in great
pain, and furious about it. This, too, was all Naomi's fault! And
the fault of the Indians. Because of them, she had to rise and
attend a meeting that should have been unnecessary, for an
advisory committee that should not even exist. There would be
people who would pay for her pain tonight; she looked forward
to seeing her own agony mirrored on their faces!

Nineteen

When Gabby opened her plastic toiletry kit in the shower, while almost everyone else was at dinner, she discovered an unfamiliar bottle of shampoo.

Holiday Inn, it advertised, in green letters.

"Where'd this come from?" she said, and the noise of the running water drowned out her whispery voice.

She saw that it was one of those free little samples, but she couldn't remember every staying in a Holiday Inn, much less packing this bottle in her kit.

"Oh, well," she said, knowing life is full of mysteries.

She unscrewed the top and turned the bottle upside down, but no shampoo trickled out into her palm. Puzzled, she turned it right side up, and peered in. When she saw there was paper inside, she quickly turned off the water. Ignoring the instant chilling she felt, she reached toward the door of the shower stall to dry off her fingers on a towel she'd hung there, and then she retrieved her tweezers from her toiletry kit. Delicately she lifted the paper from inside the bottle and held it up to get a good look at it.

She saw two little rectangles, each with a cartoon of an owl printed on it.

"Oh, my God," Gabby whispered.

Her fingers now trembling, she put the tiny owl rectangles back into their safe dry cave in the bottle, and then rescrewed the lid on tight. As she put the bottle back into her kit, Gabby felt overwhelmingly excited, even grateful. She'd viewed photographs of such things before, but as a person who didn't use intoxicants, she'd never actually seen any real ones before this.

"It's a gift from the spirit world," she told herself as she stood shivering. "It's a sign that I must do a vision quest." She experienced the cold as her conscious sacrifice, offered in appreciation for this astoundingly unexpected gift of two tabs of LSD.

She changed into fresh clothing in the empty hogan.

It was too late for her to get dinner, but she wasn't hungry anyway, at least not for food. She had originally planned to work this evening on certain story ideas she was developing. It made her laugh to think how much information she could gather by quietly moving around the campus in her moccasins, which some people laughed at her for wearing. And she had the last laugh as well, because of the many things she had overheard just by keeping quiet while all of the other women were talking to each other. She'd caught the two teachers whispering about using drugs, for instance. If they could only see her now! Gabby giggled at the irony of it. But all of the story ideas she had gathered in those secret ways could wait now.

Eager with anticipation, she grabbed the precious little shampoo bottle and ran out of the hogan toward the woods on the far edge of the meadow below the main lodge.

In a little circle of aspen trees, she bowed first to the four winds, and then she sprinkled corn pollen on the ground from the soft deerskin pouch she kept hanging around her neck, always close to her heart. She didn't know exactly what to do by way of ceremony, so she tossed in bits and pieces of ritual she'd heard about from various sources. A snatch of Navajo here, a snippet of Hopi there, a bit of Zuni and even Cherokee. Only when she felt the spirits were satisfied with her seriousness of purpose did she allow herself to unscrew the top to the bottle.

Carefully she used her tweezers to pull out the contents.

Gabby would have preferred peyote for its sacred history, but she suspected that the gods prescribed only culturally appropriate drugs. Since she was a young white woman, they must have settled on LSD as the logical hallucinogen of choice.

She placed the first owl on her tongue.

"What is she *doing*?"

Teri and Judith were still sitting on the veranda railing, facing each other but staring down into the meadow where their group had met for its first Wisdom Circle. It was dark by now; the almost-full moon seemed to turn even the most ordinary objects, like trees and cars, into strange, almost unrecognizable things.

Genia followed their gaze.

She saw Gabriella Russell running back and forth from one end of the meadow to the other. Her arms were stretched high, so the fringe on her jacket flew out behind her, and her head was thrown back at an unnatural-looking angle, so her long straight hair trailed down her back like a pale yellow wedding veil. As she ran, she lifted her knees high. It looked comic, absurd. Genia thought it also looked awfully uncomfortable. It made her feel nervous just to see it, because she sensed in it something abnormal and dangerous.

"Oh, Genia," Lillian Kleberg said quietly, beside her. "What's she doing now?"

"Is it a dance?" Teri asked of no one in particular.

"Maybe it's an Indian ritual," Madeline guessed, and laughed. "Better not be a rain dance."

Teri snickered and gave her a kick.

Beside Genia, Lillian made a small unhappy sound.

Genia immediately decided the direct approach was the best one.

"Come on, Lillian. Let's go down there and ask her."

Judith jumped to her feet. "This ought to be good. We'll go, too."

But Lillian stepped out in front of Genia and said forcefully, "No, you won't, Judy, not if you're going to make fun of her. If that's all you have in mind, you stay here."

Judith sat back down hard, as if she'd been pushed, looking surprised and abashed. Genia felt a little sorry for her; it was understandable that a person might be tempted to laugh at the herky-jerky scarecrow in the meadow. It looked like a joke, an exaggerated mime act for the entertainment of the observers. But Gabby was probably dead serious about whatever it was she thought she was doing down there. And Judith really ought to have sensed that. Genia started down the stairs with Lillian, but before they managed to traverse half the distance, the strange, bobbing figure ran off into the woods.

"Gabby!" shouted Lillian, breaking into a slow trot over the hazardous gravel in the driveway in front of the lodge. "Gabby! Wait!"

"Lillian, slow down! You'll fall on these rocks!"

Neither of them fell, but by the time they reached the edge of the woods, they were out of breath. They stepped a few yards into the deeper darkness under the trees where Gabby had vanished. There was no sight, no sound of the girl. Giving up, the two women trudged back through the meadow toward the veranda where the others waited. But at the edge of the driveway, Lillian pulled at Genia's sleeve, stopping her.

"I have to tell you something, Genia."

Her voice was spent, hollow.

It was something about Gabby, Genia supposed, but she was wrong.

"I . . . lost my daughter last year."

The awful sentence ran straight down from Genia's ears into her heart, where it instantly touched the spot where a mother's terrors live. She fought a natural urge to recoil in fear and instead reached out, wordlessly, to touch Lillian's arm. At last the awful news was out and spoken between them. Genia had waited for Lillian to speak of it, only if she wanted to, and now, here it was.

"Tonya was thirty-six, which is just the same age I was when I had her," Lillian said, in a voice so full of pain that Genia's throat began to ache and her eyes felt wet with sympathetic tears. "It was cancer, something odd and rare and awful, and there wasn't anything we could do to—save her. She died exactly one year ago this week. I thought if I came on this trip, I could get away and just think about her. I was afraid that my friends would call to console me on the one-year anniversary. I knew I'd fall apart and be miserable. Can you understand? I hoped I could come out here and feel closer to Tonya somehow."

"Oh, Lillian. I—"

"I know, please don't say it."

Genia nodded, and then thought of the one thing that had helped her the most when her own dear Lew had died. "I'd love to hear about her, if you'd like to tell me—"

"Oh!" Lillian's sad face seemed to light from within at Genia's suggestion. "Would you? Really? May I show you pictures of her, too? I've just been bursting to talk about her, but I haven't wanted to inflict my troubles on—"

"Lillian, I'd really love to hear all about her."

They ended up walking arm in arm to Lillian's hogan, instead of returning to their curious audience on the veranda.

"My goodness," Madeline Rose said in a dry tone of voice, while Teri and Judith looked on. "Everybody's leaving us. Do you think it was something I said?"

★   ★   ★

It was more than her daughter's death that troubled Lillian, Genia learned. Lillian had helped her to die—secretly, against every doctor's orders, in a manner she wouldn't confide to Genia, who didn't ask, anyway.

"It was my final obligation to Tonya, as her mother. I would do it again, too, for anyone I loved, and especially for one of my children. She was suffering, she only had a little while longer to live, and nobody would let her die, which is all she wanted to do toward the end. She couldn't do it herself. I had to help her."

Genia simply listened and held Lillian's hands. The photographs of Tonya showed a beautiful young woman with a vibrant smile and long blond hair like Gabby's. Later pictures showed her gaunt and bald, the smile fading, and a pleading look in the wide expressive blue eyes. After viewing the pictures and hearing the story, it became even easier for Genia to comprehend Lillian's attachment to and concern for Gabriella Russell.

"Gabby reminds me of Tonya," Lillian told her. "The passion, the naiveté. Tonya was like that. And toward the end, she was hallucinating, all the time, like—"

Genia realized with a start that Lillian was thinking about Gabby's strange antics in the meadow. Was she comparing the hallucinations of a terminally ill daughter with the behavior of a fully alive young woman? If she was, there was something askew in Lillian's perception of Gabby, Genia thought with a small frisson of unease. Gabby may be intense, even obsessive, but physically she looked as healthy as a horse. She was quite *alive*. Genia felt she should say that to Lillian, but she couldn't find the words to do it.

Lillian opened a second small photo album, and Genia's opportunity to say something passed, soon forgotten.

Twenty

The trees smelled of nutmeg, the ground smelled like meat, and she herself gave off a weird fragrance of straw. The sight of the moon knocked her out, because there were curlicues of light popping off of it. She heard a sizzling sound every time one of them fell into an ocean.

That was all very nice, Gabby thought, as she felt herself flung from one tree trunk to another like a pinball, but she didn't see anything unusual about it. Perfectly normal. This LSD business was a crock. There were so many things she had expected to happen that weren't happening!

Tired of being pushed around by trees, she sat down.

For the longest time she stared at the palm of her own hand, anticipating that the skin would soon part into its various layers, revealing sinew, corpuscle, and bone below, and then that her vision might rocket on down to the cellular level. Before she took the LSD, she had been terribly excited about the possibility that she might get to actually see the difference between what her blood looked like going into her heart and what it looked like when it was going in the opposite direction.

Maybe she'd have a vision of oxygen! Or carbon monoxide!

Or maybe that was carbon dioxide—she was always getting those two confused. Biology had not been one of her stronger grades in high school or college. Actually, nothing had been, she had to admit.

But for some strange reason, she had always remembered the composition of an atom, possibly because everybody in her sixth-grade class had had to make a three-dimensional model of one. She was holding out hopes—as she held out her palm in front of here eyes—of seeing an actual atom: nucleus, outlying electrons, and all.

No such luck.

For a short while a certain tree seemed willing to reveal itself: a squirrel hole gaped, and its inner light glowed as if a fire burned within. But then it was just a tree again, pushing her around. Gabby wished she'd paid more attention in botany, so she'd know what names to call these listening, human-pinball-playing trees.

Darn it, the LSD wasn't working!

Apart from a feeling of light-headedness—and of being just slightly unsteady on her feet so that she had to throw up her arms and lift her knees and cant her head back a bit in order to keep her balance—she felt perfectly normal.

Actually, she felt rather sick.

She wondered if some jerk had sold the gods a bill of goods. She was then heartened by an ever-so-vague realization that that was a very strange thought to have. If she was having strange thoughts, maybe the drug was working after all! Good. Now if only she could recall why she had taken it in the first place.

She didn't feel very good.

Gabby looked around her, although the sensation was more that the world was revolving while she sat still. "Well, would you look at that," she said. "There's a huge apple with wheels on it, and a door." This was confusing. She remembered Cinderella riding to the ball in a pumpkin, but maybe that was inaccurate. The truth was important. She must find out the truth. She struggled to her feet and commenced to skip (she thought) toward the apple (knowing better than to take a bite of it, for it was poisoned). She was thrilled to see for the first time how her shoes sparkled and shot off penetrating beams of rainbow-colored light. Funny, she had not noticed that when she bought them.

Everything was suddenly so pretty and so funny.

If only the drug would start working, it would all be fantastic!

Gabby pried open the back door of the apple, lay down upon the church pew that had unaccountably fallen there, pulled a choir robe over herself, and closed her eyes. Many centuries passed. When she next opened her eyes, after having been to a little-known planet on the edge of Mercury where it was very hot, she seemed to be moving rapidly through space. Then the whole world stopped, and she was thrown off the church bench.

But she didn't feel any pain.

Instead, she heard a haunting chorus of men's and women's voices blended in perfect harmony in her skull. Then Jesus suddenly appeared, looking worried. Mary, the Mother of God, led Him away by His hands, which had bloody holes in them. (This was quite a surprise, because she remembered having expected to see other spirits, like maybe the spirit of Crazy Horse, or the spirit of Chief Joseph.) Oh, the singing was lovely! But Jesus and Mary were leaving her!

Suddenly Gabby felt an onslaught of dreadful fear and nausea, all of it growing from the middle of her chest. Oh, God, if Jesus and Mary were getting out of here, she didn't want to stick around by herself!

Wait! Wait for me!

She was so frightened—she'd never been so scared in her whole life! There must be something very, very evil nearby, if even the gods were fleeing.

Don't leave me! Don't leave me alone!

She had to get out of there and run! Gabby frantically struggled to get out from under the blanket she had imagined was a choir robe, and then fumbled around until she got the car door open. She stumbled into open air.

The considerable noise she was making attracted attention.

"My God," a voice said, "what's she doing here?"

Gabby felt herself grabbed by invisible hands. She surrendered into them, sobbing with relief and jubilation: "Thank you, thank you!"

The spirits were taking her, at last!

Twenty-one

When Gabby did not return to hogan one by the time Genia switched off her reading light, she didn't know what to do about it. But she discovered that lying awake in bed worrying for two hours didn't help at all. She had learned that night that Lillian regularly took sleeping pills, so at least she wasn't also awake and fretting about strange young Gabriella.

When Teri and Judith tiptoed in, Genia reached for her travel alarm clock. Its luminous dial said it was almost midnight. "I'm awake," she told them. "You don't have to be quiet. Gabby's not back. Have you seen her?"

Teri yawned as she started to prod one boot off with the toe of the other one. "Nope," she said. "I wouldn't worry, Genia. She's probably just out chanting to Orion or some damn thing."

"I suppose," Genia murmured. "She didn't ever come back to the lodge?"

"I don't know," Judith answered. She was undressing in front of her bed. "I didn't see her. Is her bedroll here? If it's not, then she's probably sleeping outside tonight under that glorious moon. I wish I'd thought of doing that, but I'm too pooped now. Time for bed. 'Night, all."

Genia started to get up, but Teri did the looking for her.

"Well, you're a smart one, Judy," she said. "It's not here.

How'd you think of that? Yep, she's sleeping out tonight, Genia."

Genia fell back onto the pillow, relieved but also annoyed. She wished *she'd* thought of that possibility and saved herself two hours of tossing and turning. She also wished, with no small measure of irritation, that young Miss Gabriella Russell had thought to inform her roommates that she wouldn't be coming home tonight.

Then Genia had to smile at herself.

You sound like her mother, she chided herself.

"Did you have a good time tonight?" she called out softly to Teri, since Judith seemed to have entirely conked out. A waft of the smell of alcoholic beverages and cigarette smoke had floated into the hogan with them. Genia hoped the open windows would allow in enough breeze to waft it right back out again. "Who was up at the lodge with you?"

"Oh, everybody came and went," Teri whispered, sounding vague and sleepy. "Our group. People from other groups. You know. It was fun. We met a lot of people. Judy and I had our first cigarettes in thirty years." Genia heard a low, rich chuckle. "And I'd say that would be our last for the next thirty. We both stopped smoking when we got pregnant with our first babies. I always thought I missed the taste of it. Now I don't know why I ever liked it in the first place. Yuck, I thought I'd barf. We got them from Madeline. She's really a riot when you get to know her. She calls herself the 'designated sinner' of the group, isn't that funny? She says when any of us gets sick of all this fresh air and healthy food, we should stop down at her hogan. She's got junk food and hooch and smokes."

Poor Lillian! Genia thought privately. *All that and Martina Alvarez, too!*

"So what'd you and Lillian do?"

"Oh, we just talked for a while. Then I got tired and came on back here. It's been a long day."

"Man, you said it." Teri groaned softly. "I thought I was in shape, but my legs hurt from just the little bit of climbing we did today. How do you and Lillian do it? I mean, it really gave the rest of us an inferiority complex to see you two way out ahead of us. Especially Lillian. She must be in her seventies."

"Whereas I am a mere youth of sixty-four. I don't know about Lillian, but I get a lot of exercise on my ranch."

"Oh, well, Judy and I have decided that we both want to be just like you when we grow up."

Genia laughed, feeling completely surprised and flattered.

"Until then," Teri said, "you may have to attach pulleys to me tomorrow to get me up any more mountains."

Genia closed her eyes.

She heard Teri turn over in her bed. "Gee, I hope Gabby remembers about the mountain lion."

Genia's eyes flew open again.

Then stayed that way until the weight of gravity and exhaustion pulled them down.

Genia awoke to the sound of whispering.

She opened her eyes reluctantly, half-expecting to find the hogan still dark. But the room was light with morning sunshine. She rolled over and discovered that the source of the whispering was her roommates, Teri and Judith, who were seated on Gabby's bed, engaged in an intense conversation.

"Is something wrong?"

When they turned their faces toward her, she saw how upset they were. Teri particularly looked anxious, even near tears. Judith looked just generally emotional.

"Oh, Genia!" was all Judith managed to say. Her actress's voice imbued the two simple words with heavy drama. When she heard it, Genia didn't know what to expect. Perhaps the toilets were clogged up, or somebody had died in the night.

She found Judith hard to read, because her every word seemed to be invested with such profound meaning.

"We didn't mean to wake you up," Teri said more plainly.

She waved off the apology and struggled to sit up among the sheets and bedcovers. The temperature inside the hogan was a cool slap to her skin, waking her up entirely. "What's wrong?"

"Look at this." Teri nudged Judith off Gabby's single bed. They both stood up. Teri reached down and pulled back the covers. It took an instant for Genia to understand that she was seeing a bedroll, spread out underneath the top covers like another blanket. "Look. Gabby put her bedroll under her blankets. So if she didn't sleep here last night, and she didn't take her bedroll and sleep outside, then where is she?"

"Oh, dear" was Genia's immediate and admittedly not very helpful response. She didn't like the sound of those facts, either, but she wasn't sure they deserved quite the dramatic response they were eliciting from her roommates. After having been reassured by Teri the night before, Genia now found herself trying to calm them. "Well, she's probably in the dining hall, eating breakfast. Let's go see." She made a show of getting briskly out of bed and starting to dress, because she'd always found with her children that a steady voice and an efficient manner could sometimes dissipate hurricanes of emotion into gentle sea breezes. Not that she herself felt at all happy about this latest discovery; but getting hysterical—as Teri looked close to being—wasn't going to solve anything, either.

In the dining hall they found pecan waffles, venison sausage, Canadian bacon, hot oatmeal, omelettes, toast, biscuits with sausage gravy, an assortment of cold cereals, sliced cantaloupe, grapefruit halves, strawberries, milk, orange juice, tomato juice, coffee, and tea. But they didn't find Gabby. They located every other member of their group, including Martina Alvarez, but none of them reported having seen her. When Lillian Kleberg heard that Gabby hadn't returned to the hogan, she pushed aside her full plate of breakfast, as if she'd entirely lost her appetite. Then she insisted on accompanying the three women from hogan one on a search for Naomi O'Neal, to report Gabby's absence.

Naomi wasn't hard to find, just down the hall in her office.

They crowded in, filling what little empty space there was between the doorway and the director's desk and file cabinet. Genia saw a telephone with many buttons, a pile of pink memo pads, and a desktop computer, displaying a grid that reminded her of her own year-end profit-and-loss statements at the ranch. Naomi looked up at them in surprise but took a moment to close down the document she had been working on. Then she swiveled her chair around, looked up at them, and asked quietly, "What's going on?"

But when she heard why they had come, she grinned at them.

"Ladies, ladies," she said mockingly, "you're forgetting one thing. Gabriella is a beautiful young woman, right? And she's in love with Indians, right? And who did we have here last night?" Naomi raised her eyebrows suggestively, as the light dawned in four anxious faces. "A number of handsome young Indian men, that's who. Now, do you really want me to go wandering around the Wheel saying, 'Has anybody seen Gabby Russell?' "

"Oh, God." Judith slapped her own forehead and laughed out loud. "Are we old fogies or what?" She turned to face the others. "Come on, guys. Gabby's all right. She's probably more all right than any of us are this morning!" She laughed again. "I'm starving. Let's eat."

"Wait," Genia asked them. "What about her odd behavior last night?" She told Naomi about Gabby's strange prancing about in the meadow. "You may be right, Naomi, but it worries me, the way she was acting last night, and the fact that nobody's seen her since then."

"You don't know that, Genia." Judith was cheerful about it, almost flippant. "Maybe none of *us* has seen her, but that doesn't mean nobody has." She grinned slyly at Naomi.

"Well, that's probably true," Genia admitted.

"I don't like the feel of this," Lillian said, still looking worried.

"Nor I," Genia concurred.

"All right," Naomi said, seeming willing enough to indulge their lingering doubt. "I'll ask around." She smiled. "Tactfully."

It appeared to be the best that Genia and Lillian could do at the moment.

As she followed the other women out of Naomi's office, Genia was surprised to observe that Teri didn't look any happier than she had looked going in. Genia heard her say to Judith, "Yeah, but would Gabby have done anything like this, if it weren't for—"

Judith cut her off sharply with two carefully enunciated words: "Shut up."

There was gossip in the dining hall that morning.

At their meeting the previous night, the Native American Advisory Council had voted to continue its existence and even to strengthen its ties to the Wheel by assigning a permanent paid liaison: Lillian's friend, Robert Goode, who was a member of a Pueblo tribe living within easy driving distance. It was said by people who claimed to have talked to somebody who had been there that Martina Alvarez had hectored, lectured, insulted, and offended, managing only to turn pivotal votes in the opposite direction. Then, it was rumored, she had stormed out of the meeting, threatening "dire consequences" that all present had assumed to mean financial. A half-dozen Native

Americans—all young men—had angrily followed on her heels, muttering their own threats to "shut this place down." It was said they'd gone off alone into the mountains to convene a secret ceremony.

"Maybe Gabby went with them," Teri whispered.

But Madeline retorted, "What would any self-respecting *real* Indian want with *her*?"

Twenty-two

"We have a surprise for you today," Naomi told them as they boarded the van for their second day of adventuring.

Neither Lillian nor Genia had wanted to leave without Gabby, but Naomi had finally persuaded them. "I've spread the word among our staff to keep an eye out for her," the director assured them. "As soon as Gabby shows up, somebody will bring her out to join us." And so, amid a chorus of "Don't worry!" the two older women climbed into the van with the others.

Genia thought the director and the archaeologist seemed eager to get going and as excited about something as two girls with a secret. "It's an experiment that we're trying for the first time. You're our guinea pigs. If you like it, we'll do it for other groups. You'll see what it is when we get there."

"Where?" asked Lillian, in a sharp tone that betrayed her lingering concern.

"There," answered Naomi, and grinned into the rearview mirror. She seemed in a lighthearted mood, Genia thought, probably because Martina had remained on campus. Although, Genia added to herself, if she were Naomi, she'd be worried about what Martina was *doing* there.

"I hate surprises," Madeline grumbled as she grabbed a good seat by a window. "I like schedules. Plans. Everything nice and predictable and going like clockwork." She settled in, looking ill at ease. "Is this surprise going to involve missing any meals?"

"No way!" Susan Van Sant exclaimed as she got in and slammed the door on the passenger's side of the front seat. "We know what the priorities are for this group. First food, then history."

Even Madeline cracked a smile at that.

Naomi was their driver this morning. Genia and Lillian commandeered the back bench, leaving Teri and Judith to keep company with the irritable Madeline.

"Don't even try to talk to me," Madeline warned her seat-mates. "You let me drink way too much beer last night, and the coffee pot was empty when I got to it, and I am holding every woman in this van personally responsible."

"No coffee?" Up front, Susan glanced at Naomi. "Did Bingo leave early last night?"

Naomi grinned and shrugged.

Genia thought again how much they reminded her of two mischievous little girls this morning. She wondered what they were up to. But it was going to be an hour-and-a-half drive and a treacherous hike down the side of a mountain before she would find out. Gabby Russell was on her mind most of the way.

"This is the steepest path you'll have to manage this week," Susan called back over her shoulder to the other women. "Just take it slow, and watch out that you don't put your whole weight on a loose rock, and you'll be fine."

She disappeared confidently over the lip of the cliff.

Genia, third in line behind Naomi, peered over when she reached the edge, and saw to her relief that the incline wasn't so bad, really, only about fifty yards at about a twenty-degree slope. It would have seemed much steeper from the back of a horse. The narrow path wound around huge boulders and between trees. She glimpsed Susan, then lost sight of her again behind the first giant boulder. If there truly was any danger, Genia decided prior to planting her first footstep down the mountain, it would be the loose rocks in the path. A person who slid on one of those might keep on sliding—painfully— smack into one of those boulders or trees. Whether feet first or head first, it would be a plunge into disaster.

She started down with care.

It was awfully nice, she thought as she picked her way, to be doing this with a group of women who seemed to take for granted that she could manage quite well on her own. None of the younger ones said condescendingly, "Are you okay with this, Genia?" Nor did they demean her by grabbing her elbow to "help" her down. And it wasn't because they were thoughtless, either, because at one time or another even Madeline had displayed the rather charming courtesy of younger women toward their elders. Teri and Judith insisted on ushering her into cafeteria lines in front of them; once Madeline got up and gave her the only available rocking chair; Naomi and Susan deferred to her in small ways that, Genia frankly admitted to herself, she didn't object to at all. Being sixty-four ought to carry some perks! And going first in line was a modest one, after all.

No, it wasn't a lack of consideration that caused them to leave her to her own devices on the treacherous trail; rather, they seemed to believe in her strength and agility. Evidently they gave her credit for having enough intelligence not to start something she couldn't finish. She hoped they were right!

"Oops!" she said.

Her moment of self-congratulatory reflection had cost her, by deflecting her attention from her right foot, which immediately and independently took the opportunity to slide out from under her. Genia grabbed hold of a tree branch, which luckily held firm.

"You okay?" inquired Teri, behind her.

"Fine," she answered cheerfully.

Having circumnavigated a dozen shack-size boulders, ten minutes later Genia stepped onto flat rock—and gasped. It was just as well that nature had seen fit to plant a sturdy oak right at the place where her hand might reach out to steady herself, because otherwise a sudden wave of vertigo—and awe—might have sent her tumbling forward. And forward was not the direction of choice. "Forward" meant out and down, way way down to a dry river bed in a slickrock canyon below.

She felt as if she could see clear to her ranch.

As if that weren't impressive enough, the view to her left took her so utterly by surprise with its perfect beauty that she felt moved nearly to tears.

It was a city.

A red, orange, and golden empty city.

Cunningly built brick by brick within the voluptuous inner fold of a stunning upward sweep and swirl of sandstone.

"I've never seen anything so architecturally perfect in my whole life," Genia remarked out loud, an evaluation that included pyramids, palaces, and famous cathedrals. One by one the other women came up behind her, and one by one they also gasped, first at the altitude and then at the splendor to their left. Even Madeline exclaimed over it, although what she actually said was "Oh, my God, I think I've just found out I hate heights," as if the city of stone didn't impress her at all.

They entered the city by way of an easier incline and walked over to where Naomi and Susan were already waiting for them in front of the ruin of a three-story tower. It was only when they got really close that they realized that the artifacts scattered around the ancient "city" looked remarkably modern. Dots of bright color littered two thirds of the interior of the "city": navy blue, fuchsia, chartreuse, mauve, along with clumps of black, brown and army surplus green.

"I'll be damned," Madeline said in her dryly humorous way. "The Anasazi had bedrolls?"

They'd staged a modern "abandonment."

This was their grand surprise and experiment, and it seemed to delight the women hikers. Madeline muttered, "You mean risking my life is not enough? I have to think, too?" But her posture and her face looked alert, giving away her true feelings of interest, Genia thought.

The sixteen teenagers, led by Jon Warren and their teachers, had artfully arranged a "scene" for the women to stumble upon.

"Pretend you are Richard Weatherill and his brother," Susan said, as they gathered eagerly around her at the tower that stood at the edge of the empty city. "You've been out looking for lost cattle all morning, and you decided on the spur of the moment to climb down here, where you have never been before. And lo and behold! Look what you find!" Dramatically, smiling with pleasure at the eagerness on their faces, Susan swept her arms out wide. "You're seeing what no white person"—she made a grimace of apology at Teri Fox—"what no *non-Indian* person has ever seen before. As far as I'm concerned, it's the equivalent of stumbling across the Grand Canyon, or being the first European to see a living Indian village. Even now, knowing many other people have seen this ruin, it still takes your breath away, doesn't it?"

Except for Madeline, they nodded in agreement.

"Well, think how you'd feel if you were the first person of your civilization to see this."

Genia said, "I'd feel as if I had stumbled upon Shangri-la."

Susan smiled at her. "I still feel that way, every time I see this place. It's incredible, isn't it? Okay now, to continue with our grand experiment: Remember what I've already told you about when the Weatherill brothers 'discovered' the ruins on Mesa

Verde? They said it looked as if the people who had lived there had gotten up and left only the day before."

"Just like this," Teri said enthusiastically.

"Right. That's what we hoped you'd say. Just like this. Your job is to play archaeologist. Pick your way carefully among the belongings that have been abandoned here. Take notes. Confer with one another. Pretend, if you possibly can, that you have never seen such things as backpacks or water bottles before, and work up some hypothesis about the kind of people who must have left such things. What did they eat? What were their sleeping arrangements? Did they do any sort of work? Can you determine how many people might have lived here, and what the range of their ages might have been?"

"Wait, wait!" Lillian was scribbling notes on a pad she had pulled out of her backpack. "Talk slower, Susan!"

The archaeologist obeyed, ending her instructions with the words: "And finally, when did these people leave this site? What leads you to that conclusion? Why did they go, and where have they gone?" With a big grin, she released them, saying, "Go, junior archaeologists! You have one hour to work, and then the kids are coming back to join us for a seminar on the subject of the real abandonment."

Genia felt absolutely inspired.

"I love this!" Lillian exclaimed to her, and she couldn't possibly have agreed more. They decided to team up, one of them writing down notes and ideas, the other devoting all of her attention to the "evidence."

"We need to count the sleeping bags!" Judith called to Teri.

"Pretend we've never seen a can of Coke before," Lillian instructed Genia, who replied, "Look! Here's a photograph tucked down into this bedroll! It looks like a family. That's a good clue as to social arrangements within the tribe. . . ."

Madeline heard that and laughed. "Tribe? They grew an awful lot of polyester fiberfill, from the looks of things."

"Good point, Madeline," Teri called over to her from a few feet away. "What does that say about them, that they had the capacity to make synthetic fibers? And they had the ability to dye fabrics, too. Judith, write down all the colors you see!"

Madeline shook her head at them and wandered off deep into the empty city, poking about on her own in the far area where none of the modern "artifacts" had been scattered. A half hour later, she was way at the far edge when they heard her scream, bringing the grand experiment to an abrupt and hideous end. She was still screaming, standing on the edge of a deep, excavated hole in the ground, when Naomi reached her.

Twenty-three

She was screaming on the edge of a kiva, a traditional Native American pit that was dug out most likely for purposes of worship and community gatherings. They all hurried there and stared over the edge. And then Madeline's screams were joined by others, for down on the dirt floor lay a body—what was left of it—once clothed in fringed leather pants and jacket. There was blood everywhere, well soaked into the pit, and the body wouldn't have been recognizable if it weren't for the remnants of the clothing, which they all recognized, and for the blood-stained long blond hair.

"Gabriella!" wailed Lillian, and she sank to her knees in the dirt above the hole in the ground. "Oh, my God in heaven!"

"My God," breathed Judy, clutching her mouth, "what happened to her?"

"Naomi?" Teri seemed hardly able to breathe, much less to speak. "Could it have been that—mountain lion—you told us about?" She started to sob.

Genia thought the mutilated appearance of the body and the pattern of the dark blood smears on the walls of the kiva looked as if indeed an animal had attempted to drag Gabby's body out of the hole. Then, giving that up as too heavy a job, it had torn off what it could manage to take away. Genia was horribly reminded of a calf that had fallen into a ravine on her ranch, and then been partly butchered and hauled away by coyotes.

Her mind skittered from one seemingly irrelevant thought to another, frantically avoiding the truth that lay below in the kiva. *Gabby would hate this,* she thought desperately, *this desecration of a sacred space, and with her own blood.*

"A mountain lion?" somebody asked, sounding terrified.

"Something like that," Naomi affirmed, and Genia saw her clamp down on her lower lip with her teeth, as if to prevent herself from succumbing to the same wracking sobs that were driving Teri to her knees at the edge of the kiva. As if she, too, could focus only on peripheral issues, she murmured, "If it is, if it's killing people—"

She didn't say any more, but Genia knew how to fill in the blank: If it was now a killer, it must be executed. Her brain fastened on the animal, avoiding its apparent victim. She recalled that Naomi had told them how bold that particular creature was; Genia had thought at the time that it sounded like a pet that had been let loose or escaped into the mountains. Or even a cat that had gotten loose from a wild animal reserve or a traveling show. She wondered if Gabby, in her naive way of viewing all things "natural" as also innocent, had approached it, exactly as they had been warned never to do.

"We have to get the police," Naomi said, her voice sounding strangely cool and distant. "But we can't leave her. Whatever killed her will come back for the rest of her body."

"Oh," Teri moaned, weeping at the kiva's edge.

Her friend Judith patted her shoulder helplessly.

Madeline was quiet now, her face as pale as the bark of the aspen trees on the mesa above them. Suddenly she ran away from the dreadful sight, stumbling away as fast as she could move. Susan Van Sant was breathing hard, gulping air, as if she were going to be sick, and she, too, turned and walked away, and then sat down with her back to all of them.

"We'll stay, Naomi," Judith offered in a shaking voice.

Teri looked up at her as if she'd lost her mind. "No!"

"Yes!" Judith's patting of her friend's shoulder became a pressure, as if she were trying to hold Teri in place and keep her from going anywhere.

Genia, staring anywhere but down at the body, saw an unexpected flash of color at the bottom edge of the kiva, near a bloody hiking boot. "I'll stay with them," she said suddenly. And she remained adamant on that point, no matter how strongly the others urged her to leave with them. For she had seen what she suspected Judith had also seen: the flash of color, green and white, was a little shampoo bottle lying in the bottom of the kiva.

"I'll stay," Genia repeated firmly. "If the children return, I'll keep them from coming down here and seeing this."

"But they must have seen it!" Teri's face was horror-stricken.

"No," said Naomi, "look how their belongings stop before they get here."

"Maybe that's *why* they didn't go any farther," Teri argued, sounding frantic. "Because they saw this, and it scared them and they ran away, leaving everything behind them."

"We would have heard from them, in that case." Naomi was terse, her tone clipped. "We'll be as quick as we can. Those of you who are staying, do you have water? Here, take my bottle, too. We won't leave you alone here any longer than we have to." To the others, she said commandingly, "Come on." As they left, they all looked like ghostly images of the hearty women they'd been only a short time before.

"What if it comes *back*?" Teri wailed after them.

Naomi turned back to say, grimly, "Make noise. A lot of it. I don't think he'll bother you, with so many of you staying here. But if he shows up, don't argue with him. Are you sure you want to do this? I'm having second thoughts about encouraging you to stay here. Gabby's already dead, there's nothing more we can do for her, and this isn't worth risking your lives."

"Oh, my God, I want to leave with you!" Teri started to scramble toward them.

"No," her friend said through clenched teeth, reaching out a hand to physically restrain her, "you don't." With her other hand, she waved Naomi on. "Good-bye. We'll be all right."

If I leave, Genia thought unhappily, while she watched Naomi disappear with Lillian and Susan right behind her, *will that shampoo bottle still be there when the police come?*

She felt she couldn't take the chance, although she couldn't imagine what could be so important about it, or what it could possibly have to do with poor Gabby's death. She didn't even know why she felt so strongly that nothing must be disturbed, as if it were the scene of a crime of human against human, rather than an animal attack. The child must have tripped and fallen into the kiva, and then been attacked by some wild creature. What would a shampoo bottle have to do with that? Nothing, Genia suspected, but if that were the case, why *was* the very sight of it enough to convince Judith to stay behind, when that was the last thing any of them surely wanted to do? And why would she want to stay when her friend was so frightened and distraught and eager to be gone from there?

With the others gone, Judith half-pushed, half-led Teri several yards away from Genia, and the two of them huddled together near another kiva, whispering. They weren't otherwise trying to be quiet, however, and soon began pacing noisily up and down and clapping their hands in an obvious attempt to scare the invisible beast away.

Genia walked away, too, letting herself wearily down onto a rock where her legs could dangle and where she could gaze far out across the valley. She wasn't frightened, at least not of the possibility that a mountain lion might spring at her back. Bold he might be, but never had she heard of a mountain lion so accustomed to human beings that he would purposely come down and walk among them—not even to retrieve his evening meal. Perhaps he was satisfied for now, satiated and sleeping it off, horrible though the thought was to her. But she had to admit it was also possible that he was hidden somewhere above them, watching and waiting for them to leave.

She shifted her awareness from lion to sunset.

A shaft of pain and grief stabbed through her as she realized that Gabriella had probably never seen this beauty in the daylight; it would have been invisible to her last night, merely an empty blackness beyond the edge of the city. This death could not have been the first one that this mysterious empty city had seen in the hundreds of years of its lonely existence. And when the people who built it had lived here, who among them had died here? Was there a woman, perhaps a grandmother, who had sat in this very spot with dismay in her heart, seeking solace from the peace and beauty spread out before her? Genia felt a kinship with that anonymous woman, a shared loss that centuries and differences in culture could not diminish.

Soon she heard the sound of sniffling, and she felt a tap on her shoulder, which startled her.

"Genia? May we talk to you?"

It was Judith and Teri, standing behind her, looking as grim as she'd ever seen any two women look.

"It's our fault," Judith said.

Teri added, "That she died."

A breeze at Genia's back ruffled the stray hairs escaping from the bun in which she had captured and pinned her hair. She felt the cool gentle caress, closed her eyes for a second, and thought, *I must be asleep in my bed at home, this is a breeze blowing through my bedroom window, and when I open my eyes, that's where I will be.*

"It's so stupid," Judith moaned.

"We're so stupid," Teri snapped. "Look, Genia, here's what

we did. You know how we said at the Talking Circle that we missed the sixties?"

Genia nodded. "So you participated in protest marches, and attended a rock concert, and now you're 'doing' nature. Yes?"

"Yeah, and one of the other experiences we thought we had to have was . . ." Teri took a breath, blew it out through her mouth.

"Drugs," Judith intoned. "In particular, LSD." Her theatrical voice boomed in the natural amphitheater. If there had been anyone else around, Genia thought, they could have heard this little confession miles away. Maybe that was a slight exaggeration, but Judith was now standing, pacing, commanding "center stage." She seemed to be declaiming this information to the natural world. And to Genia. "We brought some with us, a couple of—what they call tabs—nothing more than little squares of paper soaked in 'acid.' You just swallow the paper to take it. We brought one for each of us. We thought we'd be safe, doing it one at a time, with the other one completely sober and keeping watch. We thought we'd do it out alone in the countryside, after this trip was over and all the rest of you had gone home. You know, come back to one of these sites they're taking us to, take the LSD, and have some visions."

It sounded hopelessly naive to Genia, like the ill-advised, idealistic plans of teenagers, not of mature women. But then the state of being a wild and free young person was exactly what these two overgrown adolescents were attempting to capture, she realized.

Teri, whose head had been down during this explanation and whose arms had been wrapped around her legs, said, from her muffled position, "We put them in an empty Holiday Inn shampoo bottle."

Genia had already grasped that surrealistic fact. She grasped the rest of it, too, before they said it, but she sat still and listened to them tell the rest of their tale, with its tragic, guilt-ridden climax.

Judith said, "Gabby got hold of it. Maybe she stole it, you know, just looking for some shampoo. Maybe it rolled out of Teri's bag and Gabby picked it up. But when we saw her acting so weird last night, we were pretty sure she had found it and taken it. And . . ." Judith's pauses were growing more dramatic, her enunciation more theatrical by the moment. Genia found herself disliking very much the show that Judith was making out of her own and Teri's negligence. "She came out here, under the influence. God knows what she thought she was doing. Maybe she crawled down in the hole and fell asleep. Maybe she tripped—"

Her voice rang out across the valley.

"I'll never forgive myself! Never!"

Oh, sit down, Genia wanted to say.

Judith stood poised at the edge of the cliff, arms spread wide, looking melodramatically distraught. Watching her, Genia revised her opinion of Judith's theatrical potential; a great voice did not necessarily make a great actress; that was clear. Maybe her forte was directing.

"Stop it, Judy."

Teri's own furious voice cut through all the bathos like a genuine knife through phony butter. "She's dead and it's our fault, and she wouldn't be dead if we hadn't brought the acid along and if I hadn't lost it. And you make me sick, the way you're turning it into some kind of personal drama. This isn't about you or me. Who cares if you forgive yourself? We should only care about Gabby. Gabby's dead. It's about her. So just sit down and shut up."

Her friend looked, in turns, shocked, angry, hurt, and then ashen with shame. The shame looked real, Genia thought, and if it wasn't, then Judith was a superb actress after all. She stood looking bewildered, like an actor who has forgotten her lines.

It was Teri who found the words.

"Genia, Judy wants to go get that bottle and take it out of there, so no one will ever know, except us and—you. We know you saw it. She wants you to agree with that, to save our skins. I don't want to. I mean, I do want to, but we can't. We have to tell what we did, don't you think so?"

Genia never had to answer that moral question, because at that moment a shuffling sound behind them caused all three of them to turn and look.

Madeline Rose stood a couple of feet behind and to their left. Her right arm was high in the air, and she was holding some small object in that hand. She cocked the arm back and then forward. The object whipped high, over the lip of the cliff, and far out into the air above the valley. Was it only Genia's imagination that caused her to think she saw a flash of green and white?

Madeline said, "It's a good thing somebody has some common sense around here." Then she turned and walked away from them, back toward the path leading up.

Judith ran over to look into the kiva where Gabby's remains lay. Genia saw her clap her hands over her mouth. She ran back and whispered in a dramatic show of wide-eyed disbelief, "The bottle's gone! She threw it over the cliff!"

But Genia thought: *Not one of us could swear to that.*

Had Madeline just saved the two teachers from some sort of criminal charges? Had she rescued their reputations and their jobs? Genia looked at Judith and Teri and saw comprehension and relief flood into their faces. Now there was no hard evidence to link them to Gabby's death. Even if they confessed the truth, there was nothing to connect them to the tragedy.

She glanced over toward where Madeline was disappearing around a bend in the trail. She was a cynical and hard-bitten woman, and yet she had deliberately acted to save Judith and Teri.

Genia, feeling altogether disgusted with the two teacher-friends, got up, dusted herself off, and walked off to find Madeline. But before she even reached the trail, a moment arrived when the fact of Gabby's awful death finally sank fully into her soul. She had stood at the edge of the kiva like an observer, seeing but not accepting, noticing but not allowing herself to feel it all. Now it came in a wave. Genia, suddenly overcome with sorrow and horror, stumbled into a far corner of the desolate ruin. In privacy, hidden by a crumbling stone wall, she cried and prayed for the lost girl.

In an hour Naomi returned with Martina, and a half hour after that, three law enforcement officials showed up in two cars. But at no time did Jon Warren and the Texas teachers appear with their group of sixteen teenagers.

As dusk began to drape the ruins in lavender shrouds, the sleeping bags lay as still and neglected as Gabby's body in the kiva.

It was Naomi who first asked the question that none of the rest of them, preoccupied with Gabby's death, had thought to ask.

"Where are the kids?"

Twenty-four

The deputation from the Montezuma county sheriff's department had more immediate questions.

"Who was she?"

Naomi told them what she knew. Gabriella Russell, from Santa Fe, New Mexico. Unmarried. Twenty-four years old. A freelance magazine writer specializing in Indian affairs.

"What was she doing *here*?"

Nobody answered that.

"How'd she get here?"

The women—Naomi, Martina, Teri, Judith, and Genia— looked at one another. That was a very good question. How *had* she gotten here, at least seventeen miles from campus, when her car was still parked on campus? (Naomi attested to that; she'd seen it, she said.) And when there was no other vehicle on top of the mesa, or anywhere near the ruins, that she might have driven there.

"Did somebody bring her out here?"

They didn't know.

"Would she have hitchhiked?"

Nobody could say, but they all supposed she might have.

The deputy asking the questions pointed out the obvious.

"Well, she had to get here somehow."

"Maybe one of the young braves brought her," Madeline said, an edge of contempt coloring her tone and her words.

The other women cast her hostile glances, but she made a mocking face at them. "Well! She just *loved* Indians, didn't she? And Naomi, aren't you the very one who suggested she might have gone off with one of them last night? One, or more?"

Of course, then the representative from the sheriff's department had to hear all about the advisory council meeting of the previous night, and of the young men exiting in anger with the stated intention of heading for the hills, and of Gabby's infatuation with all things Native, possibly including young men. Madeline also told him about Gabby's odd behavior in the meadow the night before.

"She never came back to the hogan," Judith confirmed, sounding as if the words were being dragged out of her. "To tell you the truth, some of us were worried about her this morning."

"She acted as if she were high," Madeline said, and her smile reached her eyes, although she did not look at anybody except the deputy when she said it.

"Last night?" Naomi asked them.

But only a tense silence followed those words.

Genia waited to see if Madeline would mention the plastic bottle, but she said nothing more. *It was she, after all,* Genia thought, *who threw it away.*

The youth group did not return.

At first, no one from Naomi on down to the cops investigating Gabby's death seemed to know whether to take it seriously.

"They're supposed to be here?" A county sheriff's deputy inquired of Naomi, within hearing distance of Genia, Teri, Judith, and Martina.

"They were supposed to be here at least two hours ago," he was told.

"So where could they be?"

"They could be at one of the other sites they were scheduled to visit this afternoon," she told him. "But they're way off schedule, if that's the case, because they were supposed to return here at three, participate in a seminar with us and the ladies—"

"The ladies?"

"A hiking group. Seven women. Gabriella was one of them."

"Okay, then what?"

"Then we were supposed to go back to the campus—"

"We?" He was patient, more than she.

"Uh, the ladies' group—our seven women—and Dr. Susan Van Sant, one of our archaeologists. And me. And the kids were supposed to pack up their belongings and move on to another campsite."

"You think—car trouble?"

"I don't know. They're in three vans, like the one we came in. Medicine Wheel vans, with our logo on them. I don't know. I guess that could be it, a flat tire, or something. But— you haven't heard about any accidents, have you?"

He shook his head. "No, but I'll check to see if anything has come in since I've been down below." Down in the ruins, he meant, with Gabby's body. "You probably got your signals crossed. Maybe they arrived here too early and you arrived too late. Maybe they're already at their campsite, cooking hot dogs."

"Without their sleeping bags?"

He frowned, seeming for the first time to consider the possibility of a problem of some kind.

"Tell you what," he said. "You take your ladies on back. We'll be here for a while, so we can wait for the kids. How many kids did you say?"

"Sixteen." Naomi's face had paled under her tan. "And three adults. Maybe they called. Maybe there'll be a message for me at my office."

172 THE BLUE CORN MURDERS

"I'll bet there will be." He was kind, encouraging. "I'm sure there will be. I mean, look at it this way, they're not lost. They know where they are, even if you don't."

"Maybe I'll drive up to their next campsite, where they're supposed to be tonight."

"Good idea."

"If there's no message."

"Right. If there isn't."

He made a movement, as if he was going to walk away, but then he turned back, as if he'd had a mere casual afterthought. "If there isn't, and if they're not at their campsite tonight, you call our dispatcher, all right? Just let us know."

Genia saw Naomi swallow, saw her chest rise and fall. "Okay." Her voice sounded weak. She cleared her throat and made it stronger. "Okay."

"Any local kids among them?"

His head was cocked to one side, his expression was calm, pleasant, his voice still casual. Too casual, perhaps, Genia decided.

"No, no. Texas kids. Honor students. From a prep school in Dallas." Naomi seemed to hear herself talking too much, because she cut off her own words and turned and hurried over to where the "ladies" were waiting.

The tall sheriff's deputy stood and watched them pile into their van, watched them drive off. When Genia glimpsed back at him, he was still standing at the edge of the cliff, watching them.

Twenty-five

They endured a long and mostly silent van ride back to the campus. The silence puzzled Genia, although personally she appreciated it, because she was feeling too overwhelmed and sad about Gabby to talk. She simply couldn't believe anything bad had happened to the teenagers—there would be a calming, logical explanation, she felt sure—but anxiety nagged at her all the same.

Silence wasn't what she would have expected from the others, but maybe they were just as exhausted and drained as she was. Some people chatter when they are frightened or upset; other people withdraw into themselves. Genia knew she fell into the latter category, and she suspected Naomi did too, judging from her actions at the Talking Circle.

It was Naomi who surprised Genia by being the first one among them to speak, as they sped along the deserted highway toward their "home." "I'd like," she said, "to hold a Talking Circle tonight. To honor Gabriella's memory. Do any of you object to that idea?"

No answer, but no objections, either. Beside Genia, Teri brought her left hand up and covered her mouth, and then raised it up to cover her eyes. She bowed her head.

"I'll take that as consent," Naomi said.

★   ★   ★

When they reached the campus and got out of the van, they discovered themselves to be the object of stares. No one came down to greet them—not that anyone necessarily would have anyway, Genia thought—but they seemed to step out of the vehicle into a bubble of isolation.

They gathered their backpacks and stayed close together as they started toward their hogans.

But Naomi stopped Genia before she could leave the vicinity of the parking lot. "Genia? We usually pass around the leadership of the circles. Would you be up to taking it tonight? It would require you to set a time, notify the rest of us, get the chairs set up, and pick a topic. I'll give you the blue corn, or you can bring a totem of your own choice. I'll bring the tape with the music. Will you do it?"

"Yes." Genia's response was quick and sure. "I'll be grateful for something to do."

"I know."

"And it sounds rather . . . healing."

"I hope so."

"Why don't you suggest the time for me, Naomi."

The director breathed deeply, which could have suggested that she felt relieved, or overburdened, or both. She seemed to be thinking of all of the responsibilities awaiting her. "It may depend on when I hear from Jon and the kids—"

"Of course."

"But let's say nine o'clock."

"In the meadow."

"Yes. Will you ask for help with the chairs?"

"I will. And if you'd bring the blue corn?"

"Yes. Sure."

"Naomi, I know this is not the time—but I wondered, at our first circle, you didn't answer the question you posed to us."

That prompted a small wry smile from the director. "You

noticed. I thought I got away with it. I didn't take my turn because you'd already seen one person burst into tears. I thought seeing me do it, too, might be a little much for your first night."

She gazed at Genia for a moment, as if deciding something.

"Things are rough around here. Even before . . . this. For the first time in my life, I'm not holding myself together very well. I may lose this job. And I've loved it. *Loved* it. That question I asked—'Why have the Ancient People called you here?'—I thought they called me to set things right for them again.

"See, unlike some people, like Gabby, I've never thought of them as perfect beings, or this existence as idyllic. I think they screwed up. Big time. It looks to me as if they lost everything except their lives. I look at their empty cities, their magnificent empty architecture, all that accomplishment, all that beauty, and I see all of that, but I see failure, too.

"They built it all up, and then they had to abandon it because they failed for some reason. All that work, Genia! Was all of their work for nothing? Was it just so that almost eight hundred years later, you and I could drop our jaws and say, *Wow?* And was there any way they could have kept it from happening? I mean, what if you put in years of backbreaking labor on building a community, and you suddenly had to leave it? If I were one of the Ancient Ones, I'd have done anything I could to keep that from happening. What they had—what they made—was so brilliant, so rare. I would do anything to save something like that.

"I hear them telling me not to make the same mistake: 'Don't walk away. Don't give up. Fight to protect everything I've done here.' But it's so hard, because—"

"I wouldn't fight to save *buildings,* for God's sake," Madeline Rose interrupted. She had come upon them without warning. "I don't care if they were designed by Leonardo da Vinci. They all fall down, eventually. I say, if you gotta go, go. Don't make a fuss about it. Just pack up and move on and build something just as good at the next place." It almost seemed, Genia thought, as if Madeline were speaking directly to Naomi, but surely even she wouldn't be that presumptuous.

"But they *didn't* build something just as good," Naomi pointed out, heatedly. "And it's not just about buildings, Madeline, it's about ideals and struggle and community and *people*."

Madeline shrugged. "So get new ones. Anyway, who says the abandonment had to be such a tragedy? Maybe they *wanted* to leave. Maybe they thought they were going to something even better. I say the real question is, what was in it for them?"

She smiled slightly, as if she knew she had dropped a discordant note into their duet, and walked calmly away from them, back toward the hogans.

Naomi said quietly and bitterly, "So easy for her to say."

Before the director could rush away, Genia reached out to touch her arm. "About the children—will you pass the word along when you know they're all right?"

Naomi's entire face contracted, as if her facial muscles had spasmed in pain.

"They have to be all right," she said in a hoarse, intense whisper. "Oh, God, Genia! I have such a sickening feeling. Is it because of Gabby, do you think? Or am I having some sort of terrible intuition about those kids?"

Genia found one of Naomi's hands—cold as snow—and grasped it, trying to pass along a little extra strength to help her bear whatever must be borne.

"Please," Naomi whispered. "Pray!"

"I will. I am."

In fact, Genia had already been doing quite a lot of praying. She felt suddenly humbled by a forgiving thought: *Maybe that was the reason for our silent ride; maybe the others were praying, too.*

As Naomi walked hurriedly toward the lodge and Genia

headed toward the hogans, she realized she didn't share Naomi's awful premonition in regard to the children. But she was worried about a certain young boy named Hiroshi, and she hoped with all of her heart that wherever he was and whatever he was doing, he was not frightened, and that he had no real cause to be.

Her more immediate concern was for the emotional welfare of Lillian Kleberg. As desperately as Genia wanted to lie down, she wanted even more to comfort Lillian. But when she knocked on the door of hogan two, Madeline wouldn't let her in. "Lillian's trying to sleep, Genia."

She retreated to her own hogan, getting there just as her remaining roommates did, too. Their first sight of Gabby's belongings—her bed, her toothbrush sticking out of her pink plastic cosmetics case—was a blow to the heart.

Twenty-six

Judith literally doubled over when she entered hogan one. She said, "Oh," in a voice full of pain, and stumbled over to sit on her bed. Then she began to cry. "I forgot—it's all here . . . I forgot." It was the first time that Genia had observed anything that looked like genuine emotion in the schoolteacher.

Teri went over and knelt down beside the bunk with the bedroll tucked inside the covers. She began to stroke the bedroll, to smooth the wrinkles, and then she put her arms on the bed and the side of her face on her arms, and she closed her eyes.

Genia slowly walked over to where most of Gabby's belongings lay piled in a cheerful heap against the wall near the bed. With trembling hands and an aching heart, she began to gather the girl's things together, to put them away in the soft-sided suitcase. At the bottom of the pile, she found an old-fashioned steno pad, folded open. Genia glanced at the handwriting. Small, legible. She saw, to her surprise and then growing dismay, her own name.

"Genia Potter: Theft/desecration due to abysmal ignorance of N.A. history and ignorance due to underlying cultural disrespect of N.A."

"N.A." must stand for Native American, Genia surmised, her breath rather taken away by her discovery. Gabby was obviously referring to Genia's artifacts. But how did she know Genia had taken them—unless she'd gone through Genia's suitcase?

Genia flipped forward, then backward through the notepad, discovering all of their names there, and a heading: *"Story Ideas to Submit to Editors."*

"Teri Fox/Judith Belove: Teachers/drugs/influence on young people/misuse of sacred medicine for selfish ends.

"Madeline Rose: Reservations as real estate. Location, location, location! The profit in cynicism!

"Lillian Kleberg: Perverting the sacrifice!

"Martina Alvarez: The only good Indian is a dead Indian!

"Susan Van Sant: White dreams mean Red nightmares!

"Naomi O'Neal:"

There was nothing written beside Naomi's name, and Jon Warren's name wasn't even on it, so Gabby hadn't gone completely around the original Talking Circle.

Behind Genia, all was quiet.

When she glanced back, she saw that Teri lay on her bunk with her eyes closed. Judith was slowly brushing her hair, staring into her own face in the mirror.

Slowly Genia closed the notebook and put it away among the dead girl's other belongings. They hadn't been people to Gabby, Genia realized with regret, so much as they had been "story ideas," grist for the mill of her profession and her obsession. She suspected that Gabby would not have hesitated to write any of those stories, at whatever cost to the target. How far would she have gone to make her point? Far enough to endanger Judith and Teri's jobs? Their reputations? Far enough to embarrass any of them, including Genia, who already felt bad enough about letting her cattle walk all over a prehistoric site for years and years?

Yes, Genia thought, *she would feel completely justified in her actions. She wouldn't give us a second thought.* She imagined how easily the pure joy, awe, and reverence of her own moment of discovery could be made to look arrogant, uncaring, mercenary. And it was true that she was "abysmally ignorant" of the people who'd left the treasures, just as she'd been ignorant of the laws now protecting them. There was at least a kernel of truth in all of Gabby's "story ideas," no doubt, and that was what made the list so unnerving.

I hadn't stopped to think, Genia thought, as she remained sitting beside Gabby's belongings, *that Gabby, as a writer with an obsession, could be dangerous.*

Dangerous?

Surely the word was too strong, melodramatic even. But Genia ran down the list in her mind's eye and thought: *No, I'm right. Dangerous is the word for it.*

She felt as if she'd had a near-miss from public humiliation, and she disliked having that feeling undermine her genuine shock and sorrow over Gabby's death. What would the other women think of this? she wondered. And then she decided: *They will never need to know.*

She piled one of Gabby's sweaters on top of the steno pad. *No need to stir up a hornets' nest of resentment. Gabby is gone, along with whatever threat she might once have posed to anyone at all.*

Twenty-seven

By suppertime, there still had been no sign of or word from the student group. An undercurrent of fear and dread was beginning to run through the campus like a stream about to overflow its banks. *Where were they?* Everyone was aware that the children were supposed to have been that day in the same vicinity where a woman had been killed. *When had she been killed?* Before they arrived? Today, or last night? After they had left? Had they seen Gabby's body? Was it true, as the hiking group had reported, that there had been no bedrolls or other kids' belongings near the deadly kiva? The kids and their adult leaders seemed to have scattered their things two-thirds into the empty city but no farther. Maybe they hadn't seen her. Surely they hadn't seen her, or they would themselves have returned to the campus and reported it.

Where were they? The suppositions and rumors flew.

At seven o'clock and again at eight, Naomi attempted to quiet things down by holding public meetings in the dining hall. She announced that according to law enforcement officers who were still waiting or working at the ruins, the sleeping bags were *also* still waiting for their young owners to arrive. As the night slid down the Rockies and covered the valley with a dark, cool blanket, the word was going out across the Four Corners area to other law enforcement agencies, ranging from federal to tribal: Keep an eye out for three golden vans carrying teenagers and the logo of the Medicine Wheel Archaeological Camp.

The first time she addressed the gathered diners, Naomi stood at the head of the large room and said, "Their schedule was that they would tour Three Pot Cave and Joseph Mesa yesterday, and then camp on top of Antelope Ridge. This morning they had a lecture at their camp, and then they were to travel to Red Palace Ruins to plant their sleeping bags for our women's hiking group to find this afternoon."

Heads turned to stare at the table of women, where Genia sat. There were about forty men and women eating in the dining hall that night; from overhearing snatches of conversation, Genia guessed they included a couple of different groups of other tourists who were participating in digs, no hikes. She intuited the presence of a handful of field archaeologists as well. They all knew about the death, about the group of teens who hadn't shown up and why they were supposed to. The campus was awash in talk, speculation, and rumor about little else. Now all of them, tourists and scientists alike, turned back toward the sound of the executive director's voice. The room was so quiet—except for Naomi's words—that the clattering from the kitchen came through clearly, like a discordant percussive accompaniment to the information being delivered. A faint undercurrent of classic music emanated from the kitchen.

"After that, they were to drive to the Long Neck digs for exploration and climbing, but they were to meet us back at the Red Palace Ruins by three. We were to combine groups there for discussion led by Dr. Van Sant. After that, our women's group would come back here, and the kids would travel to their next campsite, on the south side of Willoughby Canyon."

She paused, then hurried on. "They never showed up for the meeting at Red Palace. They also have not shown up—at least not yet—at the Willoughby campsite."

Genia glanced at a big round clock on the east wall: seven-ten P.M. Others did the same thing, and a man called out, "What time were they supposed to get there, Naomi?"

"Around five, five-thirty at the latest. I sent two interns over there with a borrowed cellular phone to wait and call us the moment they show up."

"They're only an hour and a half late," someone said, "at most."

"No," Naomi corrected him. "They're four hours late, if you start the count from three o'clock this afternoon."

Lillian Kleberg spoke up. "Doesn't Jon have a cell phone with him, Naomi?"

"No, we've been trying to avoid the expense, Lillian. If I buy one, I've got to buy twenty, one for everybody who travels away from the campus. We figured we've gotten along without them—"

"Shortwave radio?" someone called out.

"No, no." Naomi looked defensive, harried, exasperated. "They're in three vans, for heaven's sake. If one breaks down, that still leaves two others to go for help. There are still gas stations and pay phones in the world. We can't outfit every one of our vans with phones, faxes, and modems, you see."

"I was just asking," the man said apologetically.

Naomi was immediately contrite. "I know."

Her sarcastic tone had not set well in a room where her audience's questions sprang for the most part from simple concern and curiosity. She seemed to sense that now, and to hear the sound of her own explanations. She made a weary, self-deprecating grimace, as if in apology.

"Right now," she admitted to them, "I would gladly take the cost of one damn cell phone subscription out of my own salary."

It was like a press conference, Genia thought.

"Do the parents know?"

Naomi whirled toward the questioner, a haunted look appearing on her face. "I've spoken to the headmaster. I'm to call him every half hour until they show up. I am leaving the question of parental notification up to him."

Parental notification.

It sounded so formal, so final, Genia thought, with an inner shudder, and she observed a similar reaction mirrored on the faces around her.

"Jesus!" One of the men whom Genia had privately identified as an archaeologist muttered at a nearby table. "How can you lose three vans full of teenagers?"

"God, those poor parents," Judith said beside Genia. "If it were my kid, I'd be on the next plane up here. I'd be camping on Naomi's doorstep."

"I'd hate to be that headmaster," Teri said with feeling. "How'd you like to make *those* calls?"

"If Naomi were Japanese," Madeline said, looking indignant, "she'd commit hara-kiri. I mean, she is in charge, after all. It's her job to see that these trips are safe enough, especially for children."

"Accidents do happen," Teri responded. "She's only the director, not God."

"Nobody even mentioned Gabriella," Lillian murmured, though no one appeared to hear her except for Genia, who squeezed her hand. When she looked at Lillian, she was disturbed to find on the older woman's face an expression as haunted as the one on Naomi's. It looked like naked fear. And misery. "Oh, Lillian." Genia held on firmly to the woman's hand, unable to think of anything both encouraging and true to say to her.

"What about Gabriella's parents?" Lillian whispered, her eyes filling with tears. "Who made *that* phone call? What about the people who cared about her?"

"Do you want to ask Naomi?"

"Yes, I do. But not here."

But the heretofore silent woman who was seated on the other side of Lillian now spoke up, although in a surprisingly quiet tone of voice. "You don't have to ask her." It was Martina Alvarez, ramrod straight in posture, clipped in speech, haughty of expression. "I'll tell you what you need to know. It was I who spoke to the girl's parents."

To the surprised—and openly appalled—looks on their faces, the trustee shrugged, an almost imperceptible roll of her thin shoulders. "It is vital that these things be done in the correct manner. However unpleasant the implication, we do have to be always on guard against the likelihood of lawsuits."

Genia thought, despairingly: *Lawsuits!* Never before had the culture of blame seemed to her to so clearly be a corruption of the honest strength, power, and grace of grief.

Twenty-eight

"There's a Harvard Moon again tonight," Genia observed to Lillian, as they walked toward the circle of chairs that Teri and Judith had set up in the meadow.

When Lew and Genia Potter had lived in Boston, their youngest daughter—four at the time—had heard the grown-ups speaking of an unusually beautiful full moon, and the child had thought they were calling it a "Harvard Moon." It had ever after been a Potter family joke. Lew, especially, became inclined at odd moments thereafter to burst out in tuneful baritone, "'Shine on, shine on, Harvard Moon, up in the sky.'"

Genia told Lillian the family story. It made the other woman laugh, which was exactly Genia's intention in telling it.

At the Talking Circle there was one empty chair again.

But all of the rest of the women were there: Teri, Judith, Madeline, Lillian, Naomi, Susan, Genia, even Martina.

The haunting music—flutes and drums—played once more.

"I've thought of a question," Genia began, "a topic, for all of us to answer, if you like the idea of it. It's this: If you could now say anything to Gabby, anything at all, what would you say to her?" She gazed around the circle. "What do you think of that? Do you have other suggestions we might consider?"

Nobody did. They agreed it was a good question for them.

She passed the blue corncob to Teri Fox, who sat very close to her side, as if seeking comfort.

This time everyone took a turn to speak.

Teri said, "Gabby, you were one of the prettiest women I've ever seen. I'm not sure you knew that, so that's what I would tell you, that you're very beautiful. And . . . it was good of you to feel so deeply about other people's problems, and . . . I'm sorry."

Lillian also said, crying, "I'm so sorry, Gabriella. I wish I could have saved you. If I had run a little faster, shouted a little louder, maybe I would have. You reminded me in many ways of my daughter. I know life was hard for you and that you suffered things deeply, just as my daughter did. I'm so sorry it had to be this way for you."

Judith said in a carrying voice, "I wish I hadn't laughed at you, that's what I want to tell you now. And I want to say that you meant well. You cared more than any of us. You were a serious and well-intentioned person, and I think I envied your passion. I'm really sorry."

Madeline's voice was tight as she said, "I didn't know you at all, and I thought you were kind of an idiot." Across the circle Teri Fox gasped. "Well, I did. And I think you were especially an idiot to get high and end up out there in that kiva. If you'd had any sense, you wouldn't be dead." She shrugged, a gesture that was familiar to them all by now. "Nobody likes what I said. Nobody ever does. But it's the truth. Sorry, kid."

Alone among them, Martina Alvarez had been nodding approvingly. Now she said, "I also would tell you the truth, Gabriella. It is true that you were an exceedingly foolish young woman. Perhaps you didn't deserve your fate, but you might have avoided it, had you thought and behaved in a more mature, judicious manner. I make no apologies for speaking the truth, either to the living or to the dead." Her severe tone seemed to take on greater meaning as she added, "I pray your death is a lesson to others in their own dangerous foolishness."

Naomi's face wore a woebegone expression as she said, "I feel responsible, Gabby. I can't tell you how sorry I am, for a lot of things to do with you. May you find peace and happiness, wherever you are."

From Susan: "Godspeed. I'm sorry."

Genia spoke at last. "I thought you were a sweet child, Gabby, and I saw how kind and thoughtful you could be. I hope you didn't suffer. Like Lillian, I, too, wish I could have caught you and stopped you last night. I hope there's a heaven, my dear, and that you're in it. I hope you know—somehow— how much sadness there is tonight on your behalf. I will re- member you with affection."

It didn't take very long. They hadn't known her very well; there wasn't much for any of them to say, except that they were sorry. Genia thought the group as a whole sounded as if apol- ogy were uppermost on their minds. Certainly it was for Teri and Judith. Genia worried that she should have chosen a better question, something more complex and profound. She worried that she hadn't led them well enough to do justice to their lost maiden.

But Teri hugged her afterward and in a choked voice said, "Thank you." And Judith grasped her hands and murmured, "I didn't know how bad I needed to say that out loud to some- body."

Madeline didn't make any other rude remarks.

And Lillian seemed a bit soothed by the little ritual.

So maybe, Genia decided, it had been adequate after all.

She truly hoped so.

After the circle, Teri, Judith, Madeline, Lillian, and Genia congregated around each other and agreed that they didn't know whether to stay at Medicine Wheel or to go home. To continue their tour seemed callous, but to leave seemed abrupt. Nor did they have any idea what Naomi or Susan would want—or have—to do. Naomi had departed the circle quickly, with Martina accompanying her, so they couldn't ask her.

"Let's sleep on it," Lillian suggested, sounding depressed.

"No, let's go up to the lodge and have a drink," Madeline countered. "And let's talk about it up there."

At everyone's urging even Lillian joined them.

They had hot chocolate, all of them, as if they all craved the comfort of something warm and sweet.

It was just the five of them now, a sad little band huddled together around a table off in a corner, separate from the twenty or so other people in the dining hall. They were aware of glances directed their way; they were the group whose seventh member had died. They were the group who'd discovered a body. They were the group the kids were supposed to meet but hadn't. Each of the five of them had already been asked questions by other curious tourists all evening long.

Madeline took charge, as if she were leading a committee meeting and they needed to take a vote.

"Let's decide," she said to them. "Go or stay? We need to figure out what *we* want, and they'll have to do it."

"They won't have to," Teri said.

"We paid," Madeline reminded them.

"Acts of God," Judith reminded her. It was a way of saying their "contracts" for the trip could be broken—possibly with no recompense—because of Gabby's death. Genia didn't really believe that Medicine Wheel would send them packing like that; more likely they'd all be offered another tour, at a better time.

"Act of God, my eye," Lillian remarked, sounding like her old tart self. "Did God give her a ride out there?"

The others stared at her.

Madeline crudely voiced all of their thoughts. "Huh?"

"Nobody has explained how Gabriella got out there," Lillian said. "Seventeen miles from here. She didn't drive her own car. And how did she know to go *there*?"

"What do you mean?" Genia encouraged her to keep talking. "What do you mean, how did Gabby know to go there?"

"*We* didn't know that was our destination! Not until we left this morning! Why did Gabby happen to end up at the very place we were going to be today?"

Judith shrugged, as if that were easy to answer. "Somebody on the staff must have told her. Naomi. Susan. Anybody who knew our schedule could have let her know."

Lillian compressed her lips for a moment, then nodded. Compliantly, she murmured, "All right."

But Teri took up the first part of the question. "Yeah, but how did she get out there?"

They all glanced at one another. Genia asked the pertinent question:

"Does it matter?"

They shuffled uneasily in their chairs.

"She found out from Susan or Naomi," Madeline said, sounding as if she were stringing separate facts together like beads on a string, making it up as she went along but trying to sound authoritative. "She hitchhiked out. Got down inside the kiva to do some crazy Indian ceremony." She flushed a little at the reaction of the others. "Sorry. But you *know* how she was. It's likely, isn't it? And a wildcat—or something—got her. She was trapped like a bear in a pit."

It was an awful scenario.

Genia could barely stand to think of it. But it was possible that it happened that way. Madeline might have—in a moment of impatient improvisation—outlined the actual sequence of deadly events.

"And she was stoned," Madeline said then, looking around at them, with a small smile hinting at the corners of her eyes and mouth. Her glance paused a fraction longer on Teri and Judith than on Genia and Lillian. "You gotta admit it. She was stoked on something. That weird scene in the grass?" Madeline actually laughed a little. "Maybe she was *on* grass. Had to be something more, though. I mean, she acted like she was hallucinating or something. Not coke. Not just uppers. LSD, or like that." Her sharp, attractive features were arranged in a blandly knowing look.

Judith changed the subject ruthlessly.

"What are *we* going to do now?"

"About?" Madeline inquired, looking perversely mischievous.

"About . . . do we stay, or do we leave?"

It was Lillian who turned the tide toward their collective decision. "You all can do what you want," she told them, "but I don't feel ready to leave yet. It would feel like abandoning her somehow. I know that doesn't make sense—"

Genia spoke up. "It does, Lillian. I'd like to stay, because I'd like to have time to register the fact that she's . . . dead. And I don't really want to go until we know the children are safe."

"It would be wonderful," Teri said wistfully, "to be able to go out on another hike tomorrow. Where it's peaceful, where we could think about Gabby and be together in her memory."

Genia was touched.

Lillian reached over and grasped Teri's hand. Genia felt her own eyes fill.

"When should we ask Naomi?" Teri said, as if it were already the consensus. "Tonight? Or wait until tomorrow morning?"

They decided the director had enough on her plate at the moment. They'd wait, sleep on it, and be absolutely sure of their own desires when they approached her in the morning. None of them were aware that it was already too late to get any executive decision out of Naomi O'Neal.

Twenty-nine

By the next morning the children still had not been located, but the mountain lion had been found. The big cat, a male, had been tracked to its lair, shot, and killed. Sometime in its life, it had been neutered surgically, and it was wearing around its neck a clear plastic flea collar, which confirmed the suspicions that it was someone's escaped—or released—pet.

Those were the first facts Genia heard upon wakening. The children hadn't arrived at any of their scheduled campsites, she was told. The news of the lion's death only compounded her mounting sense of loss and sadness.

The parents had begun to arrive on campus.

Walking together to breakfast, Genia and Lillian spotted the parents. The mothers and fathers weren't hard to identify: all appeared of an age to have teenagers, were dressed for Dallas, not for Colorado, and showed haggard faces, as if they had flown all night, in cramped airplane seats. They stood together inside and outside the main lodge in private groups, looking self-contained, as if they wanted only one another's company and nobody else's. Several were weeping. Some looked angry, others stunned with anxiety.

"My heart aches for them," Lillian murmured as they neared the dining hall. "Do you suppose Gabby's family is here, too?"

They didn't know.

Genia kept her eyes peeled. It seemed important for her to

find Hiroshi's parents and to tell them she'd met him, talked to him, thought him a delightful boy. There was no need to confide to them his last-minute fears or his premonition of disaster, which might only make them feel worse.

Parents weren't the only ones to arrive en masse that morning. Cars—mostly four-wheel-drive vehicles—and vans with law enforcement logos, and others with radio or television station call letters, were crowding the gravel parking lot above the meadow where Genia and Lillian had last seen Gabby alive.

"Poor Naomi," Lillian whispered to Genia as they climbed the stairs to breakfast. "Imagine having to handle all this."

But Naomi wasn't having to handle the increasing chaos. That was the next thing the two women found out, when they sat down with their breakfast trays beside Madeline, Teri, and Judith.

"Naomi's been relieved," Teri leaned across the table to whisper.

"Fired," said Madeline, looking pleased.

Judith dropped the other shoe: "Martina is in charge now. The trustees are arriving, and they're taking over."

Madeline had exaggerated.

It was not true that Naomi O'Neal had been outright fired; she had been, as Teri had told them, "relieved."

"Suspended, relieved, whatever you want to call it," Susan Van Sant said to their little group a while later. She looked grim as she predicted, "That's only to keep her from suing them later. When this is all over, then they'll fire her."

"Where is she, Susan?" Genia asked with concern.

"Searching the outback" was the grim reply. "Martina ordered her off the campus. She said Naomi would be a lightning rod for the parents' anger. And for the media. Naomi told me she was going to join the search for the kids, that she wasn't coming back until she found them."

While all around her, her new friends expressed dismay for Naomi's sake, Genia found herself wondering if that was the only reason for Martina's actions. What might Martina accomplish at the Wheel if she put herself in charge, even temporarily? Would she disband the Native American Advisory Council? Banish all tourists, as she had now barred the director who attracted them to the Wheel? And then would Martina make sure the next director they hired was more to her liking?

"No offense to Naomi," Madeline said in a caustic tone that contradicted her words, "but I mean, really, what would you do if you were the trustees? Naomi screwed up. Directly, indirectly, it hardly matters. All this happened on her watch. She deserved to get her butt fired. And from what I've been hearing, maybe it's long overdue."

But none of the others wanted to hear that. Or rather, Genia was curious but decided not to ask, as Teri, Judith, and Lillian all jumped in at once either to defend Naomi or to change the subject.

Only the young archaeologist remained quiet.

She still looked pale, ill.

"Susan?" Genia asked kindly, moving to her side. "Are you all right, dear?"

The look Susan gave her was almost shockingly vulnerable. Tears filled her eyes. "I'm so worried about Jon." She could hardly say the words, they came out sounding choked with tears.

The other women heard her say it, and they stopped their arguing to stare at her.

"Susan!" Lillian tried to sound hearty and encouraging. "Jon's a genuine outdoorsman! Daniel Boone! A gold miner! A bear in the woods! If anyone can take care of those kids and keep himself safe in the bargain, you know it's Jon Warren."

Genia wondered if Lillian believed her own sturdy sentiments.

"It's not just that," Susan confided. Her eyes filled again. In a near whisper, she stepped closer to the little circle of women and confessed, "I'm pregnant. And it's Jon's baby. He doesn't know about the baby yet, but he already told me he's going to divorce his wife and marry me."

Genia put her arm around the young woman's shoulders and gave her a comforting squeeze.

Later, as she and Lillian walked back toward the rest room together, Lillian was indignant. "So am I supposed to act sympathetically toward a woman who steals another woman's husband and gets pregnant, to boot? Is that the agenda, do you think, Genia?"

"I gather that's the idea," Genia replied mildly.

"Well!" A good night's sleep, with the help of her pills, seemed to have put some starch back into Lillian's personality. "I'd like to put her out of her misery by informing that young lady that her unhappiness is entirely of her own making!"

As things turned out, the little band of women didn't need to go looking for permission to continue their hiking. Permission found them, in the person of Susan Van Sant, who stuck her head into the doorway of hogan one.

"I can't stand it around here," she announced, with the sun and Mesa Verde behind her and her hands on her hips. "I want to escape into the field, but if I do that, I know the other archaeologists and the interns will bombard me with questions."

She smiled unhappily at the three remaining roommates, who had looked up at her from their small personal housekeeping chores: making beds, folding clothes, cleaning backpacks. They waited for Susan to finish speaking.

"You're the only ones around here who understand . . . everything," she said. They glanced at one another, definitely understanding what she meant by that. Gabby. The kids. Susan's pregnancy. Everything. "You paid for the whole week. I know Martina has completely forgotten about you. And me. We can do what we want. So how about it? Want to keep going? We promised you an overnight. Want to camp out tonight? Want to take a hike with me?"

The unanimous opinion in hogan one was yes. And in hogan two a few minutes later, yes again. At the last minute Genia put her plastic bag full of artifacts into her backpack, because the way things were going, she couldn't be sure when she would get another chance to ask Susan about them.

Teri said it felt as if they'd stolen the van. Judith said they escaped just in time, because she'd seen one of the other tourists point them out to a man holding a camera with a television logo on it. Susan told them they didn't know the half of it.

"It isn't only the media who want to interview you," she said, picking up speed as she drove out past the front gate. When they asked her what she meant, she glanced in the rearview mirror, meeting Genia's eyes, and said, "I'm not going to tell you until we're a long way away from here."

She drove, Genia thought in some alarm, as if she thought they were being chased.

Thirty

A long way away it was, over the Colorado state line into Utah, where they drove deep into a slot canyon with high sandstone walls rising close on either side of a dry creek bed. It was hiking, indeed, that Susan seemed to have in mind for them, and a lot of it, moving from isolated site to site, walking off their tension until they were ready to drop.

All the rest of that morning and afternoon they hiked, first at an almost frenetic pace, until Teri pleaded for mercy, speaking for all of them. Susan allowed them to slow down then, but always she pushed them ever-winding upward. They stopped fairly often—for calls of nature, to drink water, for the views, for minilectures from Susan, and for the lunch of sandwiches, chips, and cookies she had secretly scrounged for them with Bingo's connivance.

"Bingo wanted to come. She said if Martina fires her before the day is out, she'll join us at camp tonight. Otherwise she'll send an intern out with our next meals."

Lillian exclaimed, "Fire Bingo? It'll never happen. Even Martina must know how important she is to the tourist—oh, I forgot, Martina wants to get rid of the tourists. And she knows that Bingo is a staunch supporter of Naomi."

"Yes." Susan said as they climbed. "But look at the bright side, Lillian: Bingo may quit before Martina gets a chance to fire her."

"That's bright."

Only when they were halfway up the canyon—following a route that ascended more gradually than the canyon walls suggested—did she finally tell them who else it was that wanted to interview them.

"The law." She said it seriously but with a hint of sardonic humor. "Various law enforcement agencies of indeterminate stripe." The slight English accent lent a wry crispness to her words. "Bingo warned me—she heard a couple of them talking about it to Martina." She dropped her voice an octave and posed in macho swagger. " 'We're thinking we'd better have a talk with those women.' "

"Us?" Teri's dark face looked ashen as burned charcoal. She wailed, "Why us?"

Susan looked doubtfully at each of them, as if she were afraid they might all bolt back down the mountain. "Because," she said in a carefully neutral tone of voice, "Bingo said that it may not have been wild animals that killed Gabby."

"*What?*" Teri yelled it, again giving voice to all of them.

"Bingo heard that she sustained heavy blows to her head." Susan's voice took on a sardonic tinge again. " 'Sustained.' I sound just like one of them."

"She *fell,*" Madeline said emphatically, "into that hole, what-do-you-call-it, kiva, and she hit her head."

But Susan shook her head and looked meaningfully at them again. "Do any of you remember seeing anything like a rock in that kiva? Did we see anything in there at all except for Gabby's body?"

Genia spoke first. "No."

"Right," Susan said.

Judith appeared bewildered. "But what does that mean, Genia?"

"It means," said Madeline, cutting in impatiently, "that

somebody hit Gabby on the head and either pushed her into the pit or she fell into it."

Teri's hands flew to her face, and Judith stepped back with a dramatic expression of horror on her face. Lillian looked as if she hadn't taken it in yet, while Madeline's face registered disgust. "Why would anybody bother to kill her?" she said. "She was such a gnat in the scheme of things." Then she embellished, pleased with her first figure of speech. "A flea on the dog of life."

Lillian whipped around, looking murderous.

Genia stepped in firmly. "Stop, Madeline. Enough."

"My God, I should think so," Judith said breathily.

"It's not really true, is it?" Teri pleaded.

Madeline opened her mouth, but Genia leveled her with a stern look, and she closed it again.

Susan wouldn't let them carry the discussion any further. Saying they had to make the top before sunset, she urged them on, starting off without them when they didn't begin to move.

Genia felt shocked at the news they had been given, but for some strange reason not entirely surprised. But she didn't like what Susan was doing, and she agreed when Lillian objected, calling after her, "Susan! We have to go back! If they need to talk to us, we have to be there!"

"No!" The archaeologist shouted angrily over her shoulder. "No, we don't! Anyway, it's too late now. You can't. Can any of you find your way back without me? No, I didn't think so. Not to mention that I have the keys. You'd better start moving now, or I'll be gone and you'll be lost."

"My God," Judith said. "What's wrong with her?"

"What's wrong with everybody?" Teri echoed, sounding near tears.

But they all realized Susan spoke the truth. With nervous, worried glances at one another, they shifted their backpacks into place and followed their leader up the rocky slope.

"She's lost her mind," Madeline said behind Genia. "Maybe *she* did it. Maybe she killed Gabby, and now she's leading her only witnesses to the top of the damn mountain to pick us off, too. Hell, I'm not dressed for this."

Genia almost admired her plucky humor at that moment.

"We're not witnesses to anything!" Teri cried, behind Madeline. "We didn't see anything!"

But Genia thought that Teri might be wrong. Any one of them might have seen something important, perhaps even without realizing it. Wasn't that the staple of mystery novels? The witness who didn't know what she saw, and then was killed for her dangerous knowledge? It was also the staple of real life, she reminded herself; didn't she read in the newspapers about unfortunate witnesses who were killed before cases came to trial? Fiction or nonfiction, it happened. She spoke to Lillian in front of her. "We ought to be going back."

From the head of the trail, Susan shot back, "Well, you're not! Not until tomorrow. So climb, dammit!"

Genia heard the sounds of someone beginning to cry. She dropped back far enough to squeeze side-by-side near Teri on the trail, so she could comfort the frightened woman. "I'm scared," Teri whispered, miserably, "and I'm tired, and my back hurts, and I don't know what's going on, and I *hate* this!" Again, she seemed to be the plain-spoken honest one who voiced what everyone else was thinking.

"I know," Genia said in heartfelt sympathy. "Me, too."

"This is ridiculous," muttered Madeline. "Let's jump her and hold her down and grab the keys and force her to take us back."

"You'd get your outfit dirty, Madeline," Judith said.

"Oh, well, never mind."

They actually managed to share a laugh, behind Susan's back. It was as if, Genia thought, none of them—not even she herself—could believe that what was happening was real. She knew, however, that her left shoulder hurt where her backpack was rubbing against it. That was real, and she almost welcomed the pain, which connected her to something substantial she knew she could count on: more and more discomfort before this strange and endless day was over.

There was a purpose, it turned out, to Susan's forced march. She didn't, apparently, want to push any of them off the cliff. Instead, when they reached the summit, she turned to face her mutinous hikers, who dropped to the ground on the pine needles, groaning and cursing.

"We're going to put it all together," Susan told them, looking every bit as exhausted and grim as they. "In a Talking Circle. We were the first people to see her. We're the only ones—except for Jon and Naomi—who knew her. We're going to figure it out, dammit, who killed Gabby and where Jon and the kids are."

They stared at her; she had to be kidding.

"Impossible," Madeline declared flatly. "Take us home, dammit."

"Susan!" protested Lillian. "We can't possibly accomplish that. We don't know enough. We don't know anything."

"We might," Genia said to their obvious surprise and dismay. "Truthfully though," she added, "I would be surprised if it would prove to be enough. That's a very ambitious plan, Susan. Don't you agree the police are more likely to draw out of us any assistance we could give?"

"Not the police!" Teri pleaded. "Maybe we can do it."

Lillian and Susan cast her curious glances, Genia thought, but of course they didn't know about the LSD.

Judith rushed to support her friend. "At least we could try it Susan's way. She has us here, and as she said, we can't easily leave without her. What have we got to lose by trying?"

"Quite a lot," Genia responded with some heat. "We could

pollute the testimony we will give the police. We could influence one another's memories and opinions. We could waste
time that could be spent solving this crime." She pushed herself
to her feet and looked the archaeologist squarely in the eye.
"Take us back."

"We can't get back to the van by dark," Susan said calmly.

Genia sat back down again, heavily.

But then Lillian stood up. "Susan, this is crazy. It's a mistake."

Nobody stood up and joined her, though several nodded.

"You participate," Susan told them, "all of you, or I leave
you here on your own."

"Susan!" Lillian sounded shocked.

But the young woman stood her ground, her eyes filling, her
lips set in a firm line. Genia heard desperation in her next
words. "We have to find Jon. *I* have to. And you have to help
me do it."

"All right," Genia said, thinking that the quicker they got
this exercise in foolishness over with, the faster they could go
back to the campus where they might be needed. She looked at
Lillian, who nodded in understanding. "You win, we'll do it."

"When we get back down to civilization," Madeline said to
Susan, "I'm gonna sue your ass."

Genia would have laughed, if she hadn't seen Teri Fox
crumple onto the rocky, painful ground. She was quietly and
helplessly crying as if she couldn't take this any longer.

But then Madeline suddenly recalled what the others were
too tired to remember.

"Wait a minute! We're not dependent on Susan. Bingo's
coming. With our dinner. Screw you, Susan, we'll ride back
with Bingo."

That made Genia feel better, but Susan only laughed, as if
she knew something they didn't. When the chef arrived shortly

after they crested the ridge, they saw the reason for Susan's laughter.

"Damn," Madeline said for all of them.

Bingo wasn't driving a roomy van. She had her own car: an old VW "bug," from which she had removed all the seats but the driver's, so that she could pack it with coolers and other supplies. There was no way the five of them were going back in that.

"Boy," said Bingo Chakmakjian as she alighted from her cramped little car, "is everybody pissed at you guys!"

Thirty-one

As twilight cast the slot canyon below them into purple shadows, and while a little sunlight lasted on top of the ridge, the women chose their spots to place their rubber mats, pillows, and bedrolls, which Bingo had brought along with the food. Lillian advised Genia to join her a good fifty yards away from the cliff's edge.

"You wouldn't want to get up to pee in the dark and get confused and walk off the edge."

The very suggestion gave Genia the willies. Obediently, she followed Lillian to stake a claim on a parcel of pine needles in a clearing.

Judith and Teri wandered off saying they were going to look for wild flowers. "And a taxi," Teri bravely joked.

Madeline found a thin patch of late sunshine and lay down in it, her body on the soft fragrant pine needles, her head on her backpack, her eyes closed, looking improbably relaxed.

Lillian dug a paperback book out of her backpack and propped herself against a boulder to read.

But Genia set out to do what none of the rest of them wanted to do: talk to their "captor." Her excuse was her artifacts.

"May I?"

The archaeologist sat on the very edge of the cliff, her legs and feet dangling over. In the last of the sunshine, she squinted up at Genia and nodded. Cautiously, Genia lowered herself to sit beside Susan. Then she held the plastic bag out for her to see.

"What've you got here?" Susan asked, taking it.

"It's what surfaced on my ranch."

Her treasures received a cursory glance, a shrug, and were handed back to her. "Hohokam. This red on buff is their distinctive pottery, but the seashell is the giveaway. They etched it, covering their design with pitch and then applying fermented cactus juice—probably—as an acid to eat away the shell around the design. What you are holding, Genia, is one of the first examples of the art of etching in all of history."

Genia felt amazed at her own good fortune and impressed at the talent and ingenuity of those ancient artists. "Susan, where I found these, I detected three sunken circles in the ground. What do you think—"

That drew a slightly more interested look. "Yeah? They had large communities, but they also had outlying settlements for their agriculture. Those sunken round places are indicative of a little settlement, probably a single family, maybe two or three families. Outliers. I'd say you had some farmers there a long time before the land ever saw cattle."

They had a little discussion then—temperate, instructive—about why her artifacts weren't from any other culture, not the Anasazi, the Mogollon of New Mexico, the Fremont of Utah, or the Sineaqua of northern Arizona, and of what else Genia might possibly expect to find there, along with its relative importance and what she could do to report and preserve it. When the air between the two women seemed mild enough, Genia ventured to say, "Susan? This action you've taken. I suppose you know it could be construed rather seriously."

She felt the woman beside her stiffen.

"Like, kidnapping, you mean?" Susan laughed derisively. "Genia, come on, there are more of you than there are of me.

If you really want to take the keys, you'll take them. Who are you kidding? How do you think it's going to sound when you tell the cops that one woman, all by herself and without a weapon, made five helpless little females climb that big bad mountain and eat steak dinners at the top and hold a conversation around a campfire and sleep out all night under the stars."

"Logically, that's true, Susan, but the idea of us physically tackling you? You're pregnant, for one thing. And none of us wants to hurt you." Genia's voice turned a shade wry. "Even if some of us might like to *kill* you, so to speak. No, we'd let you 'force' us to spend the night here, before we'd do anything that might harm any one of us. You know that perfectly well, I suspect, otherwise you'd never have attempted this foolish stunt." Genia heard her own words sounding braver and reminded herself that she was seated right at the edge of a thousand-foot cliff with a young woman who was not behaving in the most rational manner. "We are going back tomorrow, aren't we?"

"Sure. I just want this Talking Circle. Before everybody else 'pollutes' our memories. Can't you do this for Gabby?"

"It's not for her, though, is it?"

"No. Genia, I need to tell somebody a secret, and I need to tell it soon. You're here. It may as well be you." Without waiting for a reply, Susan went on eagerly. "Genia, I may have found the true, provable solution to the mystery of why the Anasazi abandoned their dwellings."

Genia could only stare at her. "What?"

"Yes, *please* don't tell the others, because it will come out soon enough. I'll tell you this much: It would prove the Great Gambler legend of the Navajos to be true." She smiled slightly. "You have artifacts, Genia? So do I, hidden away where nobody, not even Jon, knows where to find them. I have to get the money to launch an expedition to retrieve them, and to study them, and then—if what I think is true—I have to introduce the proof to the scientific world in just the right and acceptable way, so that my peers will respect me and my findings. I've got it, Genia, I know I have the solution and the proof of it."

"How—"

"Pure blind luck. Oh, hell, I'll tell you what it is—Jon knows this much—just not where it is. It's a pot, Genia, three feet tall, perfect condition, full of ancient gambling tokens, and it is located—completely intact—in a hidden canyon where the pictographs on the walls depict the exact story of the ancient legend and the uses of the gambling tokens in sacred ceremonies! At least I'm pretty sure that's what they depict. They will have to be studied by Native Americans, if I can get any of them to cooperate with me; and the pot, the walls, the pieces will have to be dated, all of this before I dare go public with it. Oh, Genia, it's so important, do you see?"

"Oh, yes, I do. But why tell me?"

Susan glanced at her with brimming eyes. "If Jon's . . . gone . . . even dead—then I'm the only person alive who knows. Now one other person knows."

Genia felt astonished, overwhelmed. "I feel as if someone has just told me where to find the key to the inner chambers of the pyramids."

"Not where." Even with tear-filled eyes, Susan's smile was impish. "I'm not that trusting. Or generous. As far as I'm concerned, if I die tomorrow, the location can just die with me. I'll be the legend then, the archaeologist who had the answer, and nobody else will take my credit from me."

Genia closed her mouth on comments about the fleeting quality of vanity and asked instead, "What does this have to do with the Talking Circle you want us to hold? And finding Jon?"

"I think Jon's going to be the next director of Medicine Wheel, Genia. And if he is, I'm guaranteed the money and authority I need to launch my expedition. Naomi's been backing other horses: the archaeologists who claim it was ecological conditions that precipitated the abandonment. I can't depend on her to open her mind to my ideas, or even to believe me if I tell her what I've found. She might think I'm making it up, just to wrangle grant money out of her. No, Jon's my man in every way. He has to be alive, and I have to find him. I don't want anybody else coming in to take his place, if Naomi is out now."

"So this is not about love?" Genia couldn't help saying it.

She saw Susan's face flush. "First things first."

"Science, then love?"

"I have things to do, Genia. Prove the legend. Get famous. Obtain a father for my child. It all fits together in one package by the name of Jon Warren, and I intend to have him."

Genia felt chilled both by the fading sunlight and by the naked ambition in Susan Van Sant's plan for her future. After a moment she suddenly remembered something. "Susan!" she said. "Your dream!"

"Yes."

"You've actually seen this pot with your own eyes?"

"Yes." Then she added reluctantly, "From a distance. Binoculars. There are complications. It's on a reservation. But it's there, and I saw it."

"You couldn't have seen the gambling pieces, though?"

"No. But there's an Indian who took me there. He showed me one of the pieces, and he told me the jar was packed with them. This is what I have to prove, Genia. And it's going to take money and time and patience and influence to do it, and I'll have to go about it in just the right way, not by trivializing the legend in stupid little magazine articles like that idiot was going to do."

"Gabriella, you mean?"

So that was the reason Susan had reacted with such shock the morning she had dropped her tray in the dining hall. Susan never answered Genia's question, however, because Bingo called them to dinner.

Dinner was simple: steaks dredged in fresh chopped garlic and grilled over an open flame; corn on the cob cooked in foil over the fire; green salad that Bingo had prepared back on campus; and pecan brownies iced with chocolate.

"What d'ya expect in the wilds, on a minute's notice?" she demanded, when Madeline said, half-petulantly when she accepted her plate, "I can't eat this stuff. It's fattening and it causes cancer in laboratory rats."

"Be happy," Bingo advised her, "you're not in a laboratory."

Genia and the others were vocally appreciative.

While they ate, Bingo told them what happened at the Wheel after they left. "It's a zoo back there. Dinnertime for the reporter animals. They're feasting on this. Sixteen kids missing. Parallels to ancient history. It's so dramatic, they're slobbering all over themselves. We've got cable news. Foreign press." She named two spectacularly famous network news anchors who had flown in for on-scene reporting. As if she were reading the headlines from newspapers, Bingo called out: " 'History Repeats Itself! Disappearance, Just like Nearly 800 Years Ago! Where Did They All Go?' "

The women listened, astonished at it all.

Angrily, Bingo added, "They're driving the poor parents insane. There's no place to get away from them, not if you want to stick around in case there's any news about the kids." But then she smiled wickedly. "Martina blew a gasket when she found out you guys had departed for parts unknown. I didn't tell her because nobody asked me. They didn't know I knew."

"Thanks, Bingo," Susan murmured.

"I wouldn't have lied for you," the chef said, making things perfectly clear. "If they'd asked me, I'd have told them, but nobody did." She paused, looking doubtful. "Well, maybe I would have lied. I'm not crazy about uniforms and authorities. Must be my Armenian blood."

"How'd you get away?" Judith asked her.

Bingo tore off a piece of beef fat and tossed it on the fire, where it sizzled and popped. "Why shouldn't I leave if I want to? I made sure everybody got supper. Nobody needs me until lunch, and I've got breakfast covered in the morning. I can use these few hours of time off, believe you me. I may not stay with you tonight, though. I may decide to go off on my own."

"Will you come back for breakfast?" Teri asked, and everybody laughed, because she sounded so pitiful when she said it. Bingo assured her she would.

An independent little soul, Genia thought of the chef.

When Madeline and Lillian complained about the trick that Susan had pulled on them to get them here, the little chef's reaction was only to laugh at them. "Hah. Maybe you accidentally uncovered the secret of the Anasazi," she said, grinning. Susan and Genia exchanged startled glances. "Maybe their leader told all the poor suckers they were only going to take a little hike over to the next mesa. Only when they got there and turned around to go back, he said, 'Not so fast! I say we're heading south, and guess who's holding the water?' "

Then she seemed to hear what she'd just said; her face fell into an expression of disgust. "What am I saying? Maybe they really were poor suckers, like my people. Maybe the Anasazi got forced out of their homeland, too, by murdering thugs who made them all march for hundreds of miles. That's what happened to the Armenians in 1915. Right at the beginning of World War I. The Turks tried to deport our whole population. Almost two million people. They sent them to Syria and Mesopotamia, and about six hundred thousand died on the way, starved or murdered. My father's parents. My mother's mother.

Everybody else in our family, just about. People forget about us."

Bingo took a stick and began to stir the fire until sparks flew dangerously about. "Not me. I don't forget. I figure it's my job to remember, it's the least I can do."

She looked up, saw the effect she'd had on the others. With a shrug, she laid the stick back down. "Sorry, I'm not really trying to set anybody on fire. What I mean is, so maybe something like that happened to the Anasazi, too, you know?"

There was a respectful silence for a bit, but Genia was not at all surprised when Madeline broke it.

"Great steak," she observed.

"Tell me," Bingo replied acidly, "something I *don't* know."

"Bingo?" Susan's tone was straightforward. "There's not much evidence of that, of what you just suggested. No sign, really, of a forced march, or bodies strewn along the way."

But the chef had the last word. "After another eight hundred years, there may not be much sign of any of us, Susan."

The Talking Circle looked as if it were going to be an utter failure, from Susan's point of view. She'd even brought along the ear of blue corn and the music to get things going. But her question—"What do you remember about the scene of Gabby's death?"—was too blunt and direct, Genia thought, and her participants too mulishly resentful of her coercion. The whole effort offended the spirit of the thing. They all tried, or gave some semblance of appearing to try, except for Madeline, who didn't even pretend. But nothing came out of them except the obvious things that everyone who had been there could corroborate. Genia suspected that Talking Circles weren't meant for police interrogations; they were meant for meandering gently into profound layers of consciousness. When the circle so obviously failed in Susan's intent for it, the group fell into conversation around the campfire.

"Well, that was a waste of time," Madeline complained. "I thought you wanted to find Jon. What does Gabby's death have to do with him?"

"They could be connected," Susan declared. "It's just a pretty strange coincidence if they aren't. I mean, Gabby shows up dead at the very place where they're supposed to come, but they don't. Don't all of you think they must be connected somehow?"

They were all so tired, Genia thought, it was no wonder that none of them took up the conversational baton. Instead, they all just sat and stared into the fire, seeming to be lost in their individual thoughts. Susan looked frustrated and angry. Later, Genia would never be able to say where the impulse came from, but suddenly she felt herself taking the blue corn from Susan and saying out loud in a strong voice that compelled their attention:

"What do the Ancient Ones know that we don't know? What can they tell us tonight?"

Something uncanny happened then that made no sense to her when she pondered it later; in fact, it rather frightened her because it felt so powerful, so compelling. A trance seemed to fall upon the women; something deepened and softened and seemed to pull them together, when only moments before they had been lost inside themselves. Genia quietly passed the corn back to Susan Van Sant.

The archaeologist said, as if hypnotized, "The Ancient Ones know . . . they want to tell us . . ."

She never finished the sentence.

Instead, she exclaimed, "Oh!" in a loud voice and scrambled to her feet, looking excited. "Oh, my God, I know—I know!" Susan broke out of the circle and walked off into the darkness beyond it, seemingly still caught in the trance that had held them. Genia worried she might trip and fall.

"What do you know, and aren't you going to tell *us*?" Madeline shouted in a voice that held a twist of whining in it. When that got no response, she snarled, "Well, I hope she's happy now."

They picked themselves up, put out the fire, and lumbered off to their bedrolls.

"This," said Lillian, "is certainly the strangest time I've ever had at Medicine Wheel or anywhere."

"So where is Jon?" asked Judith, flinging her arms out dramatically to the wide, starlit sky above them.

"Oh, who cares?" snapped Teri. "She must think he's safe, or she wouldn't look so happy. Now I want to feel safe, too. And clean. And I want my bed at home. And my refrigerator. And my own car that I can drive, not your car full of junk, Judith. And I want a telephone to call my kids, and—"

"We still don't know what happened to Gabby," Genia said, half to herself.

"Killjoy," muttered Madeline.

"Oh, who are we kidding," Teri sighed, sounding exhausted and ready to cry again. "We still don't know *any*thing, and I don't believe that Susan does, either."

Bingo, who had spent the time cleaning up while they were in the Talking Circle, could be heard driving off in her "bug." Genia thought she could hardly blame the chef for wanting to put some distance between herself and them.

Genia had had a long time going up the trail that day to consider the disturbing and painful bombshell that Susan had dropped on them: Gabby was murdered. Someone had struck that child's head hard enough to kill her, or to leave her to die horribly in the teeth and claws of a beast. *And which was the real beast?* Genia had thought as she labored uphill. *The mountain lion or the human?*

Instantly, back on the trail, she had connected the unthinkable with what had already been thought and even written down: Gabby's notebook. Was there a motive for murder on that list she had seen? She felt she couldn't know that, because she didn't really know the women well enough yet, not even after the intimacy of sharing shocking events. What she *could* know to some degree, however, was who among them had had the opportunity to travel to Red Palace Ruins—probably taking poor Gabby along with them—and then return, undetected by the others.

Unaccustomed to sleeping on the ground, uncomfortable and alternately either too hot or too cold in her sleeping bag, Genia pondered the question of "opportunity" for a long time. The specific time period she was considering was the second night on campus, the night before they had discovered Gabby's body.

Lillian claimed she took sleeping pills. Was that true?

Judith and Teri said they'd been partying at the main lodge with a lot of other people, but there had been much coming and going. Had *they* gone and then come back again?

Madeline was, according to them, part of the festivities, but surely she could have "come and gone" as easily as anyone else.

Susan's name had also been on the list, and Genia had no idea where she had been, or with whom, or what she had been doing that night. Nor did she know about Naomi.

I only know I didn't do it, she thought at last.

She heard rustlings in the night, an owl, distant coyotes, and she thought unhappily of Gabby's body and of mountain lions. At various times in the night, movements alerted her to women getting up to go to the bathroom. She heard long-drawn-out whispering and assumed it was the teachers talking to each other late into the night as they lay in their sleeping bags. She heard a rattling of rocks that caused her eyes to fly open and her heart to pound, because of the immediate fear that one of them had walked the wrong way and slipped off the cliff. She nearly called out to see if all were safe.

Then she heard soft footsteps from the direction of the rattling and knew someone had returned safely to a bedroll.

After a time her heartbeat slowed, her breath relaxed, her thoughts stopped beating against her skull like moths against a screen door, and she fell into a sleep of sheer exhaustion. Her last realization before dreaming was that they had all probably had an opportunity to leave the campus and return to it unnoticed on the night that was Gabby's last on earth.

She awoke to the sounds of Bingo preparing breakfast and calling out, "Everybody up! Has anybody seen Susan? Where'd she go?"

When Genia walked to the edge of the cliff to look at the breathtaking sunrise, she found Susan Van Sant. The young archaeologist's body lay sprawled lifelessly on the viciously hard and unforgiving boulders at the very bottom of the canyon. After the first shock of it, Genia remembered stones rattling in the night, and soft footsteps returning to a bedroll. And she remembered how Judith Belove had said early on that if she were staging Shakespeare among the ruins, she would have Ophelia fling herself off for love of Hamlet. Now a young, passionate lover lay dead, almost as Judith had described, but there had been no one to catch her.

Again, Judith and Teri waited with the body, despite Madeline's merciless observation, "What's the point? She's not going anywhere."

Thirty-two

Of all the things Genia might have learned when she returned to the campus with the other women, practically the last she might have expected was that Hiroshi Hansen's parents had been looking everywhere for her.

But even before she heard that surprising news, she heard amazing things. There were rumors of "sightings." Gold-colored vans were being reported from Provo to Paris. A forty-two-car pileup near San Bernardino, California, was rumored to include the kids, until the fog cleared. Stories both impossible and plausible surfaced every minute, it seemed, and the call-in talk shows were electric with guesswork and argument. The country, maybe even the world, was getting a history lesson it hadn't counted on, and even the angry young Native American men had come down from their ceremony in the mountains to be interviewed by journalists who wanted to talk to anybody who looked anything like an Indian, an archaeologist, or a parent.

Genia would have been amused, if only she knew the kids were okay, if only Gabby and Susan weren't gone. . . .

As for the campus, itself, Bingo had been too right, Genia discovered: It was a chaotic scene that appeared to have been taken over by scores of journalists. A tent city had popped up in the meadow; the perimeter of the campus was infested with trailers and campers, most bearing commercial slogans of one sort or another having to do with news gathering, generally along the lines of "the first with the biggest." There hadn't been much of an attempt to control it as yet, leading Genia to guess that most available police power was devoted to searching for the missing children. She had a feeling Gabby's death had been forgotten in the melee.

Martina Alvarez herself took Genia to meet the Hansens, picking her way over thick black electrical cords and leveling with a forbidding stare those who dared attempt to stop them. "Who's she?" Genia heard someone say, and knew the question was directed at her back. "One of those women hikers," somebody responded. And then, "They lost another one, did you hear? Very careless, I must say." Martina ignored them all, even physically batting away some hands that dared touch her or tug on Genia. She took Genia into the main lodge, through the noisy dining hall, and past a police officer who was maintaining the inner offices as islands of calm. After tersely introducing Genia to the parents, Martina then left the three alone together in a tiny office.

Genia took one of the three available chairs, feeling breathless as she sat down. The Hansens, introduced to her in Martina's formal fashion merely as Mr. and Mrs., without first names, sat across from her, but the room was so small, the three pairs of knees nearly touched.

At once she saw the racial mixture that had produced the handsome boy: his mother's small stature, straight black hair, and gently slanted eyes; his father's broad American shoulders, and a quality to the mouth and nose that he shared with his son. Genia recalled Hiroshi very well; she had stared at him as he had looked out the lone window toward Mesa Verde, struggling with his fear. She couldn't imagine how they'd known she had any contact with their son.

"Hiroshi called us," Mr. Hansen said. Genia's heart leaped, thinking perhaps that the child had called recently. His next words dashed that hope. "Just before they all left from here for that damn camping trip, he called home and talked to his mother. He had some crazy idea that something had happened to his mother or me."

Genia glanced at Mrs. Hansen, saw her eyes fill.

"Of course," his father continued, "she told him everything was fine with us." Mr. Hansen was struggling with his words, as Genia watched and listened helplessly, but he managed to get out, "He told us about you. A potter, my wife thought he said. It was Mrs. Alvarez who helped us figure out he must have meant Mrs. Potter." He stopped talking, clearly unable to go on; his eyes were pleading, as were Mrs. Hansen's.

Genia did what little she could to relieve a bit of their suffering for an instant. "Yes," she said gently. "We met on a bench. I liked Hiroshi immediately. He's so smart, isn't he? And such a handsome fellow—"

Genia's lips trembled. Feeling the deepest pity for them and very near to weeping herself, she plunged on, trying to make the boy come alive—*be* alive—in the telling of her all-too-short memory of him.

"He's so easy to talk to," she exclaimed, making sure to use the present tense. "Right away, he told me how the kids were supposed to go off by themselves and to think like ancient Americans. He developed a theory that they may not have been so different from modern teenagers."

His mother whispered, "What else did he say?"

Genia understood they wanted—needed—to hear every word, every syllable she could remember, that Hiroshi had uttered before he vanished. "Well, he figured out that they must have had to think about food most of the time, in order to survive, and then he smiled, and I remember he said, 'How's that so different from me?' "

A laugh bubbled up out of his mother, but then her face crumpled and she closed her eyes and gripped the edge of the table with both of her small hands as if to keep herself from flying into many pieces. "He's very intelligent," she whispered haltingly, with her eyes squeezed shut and tears leaking from them. "That sounds just like him."

"He told his mother," Mr. Hansen said, "that he was scared—"

Mrs. Hansen covered her face with her hands and quietly sobbed into them. "I'm sorry, I'm sorry," she whispered through her sobs.

Genia felt agony for them, and terrible helplessness. She felt as if she herself were being asked to endure terrible things— Gabby, Hiroshi, now Susan—but nothing compared with what they must be feeling. "Please," she said to Hiroshi's mother, "don't apologize. I have children and grandchildren. I understand so well. This is a dreadful time for you. I have the strongest hope that they are safe somewhere. I want to think there's been some confusion, a mistake of some sort, and they'll be back when they're supposed to be, and everything will be all right."

She was instantly furious at herself for sounding stupidly optimistic. What if she were only building their hopes for a reunion that might never happen, except in tragedy?

"I know," Mr. Hansen surprised her by saying. He was dry-eyed now, and his voice grew stronger as he spoke. "That's how I feel, some of the time—I have a lot of hope. I know my boy. I like to think I would *know* it if anything really bad had happened to him."

"We shouldn't have let him come." His wife seemed to derive a bit of strength from his conviction and Genia's hope. She raised her face again and wiped her eyes by lifting a corner of her jacket to them. "He's too young. Younger than the others. He told us he was scared to camp out. He *told* us." She cast an accusing look at her husband, who frowned at the table-top. "He's scared of heights, and—"

Her husband interrupted, as if this were an old argument rehashed many times. "It's one of the reasons we let him come here, Tomasi—to encourage him to conquer his fears."

Genia said, "He's a wonderful boy, isn't he? You must be so proud of Hiroshi."

That helped to divert the argument, and Genia was glad to sit for half an hour and listen to them tell her all about their son, his drum lessons, the telescope he set up in the backyard and how he made his dad chop down a small tree so he could get a better view of the northern sky. She heard about his nice friends; the two teachers he loved this year and the others he hated; how he was too short for the basketball he loved and not interested in the tennis at which he excelled; how he seemed to have a precocious interest in architecture, even though his dad kept telling him that, practically speaking, he'd be better off as a builder, like his dad, than as one of those tomfool designers who couldn't pound a nail if you put a hammer in his hands. . . .

When they parted company, Genia felt she knew the Hansens and their eldest child very well. She felt like an aunt, deeply concerned for the welfare of the family. As they got up from the table, Mrs. Hansen whispered to Genia, "I cannot bear to think of my son being frightened, Mrs. Potter."

Genia said softly back to her, "I think the truth is that he is very brave, Mrs. Hansen. It takes real courage—don't you agree?—to act in spite of fear. He struck me as a brave young man rather than a fearful one." And that was true, Genia realized as she said it; it is the fearful, after all, who are most likely to be experts in courage.

"Oh, yes!" Mrs. Hansen appeared to be both surprised and comforted by that revelation. "That must be so! As long as he is not harmed—" Her face threatened to crumple again, and she grasped one of Genia's hands and gripped it painfully hard. "As long as he is all right, he will conduct himself with courage."

As they parted, Genia looked at Mr. Hansen and asked sympathetically, "How are you managing to hold up?"

"Drugs," he said with a harsh air of blunt candor. "I'm tranquilized to within an inch of my life, and it still isn't enough. But at least it gets me through the day. She"—he briefly touched his wife's shoulder—"refuses to take anything, even though I keep telling her it would help—"

"I need to *feel*," Tomasi Hansen said in her barely audible, shaking voice. "I need to feel him in my heart. If I can't feel him, I will be afraid he is dead."

The two women embraced. Mrs. Hansen felt birdlike and breakable in Genia's arms. Some of the parents had been given beds in the hogans, Genia learned, and upstairs in the dormers, but apparently it was difficult for them to live on campus because reporters wouldn't leave them alone. The Hansens wanted to find a motel, but everything close by was taken—by journalists—and although kind people in Cortez were opening their homes to the families, Mrs. Hansen particularly craved more privacy than that. At the same time they wanted to be available, in case the vans carrying Hiroshi and his schoolmates should miraculously pull into the parking lot. It was a conundrum they didn't know how to solve, and Genia realized it was probably going to be *her* problem as well.

Upon leaving the Hansens, Genia desired very much to be alone, to rest, to let her feelings wash over her, to go home.

She knew it was not to be, not yet.

Now there would be no avoiding interviews with the police. She didn't mind that, it was her responsibility; it was talking to the press that she most hoped to avoid. Keeping to the back way, holding her head down, and trying to look inconspicuous, she successfully made her way back to hogan one without being intercepted by strangers.

She intended to pull out Gabby's notebook with its "story

ideas," but it was gone. The suitcase was still there, but the notebook was missing from where she herself had hidden it. Her roommates and their belongings were also missing, but they'd left a folded note on her pillow: "Dear Genia, We can't stand it around here. Martina said we're not supposed to leave, but nobody in a uniform has told us that directly, so we're going to find someplace else to stay if we have to drive to Tucson to do it." It was signed, "T & J." There was nothing else to it, no good-bye, no hint of personal feeling toward Genia. The hikers were frightened of one another now, she supposed, and suspicious. She'd felt it on the long ride back to campus. None of them knew what to think—about Gabby's and Susan's deaths, or about one another. Their congenial little band had broken up. Yet she was glad not to have to face Judith and Teri across the room. She didn't know what to think of them any more than they apparently knew what to think of her.

She concentrated on the startling fact of the missing notebook.

Had they gone through Gabby's things, found it, and taken with them the one remaining piece of "evidence" that pointed to the LSD they'd brought on campus?

Or had a reporter nosed about in the unlocked room?

It was amazing, Genia thought, that Martina had not thought to remove Gabby's things yet. It demonstrated how easily the girl's death had been superseded by the drama of the missing children, but it might also hint of a young woman who had had nobody to care deeply about her life or her death.

Genia felt herself caring very much.

It was no longer a matter of waiting to be asked to speak to the police; she knew now that she must seek them out. But she didn't want to just grab the first police officer she saw—she wanted to talk to the *right* one.

She had to gird herself to go out the door again.

Madeline Rose was still on campus, Genia knew, because she'd seen Madeline—dressed to the nines in yet another outfit—giving an animated interview to several microphones at once. The diversion had helped Genia to escape unnoticed from the lodge. As for Lillian Kleberg, Genia had lost sight of her.

Dreading the next few minutes, she slowly pushed open the hogan door. She felt as exposed as a mouse in the desert. And like that creature, she had a sense of danger, even to her own person. She needed to move quietly, watchfully, and with care. Like a mouse, Genia felt a shadow of something large moving about, something evil, moving with swift deadliness from its previous concealment into the open.

Thirty-three

G enia sought out the one person on campus who always seemed to know everything.

"May I enter your kitchen?"

With a fierce scowl, Bingo glanced up from where she had been staring glumly down into an empty bowl. She looked relieved to see it was only Genia standing in the doorway.

"Enter, Genia. Grab a stool."

Genia did that; soon she, too, was staring into the empty bowl.

"This is the most peaceful place on campus. How have you managed it, Bingo?"

"I threatened the reporters with botulism." A satisfied little smile appeared on the stern face. "It appears I am intimidating, in my own small way."

"I'll say. Where's your staff?"

"I sent them home. They needed a break from this place. So, Genia. As the kids would say, T's'up?"

"I want to talk to somebody in a police capacity, Bingo. Who should that be?"

The chef raised her glance from the bowl and fixed it on her visitor. "You *want* to talk to a badge? Personally, I can't imagine that. Well, the one you want is gone right now, but he'll be back, I imagine."

"Should I wait just for him?"

"I would. Unless you have information about where the kids are. But if you did, you wouldn't be talking to me, you'd be running to tell somebody who could actually do something about it."

"I don't."

"Neither do I."

There was a silence between them, during which Genia enjoyed the music that was playing. It seemed perfectly to fit the mood in the kitchen at the moment.

"That's lovely music."

"Hovhaness."

"I thought it might be, or maybe Dvorak."

"Dvorak? Interesting. Yeah, I can see a certain similarity, probably because they were both inspired by folk music. American, especially Negro and Indian. Eastern European. I'm Armenian by ancestry, like Hovhaness. There's a parallel, you know, between my people and the Anasazis, or maybe I already gave this lecture? My staff says it's practically the only thing I ever talk about except recipes, but that can't be true. Now and then I'm pretty sure I mention the weather."

A very slight smile cracked the somber young face.

"Anyway, what you're listening to is the music of tragedy, and of longing and of memory."

Genia listened, nodding. "I can hear it. Do you think the Ancient People had music like that, full of longing for their old cities and homes?"

"Interesting thought, Genia. Why not? You can certainly hear it in contemporary Indian music. All that pain. The deaths. The anger. The melancholy. I love that kind of music. My staff says it depresses them. I tell 'em to grow up, life's like that."

"When you get older," Genia surprised herself by saying,

"and if you survive fairly intact, you'll be able to hear the notes of gratitude, too, and of the kind of joy that surmounts all odds."

"I'll have to take your word on that."

They stared at the bowl again, while the music played.

"You've probably answered this a million times, but where'd you get your nickname?"

"It's my real name. My mom had five sons, and she really wanted a daughter. So when I popped out, the obstetrician said, 'Bingo.' "

Genia smiled. "It suits you."

"I guess it does. Could have been worse."

"Eureka? Hallelujah?"

"I was thinking more along the lines of Blackjack or Royal Flush."

The gambling terms brought vividly to Genia's mind her last conversation with Susan Van Sant. Now she, Genia, was the repository of Susan's discovery. And what good did that do anybody? She didn't know how to find it. She should tell someone—shouldn't she?

"What shall we do, Genia?"

She felt startled, so close to her own thoughts were Bingo's words.

"Do?"

"Was Gabby murdered?"

"I believe so."

"Yeah. How about Susan?"

"Oh, my." She sighed unhappily. "That would mean—"

"One of you guys."

"She may have tripped."

"Right." The word was sarcastic. "About as likely as suicide."

Again, they just sat there.

Then Bingo seemed to brighten. "Let's cook something. You want to cook with me? You want to help me fix something?"

"Bingo, I'd be honored."

"You should be."

They both laughed a little. Together, guided by Bingo's barked instructions, they prepared batter for three different colors of cornmeal: white, yellow, and blue. Carefully, like artists mixing colors, they poured the separate batters on top of one another into baking dishes. At Bingo's urging, Genia tried any combination of colors she wished: blue on yellow on white; yellow on white on blue; blue between yellow and white. While they were companionably working side by side, Genia told Bingo about Gabriella's "story ideas." Bingo wasn't named on the list, so it seemed all right to Genia to trust her with the information.

"That girl got herself killed," Bingo declared, when Genia finished talking.

"Because of one of the articles she was going to write?"

"I don't know about that, Genia. I can tell you how hot to preheat the oven, I can tell you to sift the cornflour until it's fine as baby talcum, but I can't tell you why anybody in her right mind would want to kill that silly girl. I just think she put herself in the path of evil."

Genia heard Bingo's words reverberate among the pots and pans: *her right mind,* she had said. *Her.* The pronoun seemed to harden the cement that was forming relentlessly around Genia's own suspicions about the little group of women hikers.

"Have you heard from Naomi?" she asked the chef.

Bingo, busy with a hand-held sifter as big as her head, did not reply.

Genia didn't wait around for the tricolor corncake to bake. For one thing, the kitchen workers began to trickle back in to start supper preparations, and she was in the way. For another, and as much as she hated the idea of it, Genia determined that the person to whom she must tell Susan Van Sant's "dream" was the irascible trustee herself, Martina Alvarez.

Thirty-four

Genia bearded the lion in its borrowed den.

She located Martina Alvarez in Naomi's vacated office. As Genia expected, the trustee was at first uninterested in "having a word with" any member of the women's hiking group that had caused the Wheel so much trouble and adverse publicity. But she became very interested, indeed, upon hearing of the late archaeologist's claim.

"Dr. Van Sant has to have written something down somewhere," the trustee stated unequivocally. "She didn't have her own office here. Naomi was far more willing to give offices to cooks than to scientists." This last was said bitterly. "Her home would be the logical place to look. Let us go there and determine if she adopted Naomi's no-lock policy and took it home with her." The latter was even more caustically said.

"What? You want me—?"

"Mrs.—what is your name?"

"Potter. Eugenia."

"Mrs. Potter, I cannot easily move around. I have an especially difficult time stooping and bending over. Ordinarily I would not inflict my personal problems on you, but someone has to search for that information before it is scattered and lost, and I cannot do it without assistance."

"The police—"

"What about them? The careless woman turned in the

wrong direction on that cliff last night and stepped off the edge. It is of no concern to the police, any more than is the accidental—though entirely preventable—death of that other young woman by a wild animal. Both are regrettable incidents, I'm sure, at least as far as their families are concerned, but not matters for police investigation."

"The fact that Gabriella was struck on her head—"

"She hit her head on a rock, which the animal must have carried away with it."

That amazing hypothesis left Genia speechless. A quiet little voice speaking in her own head, however, was telling her in equally certain terms not to allow this old bulldozer of a woman to meddle about in Susan Van Sant's house without a witness. So Genia, who did *not* feel anywhere near as cavalier about the police as did both Bingo Chakmakjian and Mrs. Alvarez, permitted herself to be pushed into Martina's car and driven off the campus.

It was a sweet little two-story Victorian house on a Cortez side street, with many neighboring dogs barking at the intrusion of two unfamiliar women on the block. It occurred to Genia to worry, for the first time, whether Susan had kept pets that would need care, and she was relieved to find no evidence of them, either in the unfenced yards or inside the house.

At Martina's unnecessary bidding, Genia rattled the loose front doorknob and pushed.

"Hmmph," said the trustee when the door opened.

The rooms that were revealed to them looked as if the occupant had priorities other than picking up or cleaning.

Feeling like a maidservant, Genia cleared off a chair for Martina, who sat in it for the next two hours, imperiously issuing orders.

"Bring me those files over there, Mrs. Potter."

"Mrs. Potter, put this back where you found it."

"Look in that cabinet. Open those drawers. Search the closets."

Genia would have rebelled had she not known what might be at stake: American history, a mysterious chapter explained, nothing less than that. She still might have refused to be treated in such a manner, if not for her being the repository of Susan's dream come true.

There were two computers, but she couldn't get into them. Where was her computer-whiz offspring when she really needed him?

She noted, with sadness, the evidence of Jon Warren's presence in Susan's life and was glad Martina wasn't with her in the bedroom to cast a contemptuous eye on it. The left side of the unmade double bed must have been his, she guessed, if the shirt lying across it was any clue. It was the same shirt he had worn at the first Talking Circle, so he must have spent that night with his lover. She noted a few of his hairs on the pillow.

Feeling awful for the lost mother and child, Genia looked at the book Jon had been reading the last evening he saw Susan alive: *Legends of the Little People: Tales of the Fremont*. Without even waiting for Martina to bid her so, she opened a manila folder on his side of the bed and noted within it the copies of tourist registration cards, including her own. She saw a paper with a list of dates (and assumed them to be future tours) with names and addresses beside them, and she wondered if Jon would ever be able to come back to get them. Obviously, he was a man who took his work home with him. How awful the moment of return would be for him, she thought sympathetically, when he learned of Susan's death.

If he himself was still alive.

Genia had, unfortunately from her point of view, had previous experience with police investigations, and she knew that once "evidence" was impounded, it could take forever to be returned to its rightful owners. This folder looked as if it contained registration information that the Wheel would really need in the near future. If they didn't have it, would they even know who was coming to their tours?

Hardly believing she was even doing it, she tucked the folder under her arm. What possible use could it be in an investigation of Susan's death, anyway? She would give it to Jon when he returned, or to Naomi when she reclaimed her job.

Genia, old girl, you are an optimist, she informed herself.

Underneath the folder there was a huge pile of new catalogs, including the very latest from Neiman Marcus, the fabulous store in Texas. Genia, who did most of her personal shopping by mail rather than drive all the way to Tucson or Phoenix, filched it, sticking it into the folder. She would give that back to Jon, too, she virtuously promised her conscience, which retorted in skeptical and impolite terms.

She found evidence of the life of a vital young woman, a dedicated scientist, an ardent lover. But she didn't find any map, photo, drawing, or description of a hidden wall of pictographs with a three-foot-tall pot standing intact in front of it.

"Mrs. Potter, now look—"

"No, Mrs. Alvarez. We're finished here, or I am. Will you drive me back, or shall I call someone to come and get me?"

The pot had crumbled in Susan's hands, Genia thought sadly, as Martina grudgingly drove them both back to the campus. It had turned to dust, just as it had in her dreams when she was only ten years old.

Genia's interview with the "right" law enforcement officer early that evening was swift and businesslike. She told him about the list in Gabby's notebook and who was on it, and—up to a point, beyond which she found herself unable to go—why. She confided how, during the night when Susan died, her heart had pounded at the frightening sound of rocks falling down the cliff and how soft footfalls had made her think someone had returned safely to their bedroll after that. Now she wondered: Was it Susan's fall she had heard? And whose footsteps after that? In retrospect, she told him, they seemed stealthy.

There were things she didn't have to tell him because others already had: Susan's liaison with the missing assistant director; her pregnancy and her claim that they would marry; the contretemps between Madeline Rose and Gabby; and the lesser tension between Gabby and Teri Fox over whose people had "suffered most." The officer already had in his possession the notes that Lillian Kleberg had written down when she and Genia had formed a team to "investigate" Red Palace Ruins, and he had Teri and Judith's notes as well.

"This is the first time," he said with grave humor, "that potential suspects have so thoughtfully provided lists of everything at a crime scene. And what about you, Mrs. Potter? How did you get along with the two dead women?"

She wondered how Madeline Rose might have answered that question. *Better than when they were alive, officer.*

"Fine," Genia told him mildly, and then she also told him what Susan Van Sant had confided to her about the Anasazi pot and pictographs.

He inquired, as if he were only making casual conversation, "She didn't tell you where to find this alleged proof? It would be worth quite a bit of money, I would think."

"Millions, do you think?" Genia asked him.

"I wouldn't be surprised." He smiled at her in his rather starchy fashion. Genia could see why Bingo had advised waiting for this one officer: He appeared quite intelligent and efficient, but also thoughtful, as if he would not jump to wrong conclusions. Nevertheless, he raised an eyebrow and asked her, "Would you be surprised to learn it was worth that much?"

Do you think I killed her for it? Genia thought wearily. But she merely repeated, "No, I wouldn't. But she didn't tell me."

When he dismissed her, he directed her to a phone that was being kept free. She made a quick call to each of her children and also to a certain phone number in the Boston area, to let everyone who loved her know she was fine. After all, if the news from Medicine Wheel was going out to London, Tokyo, and Cape Town, it might well be going out to her children and to Jed White, he of the massive long-distance phone bills. After answering their worried questions as well as she could, she assured them there was no reason for them to worry about her. Of course, not one of them believed her, and one or two of them threatened to hop on a plane to come out there to be with her. "There's no place to stay," she warned them, "from here to Colorado Springs." She told them the truth, that the police didn't want any member of the women's group to depart the area yet, and that she didn't want to go until she knew the fate of the children.

She returned to hogan one, where she fastened the windows with their weak latches, then struggled to shove a chest of drawers against the door. After that, she lay down and tried to sleep.

A boy sat alone on a flat rock at the tip-top of a mountain. He was thinking, not of the home for which he longed and that he worried he might never see again, or of the parents who he believed had too much faith in his ability to cope in any circumstances. He missed them; he would like to see them again at least one more time. Was he being melodramatic? "How would I know?" he asked himself in his practical fashion. "I'm too young to know things like that about myself."

There were many immediate concerns he could have been thinking about, but what he was actually thinking about—who he was thinking about—was Frank Lloyd Wright, odd as it seemed even to him. The great architect. One thousand building designs in a seventy-year career. Five hundred of them actually built, as far as the boy knew. An incredible record for one person. A monumental achievement of beauti-

ful, *singular architecture that stood out like buildings from another planet in the landscape of masses of city skyscrapers and suburban tract homes.*

The boy had a theory. If he ever got home alive, he'd tell his mom about it, and his dad, too, if his dad would ever stop talking about how he ought to be a builder instead of an architect. And he might tell that nice Mrs. Potter, too.

He reached for the silver circle and rubbed it.

It had become his talisman.

The boy's theory was that the Hisatsenom had had their own version of Frank Lloyd Wright. An ancient architect of singular vision, towering ego, and magical charisma. That was why those buildings went up in the space of one man's lifetime and why they were all of a similar, astonishingly original design, like nothing that had ever come before or ever came again. And that was also why they stopped being built, all of a sudden, bang.

He laughed, sitting on his rock. It was also why they had to be abandoned. Frank Lloyd Wright's roofs leaked, too. Like the great American architect, the great Anasazi architect was stronger on artistry than on mechanics! And when he was gone, dead, nobody else could carry it on or do it quite right. Just like Frank Lloyd Wright.

It was a good theory, the boy decided, and he sure hoped he got a chance to tell somebody about it sometime.

Late that afternoon the parents were allowed to sort through the bedrolls and other objects left at Red Palace Ruins to pick out what belonged to their children.

But none of the items did.

These were not their children's belongings, the parents said. Everything was brand new, never used. Nobody knew to whom the things belonged. If they weren't the property of the young people, whose were they? Where had they come from, and who had left them there, and to what purpose? Had the teenagers even been to Red Palace Ruins?

Thirty-five

Genia awoke that evening with one clear thought: *I can't stay here.*

With trepidation, she crept around shrubs and trees and people's backs to the kitchen door. She stood there until somebody inside noticed her and pointed her out to the busy chef.

Bingo came to the screen door.

"You look like a woebegone puppy somebody left outside. What's the matter, Genia? Apart from death and disaster, I mean."

"I need to find somewhere else to stay, Bingo. Could you suggest something for me?"

The little chef opened the door.

"Come in here while I think about this. If you're a good girl, and you stay out of our way, I'll get a plate fixed up for you, so you can eat supper in here with us."

"Oh, thank you."

An hour and many happy and full stomachs later, Bingo came over to the corner where Genia sat on a stool, her back to a wall, slopping up a delicious spaghetti sauce with the remnants of the five pieces of garlic toast she had devoured. She had obediently and gratefully bothered no one. The chef came over, wiping her wet hands on a dish towel.

"Stay with me," she said.

"Bingo, I couldn't—"

"Please." That uncharacteristic word alerted Genia to examine the other woman's face carefully for a hint of what lay behind the unexpected invitation. But the deadpan expression gave no clues. "I have room. You need a room. It's free. Best food in town. What a deal. Say yes. Please."

"Yes," said Genia humbly.

"Come," said Bingo to the "woebegone puppy," and the puppy went, feeling for all the world that if she had a tail, it would be dragging disconsolately on the ground behind her.

Bingo's home in Cortez was no romantic, charming old Victorian like Susan's. The chef ushered Genia and her belongings into a plain and practical new ranch-style house set amid neat labeled gardens of herbs and vegetables.

None of that particularly surprised Genia.

What did take her utterly by surprise was the presence of the two women sitting, over coffee and pie, at Bingo's kitchen table: Naomi O'Neal and Lillian Kleberg.

Naomi smiled warmly. "Surprise. Welcome to our little sorority, Genia."

And Lillian said tartly to Bingo, "Is this a new pledge?"

"There is a pledge, actually," Naomi said, standing up to pull out chairs for the newcomers. "A pledge of secrecy. Will you take it, Genia?"

Thinking it was that or be turned out to sleep in her car, she naturally said she would. In fact, so grateful was she for lodging away from the campus that she very nearly asked for a Bible and raised her right hand to swear to it! "Give me a piece of that cherry pie," she bargained, as she sat down between Lillian and Bingo, "and I'll keep any secret you've got! Hello, Lillian, Naomi. I'm awfully glad to see you. I've been worried about both of you."

As well she might be, she soon learned from them.

★   ★   ★

Before Genia even raised a fork to slice into pie, Lillian growled at her, "Rat fink."

Genia smiled down at the flaky crust and runny cherries on her plate. "Gabby's list of story ideas? They told you? You know I had to tell the police. You would have, too, Lillian."

"Yes, I would" was the reply, "but you're still a rat fink. I had a terrible time with that starched cop—you know the one I mean. Did he interrogate you, too?"

"Interrogate? I talked to him, yes."

"I'll bet you didn't make the mistake of bursting into tears."

"Well, no."

"I did," Lillian said, while Naomi looked sympathetic and Bingo swiped at the table with a clean wet rag. "All the man had to do was say Gabby's and Susan's names, and I blubbered like a fool."

"Lillian, that's understandable."

"He certainly thought so," she agreed, but her tone was biting. "He sure decided he understood me. 'Tell me, Mrs. Kleberg, did you think Ms. Russell was suffering from mental illness? Did you think she should be put out of her misery?' "

"Oh, Lillian! No!"

"Yes! And then he said, 'And what about Ms. Van Sant? Did you condemn her pregnancy out of wedlock? Did you try to solve her problems the way you helped solve your own daughter's?' "

"Oh, no! Lillian, I didn't tell him that much. I didn't say a word about—"

The older woman relented. "I know you didn't, Genia."

"Then, who—?"

"Guess."

"I don't know who else you told. Madeline?"

"Bingo."

For a moment, Genia was confused. Was Lillian telling her that Bingo Chakmakjian had "ratted" on her? But the confusion cleared up when Bingo herself said indignantly, "Hey! Now don't be taking my name in vain like that."

"I didn't know Madeline knew," Genia said.

"I told her," Lillian admitted, "in a moment of weakness. I've been having a lot of those lately." She didn't look weak at the moment, Genia thought; she looked like a strong-minded and determined woman. "But no more. Tonya would disown me to see me blubbering all over perfect strangers. Besides, I may have to get tough in order to save my own skin—or yours, or yours, or yours. What's *your* motive supposed to be, Genia?"

"I don't think I have one for the death of poor Gabriella. But they do think that Susan may have passed on valuable information to me, which I suppose somebody could want to kill for." Doubtfully, she added, "I suppose. Although it's not very good information. . . ." She trailed off to find three faces staring at her curiously. "More than that, I can't say."

Luckily, they seemed to take that to mean she didn't have anything more to add. Before they had time to think about their mistaken interpretation, she said, "Naomi and Bingo, are you supposed to have motives?"

"Not me," said Bingo, raising her hands defensively in the air. "I'm just the chief cook and bottle washer 'round here. Like to keep it that way, too, but I won't if Naomi leaves."

"If I leave?" Naomi's smile was crooked. "Hasn't anybody noticed that I'm already gone? It will take a miracle to get my job back. The consensus seems to be that I've gone completely off my rocker—that I'm running the Wheel into bankruptcy. It isn't true, by the way, in case you wondered; we're just slightly over one year's budget, for heaven's sake. But I'm supposed to have lost my grip on the Wheel and somehow then lost a whole group of people and also probably killed Gabby and"— her eyes filled—"Susan. My employee. My friend." She shook her head sorrowfully. "Maybe I am losing my grip on reality. How did it all get so bad? So fast? It'll take a miracle."

Lillian patted her hand consolingly. "That's what we're here for, dear." She looked across at Genia. "Got any ideas?"

"I know just what we need," Genia responded. She got up and left the kitchen, returning a few minutes later with a ballpoint pen and a yellow legal pad that she had packed at the bottom of her suitcase. She never went anywhere without one. Slapping it down on the table, which Bingo had already cleared of dirty dishes, she told them, "I can't think without my yellow legal pad. Now, where shall we begin?"

They started with the three main questions:
Where are the children?
Who killed Gabriella Russell?
Did somebody kill Susan Van Sant? Who?
And then they started brainstorming wildly, tossing out every "fact" or fantasy they could think of, filling the empty yellow pages with their ideas, their fears, their theories.

Naomi said, a glimmer of hope appearing in her eyes, "We're four smart women. We ought to be able to figure *something* out!"

Soon the "facts" began to organize themselves under the three main headings. And then there were pages headed with particular names, and long observations about those specific people, their activities, their lives. And then there were lists of "things to do," with assignments for each of the women to take on. They worked long into the night, comforted and inspired by one another's presence, fortified by Bingo's nonstop supply of wonderful food, and congratulating each other on having observed this or overheard that or gotten a glimpse of something else that might be helpful or even incriminating.

Hours later, they stopped for a review.

"I don't know what any of this means," said Lillian.

"It's hopeless," moaned Naomi.

"I've got to get up in four hours," complained Bingo.

"Let's sleep on it," Genia suggested. "Maybe it will come clear in the morning."

It didn't.

Their breakthrough didn't come until Friday night.

The children had been gone since Monday; if they were all right, they would have been expected back on Saturday.

The women had been idly talking about Martina Alvarez, how difficult she could be, and the changes she might put into place at the Wheel. Lillian was in the middle of telling them a grimly humorous story about how Madeline Rose never took any guff from Martina, when she suddenly looked up with a puzzled expression.

"Naomi," she said, "when you put Martina in hogan two with Madeline and me, how did you know Madeline could survive it?"

"What, Lillian?"

"You said, 'Madeline's a tough cookie.' Didn't she say that, Genia? We were climbing the trail to Last Man Standing, just before Madeline got in that tussle with poor Gabby. Remember, Genia?"

She nodded. She did, in fact, remember that very well.

"So," Lillian continued, "how did you know, ahead of time, when you were making our hogan assignments, that Madeline would be such a 'tough cookie'?"

"Oh." The director appeared nonplussed. "I can't tell you that."

"Naomi!" It was a vehement, demanding chorus.

"Oh, all right. I guess we all need to know everything, even if it's not important. Madeline Rose is Jon's wife."

She gazed into three faces all registering shock.

"What?" Naomi asked them. "Should I have said he's her husband? Is that better? I know you're probably surprised—"

"Probably?" Bingo screeched at her.

"—but you knew he was married to somebody."

"How do you know this," Bingo yelled at her, "and we don't?"

"Good grief, Bingo. I found out when I ran the background check on him before I hired him. But even then, Jon said they weren't really married—not *really*—and they just hadn't gotten around to filing for divorce, and they preferred to keep quiet about it. He said, very nicely, that this was intensely private information about him and would I please not reveal it to anybody, ever."

"But he told everybody he was married," Bingo objected.

"Oh, that was just to keep the horny tourists away." Naomi laughed. "He is a cutie, you have to admit. It was protective coloration. But if he did get involved with a woman—like he did with Susan—he didn't want his wife to be embarrassed by it, so he wanted her name kept out of it. Very chivalrous, you might say, in his own unique way."

She noticed they were still staring at her in the same shocked manner. "What? You don't think so? Why are you all still looking at me as if I've grown horns?"

"You weren't there, were you?" Lillian spoke slowly. "When Susan told us she was pregnant—that Jon was going to divorce his wife . . . and marry Susan."

"What?" Now it was Naomi's turn to look stunned. "No, I wasn't. She heard that, Madeline did? But wait a minute, why would she care, if they were married in name only? And not even in name, really, since she kept her maiden one."

"That's Jon's version," Bingo pointed out. "We don't know how his wife—Madeline—felt about it. Anyway, jealousy's a weird thing, don't you think? It can pop up real violently just when you think you've got it all tamped down."

"Violently?" Naomi echoed.

"What was Madeline doing in this women's group?" Bingo

demanded. "What did you think, Naomi, when you took her reservation?"

"Oh, I didn't. Jon did. You know he takes care of all the reservations—that's entirely his job. To tell you the truth, I didn't even recognize her name when I did see it. But when Jon disappeared and I looked up his next of kin, there she was."

"My God, what'd she *say*?" Bingo asked.

"Nothing. And since she didn't, I figured I'd better keep quiet, too, since nobody was supposed to know. I really don't know if she knows that I know, if you can follow that."

"I think," Genia said slowly, speaking up for the first time, "you'd better hope she doesn't." When they asked her what she meant, she just shook her head, unwilling to go any further than that for the moment. Instead, she said, "We didn't have a clue about Madeline and Jon, Naomi. She didn't say anything, didn't give us a hint that it was her husband who was missing."

"And Jon didn't say," Bingo persisted, " 'Oh, hey, Naomi, my wife's coming along for the hiking tour'? He never said that to you?"

"No, he would have made the reservation for her—"

Genia interrupted. "Naomi, I took something from Susan's house that I thought you might need sooner than the police would give it back to you."

Bingo raised her eyebrows and grinned. "Why, Eugenia Potter!"

"I'll go get it."

When she returned, she placed a manila folder in Naomi's hands. "I guess Jon was working on reservations for future trips."

Naomi opened the folder and looked through it, then held up the paper that Genia had seen: the list of names and addresses and dates. She laid the Neiman-Marcus catalog aside and Genia noticed only then that little white pieces of paper

were sticking out of it, as if somebody were planning on ordering items.

"These aren't our program dates." Naomi looked bewildered. "And I know some of these people—they've been on
recent tours. But these addresses are not where they live. These
addresses are all in Denver, but these people are not even from
Denver, any of them."

Naomi looked from face to face.

"What *is* this?"

Genia looked at the list, and then at the copies of the reservation cards. She picked up the Neiman-Marcus catalog and
leafed through it, and she thought about the big pile of other
catalogs on Jon's side of the bed. She recalled her son's dictum
about computers: "Mom, it will pay off. You'll begin to chart
patterns and trends over a period of years." Genia didn't need a
computer to see the pattern that was unfolding here. And she
said to them:

"I think it has to do with my expiration date."

Thirty-six

Saturday afternoon the impossible, the miraculous happened. "They've been sighted! They've been found! The vans are coming in!"

The incredible news went up from person to person like sparks lighting the gloom. Stunned, half-disbelieving, weeping with relief and joy, everyone on campus seemed to go wild at once. Generators began to hum as television cameras got switched on. The on-air talent ran combs through their hair, in anticipation of covering the return live.

"Is it true? Is it true?"

It *was* true, and the truth became a parade—led by highway patrol cars with their lights flashing, and filmed overhead by jockeying helicopters, and followed by cars, trucks, motorcycles. Everything that had a horn was honking like mad for the sheer joy of it.

And cuddled safely amid it all, carried tenderly—if loudly—home like nineteen precious jewels on three golden pillows were sixteen dirty, smelly teenagers and three grimy adults, staring out of their van windows in sheer openmouthed amazement.

Seated right behind Jon Warren in the first van, Hiroshi Hansen asked him, "So, Jon, do you do this for all your tours?"

At that, Jon got the giggles and laughed so hard, the kids had to yell at him to keep driving straight.

Above them, a radio reporter said to his listening thousands, "My God! The lead van just swerved nearly off the road! Is the driver ill? Are the children safe, even now?"

In the lead van the kids were listening to the radio. Slowly they were getting a glimmer of what the fuss was all about and just how very much fuss there was. When they'd driven through the first little town after coming down from their canyon hideaways, the people on the streets had pointed at them and screamed, "It's them! It's them!" Soon a police car had pulled them over, and an excited cop had asked them questions, and then the highway patrol for one state had arrived to tell them not to say anything more to anybody and that he would accompany them from that point on. And now the highway patrol for Colorado had taken over. The whole world had thought they were missing, maybe even dead. They grasped that a massive search had been under way for three days. They were astonished. At first they thought it was funny and rolled about on each other in the laughing camaraderie they had achieved in their six days and five nights together in the wilderness.

But then something began to dawn on some of them, and then all of them.

"My mom!" One of the girls, full of the emotions of the recent, arduous, challenging, voyage into self-discovery, burst into tears. "Oh, my poor mom!"

"Hurry!" the teenagers urged their drivers. "We have to see our parents! We have to show them we're okay. Drive faster! Damn those cops! Drive over the top of them, Jon!"

He responded by taking advantage of the unique opportunity to lie on the horn and tailgate a highway patrol car. It brought the whole procession to a halt, which sent the hovering journalists into a frenzy of surmise.

"What's the problem, Mr. Warren?"

"Can we go any faster? The kids are anxious to see their folks."

But the plea was to no avail; at a safe, sedate, exact fifty-five miles per hour, the long parade carried home the children the nation had been losing sleep over. Nothing would rush their caretakers now, not if even one extra mile per hour might endanger a single greasy hair of their unwashed heads.

Martina Alvarez stood, at her usual rigid attention, on the steps to meet the prodigals, her entire board of trustees behind her.

A great cheer went up as the first golden van nosed through the gate. The vans were rushed then, swarmed by weeping, smiling parents, so that the occupants could barely manage to get out. One of the girls reached through an open window to her parents, and her father grabbed her and pulled her right out of the van into his embrace.

The three adult drivers were the last to alight onto the gravel.

At their appearance, a semisilence descended on the crowd.

Jon Warren seemed to look around for someone, but then walked smilingly toward Martina and the other trustees.

She stopped him with an upraised arm, a pointed finger, and an outraged question:

"Where have you *been*?"

He looked at her as if she were speaking another language. "We've been exactly where we were supposed to be, Mrs. Alvarez. Exploring sites in northern Utah—"

"Utah!"

The cry went up from the listening crowd. *"Utah!? But they were supposed to be in Colorado; we've been looking for them all over Colorado!"* In truth, the search had covered several states, including Utah, but it was a huge state with many, many isolated, nearly invisible places. A group of nineteen people might have wandered unobserved for a very long time.

"Yes, Utah," Jon said with a frown, as if they were all being obstinately dense. "Following the last schedule Naomi gave us."

Martina Alvarez knew in that moment that she had failed to follow her own best counsel: She had taken Naomi O'Neal's word for the purported whereabouts of the three vans.

Behind her, the real president of the board of trustees knew it, too, and he sensed a chance that might never come again. Stepping forward, he said calmly, "I'll take over from here, Martina." He beckoned to Jon. "Come on up. We need an executive director, and we need him now."

As the celebration continued, the explanation seeped out.

The very morning of the trip, Jon had been handed a new schedule by Naomi. It was one that would take the kids into isolated pockets of Utah. They would stage the "abandonment" at Red Palace Ruins, but they would not return for the seminar with the ladies. Having a long drive to Utah ahead of them, they would get going on that instead. Jon had had to leave the kids and their teachers at the first exploration site while he drove back into Cortez to purchase brand-new sleeping bags for the staging, and new water bottles and backpacks, too, all at Medicine Wheel's expense, which sounded absolutely outrageous to everyone who heard about it.

"What a waste of money!"

"Imagine leaving inexperienced adults in charge of those kids like that, even for an afternoon!"

"Who are these women, anyway, the Queens of Sheba, that they should get such gold-plated treatment?"

Why Naomi might have issued those directions, nobody knew. Jon told the trustees she hadn't really told him why, just handed him the new schedule and said, "Do this instead." And it was so much at the last minute, there wasn't even time to argue with her; he said he just went ahead and followed his boss's directions, never dreaming of the upheaval it would cause. "We've used the Utah itinerary a lot of times," he said. "It's a good one, and I was familiar with it, so it wasn't really a problem. It was just weird that she'd do that at the very last minute."

But no weirder than other things the executive director had been doing for the past several months, so the gossip went. Everybody knew she had been losing her grip on, well, everything. But nobody knew where she was right now, to ask her about it. Now it seemed that Naomi O'Neal had disappeared. A search went on for her, because it was obvious to everyone that she was to blame for everything. From parents to trustees to press, people were in a hanging mood. "That O'Neal woman better be able to prove she is certifiably insane," one angry man said, " 'cause if she can't, she ought to be lynched."

Jon Warren stepped into the interim role of executive director with tactful hesitation, saying he felt disloyal to his boss for doing it. But when he finally was told of the deaths of Gabriella Russell and Susan Van Sant, and of how they were at the very least indirect consequences of Naomi O'Neal's actions, his face set in grieving, unforgiving lines. With the president of the board, he set to work that very hour to bring the Wheel back to some semblance of order and normalcy, confiding to the president of the board of trustees that "I will do my grieving later."

Thirty-seven

The women at Bingo's house were absent for the home-coming.

On Saturday morning they had flown together to Denver, where they rented a car, Jon's list of names, addresses, and dates in hand. In the car, which Lillian insisted on paying for, they drove one by one to each of the addresses on the list.

They discovered on each lawn a "sold" sign with a realtor's name: Madeline Rose.

At several of the homes, either Lillian or Genia went to the door and rang the bell or knocked. If somebody was at home, she said, "Excuse me. I'm sorry to disturb you, but would you mind telling me what date you'll be moving out? And how long will your house be empty before the new owners move in?"

"Why?" she was naturally asked.

"I'm looking for a short-term lease on a house to rent."

Several of the homeowners laughed. "It would have to be *very* short, like about twenty-four hours."

". . . forty-eight hours."

"A week."

"A month! Would you like to come in and discuss—"

Tactfully, Genia disengaged herself from that eager "seller." "Oh, dear, I really need three months. So sorry. Good-bye!"

On the plane ride back to Cortez, they put it all in order. Naomi sat next to Genia, who was writing it all down on her yellow legal pad, and Bingo leaned over Lillian across the aisle.

Jon Warren and his wife Madeline Rose had worked a credit card scheme. He took the reservations that had all the credit card information; the two of them then ordered everything they wanted from catalogs; they had the items delivered to empty houses that Madeline had sold.

She had to be there only to accept delivery.

The list contained names of Wheel tourists whose card numbers they intended to use next; the addresses to which the orders were to be delivered; and the dates the houses would be empty.

"My God," Naomi breathed. "It's so easy. If only they hadn't gotten greedy, they could have kept this up forever."

It was Naomi and Bingo who told the other women about the higher stakes for which Jon and Madeline had evidently begun to play: the millions of dollars in governmental and philanthropic grant money that could be siphoned off by a corrupt executive director.

"They had to get rid of you," Bingo said in her blunt way.

"But you have been a spectacularly successful director," Lillian observed. "Not even Martina could get rid of you through ordinary channels."

"So," Genia contributed, "they had to cook up a scheme to humiliate you in the most public way possible." A couple of hours later, they learned what Jon was claiming—that Naomi had handed him a last-minute schedule change that took them into Utah. And finally, when his subterfuge had come out into the open at last, Naomi knew—*knew*—she hadn't done that. Genia summed it up; "They started small and quietly, with Jon faking memos that contradicted your orders, probably using actual old orders in your own handwriting. And then as the distrust escalated and even your own faith in yourself began to ebb, they struck with their big scheme."

"And Gabby?" Lillian asked, sadly. "And Susan?"

"We may never know exactly how Gabby got in their way," Genia said gently. "She must have accidentally found out, or caught them in the act somehow. As for Susan, she knew that Jon was already planning to take the kids into Utah, the night *before* Naomi was supposed to have handed him a changed schedule. He was reading about the Fremont people of northern Utah, in bed, the night before he left."

"Why would he tell Susan he would marry her?" Bingo asked.

It was Lillian who said in a voice shaking with anger and sorrow, "He could have been lying about that, too."

"No," Genia said, "I think that maybe he thought now he wouldn't need Madeline anymore. He needed her for the credit card scheme, which may have been her idea, I wouldn't be surprised to learn. But once he was executive director, what role would she have to play? I suspect," she added grimly, "it is not a good idea to try to cut Madeline Rose out of any profitable deal."

It appeared that Susan Van Sant had, all unknowingly, paid the price for Jon Warren's greed.

They drove straight from the airport to the Wheel.

When the four of them walked into the dining room, with Lillian, Genia, and Bingo keeping Naomi in the middle to protect her, people started crowding around them. Martina Alvarez came forward, along with the "starchy" law enforcement official who had interviewed the women, and then Jon Warren came striding out of Naomi's office.

"I'm taking over," he said firmly.

"I don't think so," Naomi said, as she tossed a Neiman-Marcus catalog at his feet. "Pick out something you'd like, Jon. And maybe a little something for your wife."

Thirty-eight

Judith Belove and Teri Fox called to say they were going to Esalen for their next school break. "They have hot tubs," Teri told Genia over the telephone from where the two friends had found a motel room in Montezuma. Genia was still at the Wheel, but due to leave that afternoon. "And I don't have to take any hikes unless I want to." Esalen, Genia knew, was a famous retreat for counterculture gurus, which had reached its peak of fame in the sixties. It was a natural for the teachers, she thought. She might even like to go there herself sometime.

She wished them both good fortune, then hurried outside to catch the Hansens before they departed for home.

"My mom says this is sterling silver," Hiroshi said, coming up to her. "I can't keep it."

"Did it work for you?" she asked him.

"I'm still alive and kicking." He grinned at her.

"Then you'd better keep it. Tell your mom I've already bought myself a new one."

"Is that true, or are you just saying that?"

She fished in one of her pockets and then held up for him to see the object she located there. It was a tiny Dream Weaver web enclosed in a silver circle. "I only have one set of keys, Hiroshi, so I can't use two rings. If you give that one back, it'll be wasted."

"Thanks." They smiled conspiratorially at each other. "Did

I tell you my cool theory about the Great Anasazi Architect . . . ?"

They chatted happily until his parents called him to go.

She hugged Bingo, Naomi, and Lillian good-bye, and knew
they would all stay in contact because something special had
been formed among them: they were individuals fully revealed
to one another who fit together into a remarkable little group.
Maybe she'd come back next spring and bring Jed White with
her. Or maybe she'd just come back alone to be with her
friends again.

"You write to me!" Lillian instructed her.

Genia promised that she would do that soon.

As she opened her car door, a shiver down her back caused
her to turn and look toward the shadows of Mesa Verde to the
east. It occurred to her then to think: How odd that the only
two people to die were the two white women who espoused
the Great Gambler theory and wanted to spread it worldwide.
Gabby, high on LSD, had hidden in Madeline Rose's car just
before Madeline drove out to Red Palace Ruins to help Jon
arrange the scene for the women to find the next day. When
they thought she was a witness, they killed her but were forced
to leave her body there when the mountain lion scared them
off. They couldn't even finish scattering the "evidence" all
through the ruins. As for Susan, it was she and Madeline Rose
whom Genia had heard whispering, about the fact that Susan
believed Jon was in Utah with the kids. It was Susan whom
Genia had heard falling, and Madeline's footsteps coming back.

For a moment, looking at the summit where so many secrets
lie, Genia felt almost frightened, feeling as if ancient eyes were
watching her from up on Mesa Verde. But then she made herself shake off the feeling that other forces had been at work all
along; no, it was coincidence, that was all.

Thirty-nine

Genia arrived home to an "urgent" message on her answering machine from her neighbor.

"Genia!" The old rancher's deep voice boomed genially at her. She turned down the volume. "Welcome home! Call me before you even sit down. I've discovered something to put those little bits of pottery to shame. Just wait until you see, and on your own land, too. You'll say, forget that little ol' pasture with its measly ol' seashell. You've got something better, Genia, and I can't wait to show you. Give me a call, soon's you can."

As a postscript, he added, "Have a nice time on your little trip?"

Her curiosity—and suspicion—aroused, she did call him, only to have him pick up on the first ring, as if he already knew she was home and he were waiting right by the phone. He wouldn't tell her what it was he had "discovered," or how it was he had happened to be traipsing about on her property in order to find it. He insisted she meet him, right *now*, to see for herself.

"Look at this, Genia." He swept his cowboy hat off his head and through the air as if taking a big bow. "There I am, just chasin' one of my bad boys that got into your pasture—"

A bull, he meant, Genia knew, which had breeched the fence line between their properties.

"And I've just about got him squeezed up between this here

tree and that there fence, when I happen to look down, and looky what I see!"

Genia obliged him by looking where he was pointing.

There, spread out in large chunks, was pottery of a distinctive black and white design. She glimpsed geometric shapes, broken but not shattered. Counting, she found forty pieces on the ground around her, most of them at least partly covered over by dirt.

Her first response was fury.

"Amazing," she said, barely controlling her voice, "that none of us ever noticed this earlier."

"Well, looky how you only just detected those little nothing bits in that other no-count pasture that ain't good for anything but leasin' out to some fool like me. Anyways, I 'spect my old bull kicked these up out of the ground. He's a feisty old boy, like me." He grinned flirtatiously at her. "He's always apawin' at the ground, you know how they are."

"An archaeologist."

"What?"

"I say your bull is an archaeologist."

"Well, I guess. So I'd say this here pasture is what you want to pay attention to, get your official people down here to look at this. Forget that other little bit o' nothin'. They'll be amazed, they see this."

"They would be surprised, all right."

He grinned in a pleased way. "Yeah?"

"Yes, they would consider this quite an extraordinary find. You see, this black and white pottery and these designs are indicative of Mimbres pottery, which was created exclusively by the prehistoric Mogollon people of"—she paused and looked squarely at him—"New Mexico."

There was a silence, during which she could see the cogs in his brain roll over. "New Mexico, is that right? Well, that's not so far away from here."

"It was then."

She wanted to strangle him. How had he gotten his greedy hands on examples of such treasure? And to *break* them, just to try to fool her into leasing her land to him—oh, it made her want to rage and cry at the same time. Genia walked over and picked up a chunk of the pottery and brought it back to where he stood, still looking as pleased with himself as a bull after mating. She rubbed off the dirt, and then she turned the piece over in her hands.

It said, "Made in the Philippines."

Genia smiled and then began to laugh. The old rancher laughed, too, reading in her humor a signal of a good and prosperous future.

Suggested Reading

The following books proved most helpful to me in my research:

Bordewich, Fergus M. *Killing the White Man's Indian: Reinventing Native Americans at the End of the Twentieth Century*. New York: Doubleday, 1996.

Coe, Sophie D. *America's First Cuisines*. Austin: University of Texas Press, 1994.

Crown, Patricia L. and W. James Judge, ed. *Chaco & Hohokam Prehistoric Regional Systems in the American Southwest*. Santa Fe: School of American Research Press, 1991.

Gabriel, Kathryn. *Gambler Way: Indian Gaming in Mythology, History and Archaeology in North America*. Boulder: Johnson Books, 1996.

———. *Between Sacred Mountains: Navajo Stories and Lessons From the Land*. Chinle: Rock Point Community School, 1982; Tucson & London: Sun Tracks and the University of Arizona Press, 1994.

Gumerman, George J., ed. *Themes in Southwest Prehistory*. Santa Fe: School of American Research Press, 1994.

Gwaltney, Francis. *Corn Recipes From the Indians*. Cherokee: Cherokee Publications, 1991.

Matthiessen, Peter. *In the Spirit of Crazy Horse*. New York: The Viking Press, 1983; Penguin Books, 1991.

———. *Sacred Images*. Salt Lake City: Gibbs–Smith Publisher, 1996.

Miller, Lee, ed. *From the Heart: Voices of the American Indian*. New York: Alfred A. Knopf, 1995.

Time-Life Books, ed. *Mound Builders & Cliff Dwellers*. Alexandria: Time-Life Books, 1992.

Thompson, Ian. *Houses on Country Roads, Essays on the Places, Seasons, and Peoples of the Four Corners Country*. Durango: The Herald Press, 1995.

————. *The Native American: An Illustrated History*. Atlanta: Turner Publishing, Inc. 1993.

Acknowledgments

Several years ago I participated in a wonderful week of hiking and exploration sponsored by the Crow Canyon Archaeological Center near Cortez, Colorado. That trip inspired this novel. So many people at Crow Canyon said, "You ought to set a mystery here," that I finally did it! And so the gorgeous setting of Crow Canyon became the physical model on which I loosely based the campus of the fictional Medicine Wheel Archaeological Camp. Everything else in this novel is strictly a product of my own warped imagination; any mistakes I have made are my own; and none of the characters are based on anyone living or dead.

In real life I would urge anyone who is fascinated by the culture of the American Southwest to investigate the many programs of exploration, education, and discovery that are offered to the public by the Crow Canyon Archaeological Center, where the staff is terrifically smart, patient, fun, inspiring, and kind. (And the food is heavenly!)

For help with recipes, I am grateful to Barbara Kaufman, Richard E. Keith, Jill Churchill, and Sally Goldenbaum.

Uncle Dick's Chicken

(BRAISED IN MILK)

Your favorite chicken parts, enough
for 4 persons
Oil
Salt and pepper
1 quart milk

Pour enough oil into the bottom of a large pot and brown the chicken in it until it's a deep golden brown. Pour off excess oil if desired. Add enough milk to cover the chicken. Salt and pepper generously, as these are the only seasonings. Simmer at low heat, uncovered, until the chicken is fork-tender, its juices run clear, and the liquid cooks down nearly to gravy. Tasty served over rice. Serves 4.

Colorado Pine Nut Orzo

2 cups orzo
⅔ cup fresh parsley, minced
⅔ cup fresh dill, minced
¼ cup lemon juice
Salt and fresh ground pepper to taste
3 cloves garlic, minced
¼ cup olive oil

1 tablespoon butter or margarine
2 medium Portobello mushroom caps,
sliced and quartered
3 tomatoes, chopped
¼ cup white wine
¼ cup pine nuts
1 cup crumbled feta cheese

Cook orzo according to package directions, drain, and put in large serving bowl. Toss together with parsley, dill, lemon juice, salt, and pepper. While orzo is cooking, sauté garlic in the olive oil, using a medium-sized pan. Add butter. Add mushrooms and sauté until tender. Add tomatoes. Heat through. Add wine. Bring to a boil. Remove from heat immediately. Pour sautéed mixture over orzo. Sprinkle pine nuts and feta on top.

Archaeologists Corn Bread

You will need one large and two small bowls.

1 cup all-purpose flour
¼ cup sugar
4 teaspoons baking powder
½ teaspoon salt
2 eggs, slightly beaten
1 cup milk

½ cup vegetable shortening
⅓ cup yellow cornmeal
½ cup sour cream
⅓ cup blue cornmeal
⅓ cup white cornmeal